STARJUMPER LEGACY
THE VANISHING SUN

To the Puyallup Public Library

Christopher
Bailey

BY CHRISTOPHER BAILEY

Published by Phase Publishing, LLC

Starjumper Legacy:

The Crystal Key

The Vanishing Sun

Others:

Without Chance

Coming Soon:

The Plague of Dawn

STARJUMPER LEGACY

BOOK TWO
THE VANISHING SUN

CHRISTOPHER BAILEY

Phase Publishing, LLC
Seattle

Cover art by Tugboat Design
http://www.tugboatdesign.net

Phase Publishing, LLC first paperback edition
December 2014

Starjumper, Starjumper Legacy, and all related characters and elements are trademarks and/or registered trademarks of Phase Publishing, LLC
https://www.facebook.com/StarjumperLegacy

ISBN 978-0-9899734-6-5
Library of Congress Control Number 2014954278
Cataloging-in-Publication Data on file.

For Ferrell and her amazing crew for all your hard editing work. For Jeff and Brandy, Jo and Adam, and Chantelle and Shane for all your support professionally and personally. For Doug, for reminding me what's important in life.

And for my Angel.
For you, always the stars.

CONTENTS

PROLOGUE

UNDER THE SEA

"Are you sure this is it?" Allie asked, her doubts clear. Dav gave her a sidelong grin.

"This is it," he replied simply, his intense blue gaze cast out at the vast expanse of ocean spread out before them, the clear moonlight rippling almost lazily across the water. The night sky was speckled with clouds, though none seemed inclined to try and darken the moon. Standing atop the ridgeline of a small cliff, the view was impressive.

They had been on the road for two days, and it was a huge relief for Allie to finally be out of the back seat. Now she knew why her adoptive mother had never wanted to take Allie anywhere they couldn't reach in less than a day's travel. She couldn't imagine how professional truck drivers did it, day after day in their trucks, the same old scenery passing by over and over again.

Allie had to admit though, this particular type of scenery was new for her, and absolutely beautiful. Her lack of enthusiasm certainly didn't come from a lack of appreciation, more from a lack of understanding.

"Weren't we going to visit the Uhran colony?" She thought that's what Dav had told her. He'd also mentioned they lived in the Mariana Trench, which she knew was in the ocean. She didn't think it was anywhere near the coast of California though.

"We certainly are. They have an outpost here. They like to keep tabs on the comings and goings of other races on this planet," Dav replied. Artus nodded, standing on her other side.

"There aren't a lot of those though, don't worry," Artus told her as he saw her expression, "just a few visits a year is all." Allie turned to stare at him.

"A few visits a year? This planet? How many races even know about this planet?" she asked in disbelief. She'd come under the impression since spending a little time off world that Earth was a relatively backwater planet, as far as the rest of the galaxy was concerned.

"Oh, quite a few. Only a couple of them come here though. The Uhran have their colony, they get visits from time to time. The Em'l have a scientific interest in your species too, they visit most often," Artus clarified. "You know, UFO sightings and that sort of thing." Allie shook her head.

"How does nobody know about this?" she asked. Dav laughed.

"Some people do, but they're sure not sharing," he said, glancing over at her again. She couldn't think of an intelligent reply, unable to put her disbelief into words. How narrow the vision of the human race she thought, so unaware of anything beyond their own small little planet. Most of them were totally unaware of anything beyond their own televisions for that matter, she added.

"I'm going to go down to the outpost and let them know we're here," Raith told them. Before Allie could reply, he stepped forward and gracefully dove off the top of the rocks, falling for what seemed to be a very long time before splashing into the water below. Her heart leapt up into her throat and she gave a small squeak of surprise.

"Some advance notice would be nice," Allie muttered as she regained her composure. "Dav, don't ever jump off a cliff without warning me first."

"Don't worry, I'll be sure to let you know first," Dav grinned over at her.

After a long while watching the rippling light dancing across the waves, listening to the surf hissing its way up and down the rock face below, she started to get a little worried.

"Shouldn't Raith be back by now? He's been gone quite a while," she asked. "How far is the outpost?"

"Dozen miles or so," Artus replied offhandedly. She blinked in surprise.

"What? And Raith is going to swim there?" Allie wasn't at all sure how long it would take someone to swim that far. She wasn't sure anyone actually could swim that far, come to think of it. Raith wasn't just anyone, and the usual rules for people didn't really apply, but still...

"He swims fast," Dav said simply. Artus just nodded as she looked up at him. Dav shrugged. "Androids," he said, by way of explanation.

"What if he gets attacked by a shark?" she asked, trying to shake the too-relaxed pair. Dav turned an expression of mock sympathy her way.

"Poor shark…" he replied. Artus laughed, leaving Allie feeling a bit foolish. Of course she shouldn't. If Raith could take on a Maruck, a shark wouldn't be much of a threat. Nothing on this planet would be much of a threat to Raith she knew, though she still struggled wrapping her head around the fact that he wasn't actually human. She had to keep reminded herself that Dav and Artus weren't either.

Looking between the pair, she couldn't help but marvel at how simply human they appeared. The pair stood with similar smiles, their identical brown hair waving in the slight sea breeze, matching clear blue eyes looking out over the water and reflecting the moonlight as a liquid shine. They looked like extremely good looking humans, Allie clarified, but like humans just the same.

A faint sound from the gravel road's shoulder some distance behind them caused Allie to glance behind, but she didn't see anything. Artus' car was still parked alongside the road, just in front of an unpleasant-looking thorn bush that Raith had threatened to shove Dav into during a bout of good-natured insults the pair had been throwing around.

They'd been getting along quite a bit better since the escape from Tyren's station, she thought to herself as she turned back to the sea. They still seemed determined to make her think they weren't friends, but she knew Dav well enough at least to see that he was actually having fun joking around with the young-looking android.

"He doesn't need to breathe, does he?" she asked curiously.

"Nope," Dav replied. "No need to breathe, eat, or sleep. I envy him a bit, actually. He never gets tired, never gets hungry or thirsty, never hot or cold."

"He doesn't really feel anything like we do though," Artus pointed out. "Physically or emotionally. He is a machine, remember."

"Technically, so are we," Dav argued. "All life is mechanical in nature. The only difference is what the machine is made of. For us, it's organic cells. For him, it's circuitry. That difference aside, brains are nothing more than complex organic computers, our bodies nothing more than an organic system designed to convert energy into movement in one form or another. You could argue that organic life forms are nothing more than bio-robots."

"Now there's a cheerful thought," Artus said wryly.

"Why don't you like androids?" Allie asked him. He glanced down at her, and she could tell he was deciding exactly what to tell her.

"Androids are... dangerous," he finally said, looking back at the sea. "They do what they're told. Exactly what they're told. They don't feel guilt or remorse, they don't understand pain, and have no conscience."

"Raith isn't like that," Allie protested. "He fought against Tyren right alongside you and Dav. He did everything he could to help us even before then. Why would he turn against his master if he didn't have a conscience?" Artus was silent a long moment before answering. Allie had nearly decided she'd won the argument when Artus finally spoke.

"I don't know. I'm still trying to figure out what he's up to," Artus replied quietly, "or what's wrong with him."

"What do you mean by that?" Allie asked, getting annoyed and letting it show in her voice. She wasn't about to sit by and let him insult her friend. Dav put a hand on her arm to stop her. When she looked his way, he gave her a gentle shake of the head, a warning to let the subject be. She bit her tongue, though it took an effort of will. Artus didn't respond.

Another sound behind her caused her to look around again. A sudden burst of movement from the thorn bush made Allie jump, but she recognized the small form pretty quickly. Tic ran along the gravel toward her, holding something in one hand and running on the three available limbs, forked tail standing up almost straight. Allie recognized it as a happy and excited posture. She smiled and held an arm out. Tic leapt up easily as she reached her, climbing her arm to her shoulder.

"What have you got there, Tic?" she asked. Tic chirped happily, and promptly bit the head off the startlingly large grasshopper she held with a stomach-churning crunch. Allie grimaced. "Tic! That's disgusting!" she exclaimed. Tic didn't seem to care, happily taking another crunchy, but disgustingly juicy bite of the insect.

Well at least she was eating, Allie thought. Tic hadn't expressed much interest in their food on the trip. She knew Tic would eat fruit, though she was pretty picky about it, and she liked nuts only if they were raw and unsalted. Allie hadn't known the little jicund liked bugs though.

"Allie," Dav said, pulling her attention back to the water. She turned to look where he was pointing, and spotted it immediately. A divot was forming in the rippling surface, the current seeming to shift into a spiraling pattern around it as the bend in the water broadened.

Abruptly, the surface of the water seemed to fall away into the depths, leaving a large, oddly slow-moving whirlpool. Allie could see almost twenty feet down into the center, and it looked like nothing so much as a tunnel burrowing directly down into the water. It stopped growing when it was just about large enough to swallow a car width-wise.

Allie waited for something to emerge, but nothing seemed to happen. The whirlpool just sort of hung there in the ocean, encircling a large hole that vanished quickly into the depths of the ocean. She opened her mouth to say something, but of course at that very moment something appeared, interrupting her thoughts.

A faintly shimmering blue object seemed to surf rapidly up the side of the vortex, cresting the edge of the whirlpool and clearing a good ten feet of air before splashing down on the calmer waters outside the circle. Without slowing, it slid smoothly along the water toward them.

It was longer than their car was, and looked almost like an upside-down, silvery blue speedboat. It was hard to make out any more detail than that, as difficult as it was to see clearly on the water. If it weren't for the odd shimmer rippling across the liquid-smooth surface of the object, she suspected it would have been easier to see, but the shimmering perfectly matched the rippling moonlight on the surface of the water, creating a nearly-perfect camouflage. Allie focused on it, worried she might lose track of the strange craft if she glanced away for even a moment.

It reached the base of their short cliff, and a crease appeared along the outer rim, the top of the strange object rising smoothly up like a flip-top lid. Raith stood up from within and waved, the moonlight catching the silver scar on his face with a glint, giving him an appropriately otherworldly air.

Allie smiled and waved back as Raith gestured for them to come down. She glanced around, unsure how they would manage that. Dav turned toward her and smiled.

"Feeling adventurous today?" he asked with a mischievous grin. She eyed him nervously. When he grinned like that, it made her worry.

"Why?" she asked.

"Remember that promise you just had me make?" he asked.

"What?" Allie asked confused.

"Consider this fair warning," he replied with a wink, then turned and dove from the cliff in one smooth motion. Allie started to scream, but clamped her teeth shut in time for it to only come out sounding like a short yelp. She looked to Artus, but he just smiled and gestured her forward.

"After you," he said with mock-chivalry, sincerity betrayed by the glint of amusement in his eyes. She scowled back at him.

"You'd better be right behind me, making sure I don't get eaten by a shark," she retorted, looking down over the edge. It hadn't looked too far when she'd been standing up here looking out over the ocean, but it seemed taller than a skyscraper now that she knew she'd have to jump off of it.

She watched Dav easily climbing into the small ship below. He looked up and gestured her down. Come on Allie, you can do this, she told herself. You've Jumped across the galaxy, jumping twenty feet into an ocean won't kill you. Probably. Unless there really were sharks.

Allie took a deep breath, a step back, and then went for it. Allie threw herself out into empty air, fighting to control her impulse to scream. Barely containing her preciously-held breath, she tried to keep her feet pointed downward. Not as pretty as Dav's headlong dive, but as long as she didn't hit the water sidelong or face-first, she knew she'd be okay.

The water hit her feet harder than she'd expected, but not half as hard as the icy cold did. The chill cut through her clothes and skin like a razor blade, threatening to tear the air from her lungs.

Allie struggled to the surface once she felt her downward momentum run out. Several long seconds later, though it felt much longer, her head broke the surface. She released her breath and gasped, unable to stop her teeth from chattering the moment she stopped clenching them together.

She splashed about a bit before regaining her bearings and spotting the ship. Dav and Raith both leaned over the side, each with one arm out to help her in. They were about ten feet away, so she swam toward them as fast as she could, willing her frigid muscles to obey.

The moment she got within range, Dav and Raith each grabbed one of her arms, and lifted her into the boat so fast she was afraid she was going to be flung over the far side. As her body crossed the invisible threshold over the small ship, an odd sensation passed over her. It was like a faintly electric tingling across her entire body, like she was passing through an extremely low-voltage barrier.

When her feet touched down, she realized she wasn't cold anymore and that Dav was completely dry. Looking down at herself in surprise, she gasped in wonder at her suddenly dry clothes. Looking up at her friends, Dav and Raith grinned at her.

"Cool trick, huh?" Raith asked.

"I'll say," she agreed. "I could use one of those in the doorway to my shower." Raith chuckled, turning to help Artus in. Artus practically leapt out of the water and into the boat of his own accord, completely ignoring Raith's offer of help. Allie resolved to try and figure out what his problem was and get him to relax about Raith. Raith was as trustworthy as any of the others, and she had no doubts at all that he was a true friend to the group.

"Come on," Artus said a bit gruffly. "We should go. The longer we're on Earth, the more likely Tyren will find us." Raith rolled his eyes, or his good one at least, and moved to the front bench seat.

"What about…" Allie began, meaning to ask how Tic was getting down, then yelped as the little fur-ball came plummeting out of the sky, landing directly on the seat beside her with a thump. She took a steadying breath as Tic scurried to her shoulder. "Don't do that!" she admonished her furry friend. Tic chirped happily.

Dav sat in the back by his brother, and Allie moved to sit beside Raith. Looking around as the roof lowered over their heads, Allie was amazed. The outer surface was almost completely transparent, giving her an only slightly blue-tinted view of not only the sky above, but into the water below her feet. It had a pair of bench seats, like Artus' car, and a single control bar and display in front of Raith's seat. Raith took hold of the bar, and the ship spun about, gliding effortlessly and soundlessly, across the water.

Allie braced herself as they crested the lip of the whirlpool, the nose of the craft dropping abruptly. Oddly, she felt no movement at all. In fact, she would swear she wasn't moving at all, if she hadn't been able to see the water rushing past her.

The craft picked up speed, almost like it was surfing the spiral down the side of the swirling torrent of water. In seconds it had straightened out and was traveling far faster than any boat she'd ever heard of could possibly move, racing along the tunnel through the water like a bullet down the barrel of a gun. That image unnerved her somewhat, so she tried to push it out of her mind.

Allie was a bit disappointed that they were moving too quickly to really see much in the water outside. It was too dark to see much anyway, she knew. It would have been an incredible experience, watching as they surfed down a spiraling tunnel of water under the ocean in a transparent submarine.

Instead, all she saw was a rush of bluish gray, darkening quickly until she couldn't see anything at all, except the light from Raith's navigation display. The display gave off a warm blue light, casting an odd shadow across Raith's face, and Allie found herself studying his features.

He looked almost nothing like Dav, also handsome but in a more rakish, kind of mischievous way. Something about the tilt at the corner of his eyes and the quirk to his lips made it look like he was perpetually about to break into a conspiratorial grin.

His skin and hair were both darker than Dav's as well, but they both had deeply intense eyes that reflected a razor-sharp awareness and intelligence behind the boyish charm. Both of them looked at her like she meant something to them, like they cared not only about her safety, but her happiness as well. There was something absolutely enchanting about that, Allie thought.

He noticed her watching, and glanced over to smile at her. The blue light reflected off the silvery scar on the side of his face, sending a metallic gleam gliding across it, looking eerily like the outer surface of the water craft. She smiled back, again surprised slightly by the appearance of the scar, but even more by the fact that it didn't make him any less attractive to her. Quite the contrary, she again found herself admiring it.

It was probably strange how cute she thought he was, despite the knowledge that he was a machine. Dav said we all were though, just made of different materials. A person is a person, she supposed, it didn't really much matter how they were defined. Grown or constructed, either way Allie still thought Raith was incredibly attractive.

Dav cleared his throat loudly in the back seat, and Allie realized she was staring. She turned her eyes outward again, despite not being able to actually see anything.

Allie could tell that it bothered Dav that she was drawn to Raith, but she couldn't help it. It probably concerned him that she was attracted to an android. You can't pick who you think is cute, she thought defensively as though arguing with Dav out loud over it, it just happens. Her thoughts were interrupted by Raith's voice.

"We're here."

CHAPTER ONE

EYES ON IMBER

She looked forward to see where exactly they were, and froze in shock. Ahead of them was a light, a bright one that rapidly grew as they approached until it split apart into thousands of smaller lights stretching over what must be miles of ocean floor, framed by the faintly-illuminated walls of a colossal canyon they seemed to be traveling down.

Her mind began to wrap itself around what she was seeing and she suddenly realized it was a vast city, lit up and spread out before them like those helicopter tourist photographs she always saw on postcards in gas stations.

As they neared, she began to see more detail of the buildings, and noticed some distinct differences between those photographs and the city spread out below her. These buildings all seemed to shimmer, made of some highly reflective material, probably metallic she thought. None seemed to have windows either, though the most notable difference was the shape. Every building she could see was round, as spherical as beach balls, though they varied a great deal in size.

"Why are they all round?" she asked. Raith glanced over at her and smiled again, something intense in the gaze of his good eye making her blush.

"Most efficient shape," he told her. "Spheres have an amazing resistance to pressure. We are almost seven miles down after all. At an extra atmosphere of pressure every twelve feet, it sure adds up. Granted, the inside of their buildings are generally the same pressure as the outside and they come and go just like we do in our buildings, but the spheres withstand a lot of things better."

"That makes sense," Allie said, then paused. "Wait, if there's that much pressure down here, how are we going to survive?"

"Pressure suits," he replied. She wasn't sure that would be enough as she tried and failed to do the math in her head to figure out how many atmospheres of pressure they were under right then. Ahead of them, Raith followed the tunnel of water to a round port door in the side of one of the larger buildings.

As the port door opened with their approach, she realized that no water was passing through the doorway. The interior seemed completely empty of water. The little craft passed right through the invisible barrier though, and looking down she could see no trace of drops falling from the craft, or moisture beading on the outer shell at all. That really was a cool trick. The craft hovered in the air a moment before gently lowering to the floor.

The room was fairly large, a row of half a dozen heavy pressure suits lining one wall. As her eyes scanned them, it took her a moment to realize the suits were inhabited. The clear helmet faceplates showed faces peering out at her that were definitely familiar.

"Wait, are these Harelo's people?" she asked.

"The Uhran," Artus replied from behind her. "These are the people Harelo is imitating, yes."

"Why are they in suits? Harelo didn't wear one," she asked.

"They've lowered the pressure and oxygenated the room so that we can survive here without suits ourselves," Raith told her after a quick glance at the holographic display in the water craft. "They probably did it to the whole building, as a courtesy. It's difficult for them to adjust their bodies to live at an atmospheric pressure that's comfortable for us, though they can do it with enough time. Most of their people who live on other worlds do, unless there are oceans as deep as this one on the world they're inhabiting."

Allie nodded, looking around in amazement. The room itself was undecorated, with only a few racks against the far wall by the door. The gently curved walls were left bare, leaving the room looking like nothing so much as the inside of a giant soap bubble. The walls all around looked completely clear from the inside just like glass, though Allie knew it had to be something much stronger than that to withstand the pressure down here. They also shimmered faintly in rainbow hues as the light played across the curved surface just like a soap bubble. What really amazed her though was what was beyond the walls.

Allie could see the pathway between the buildings to the bubble across the way. You couldn't properly call it a street she thought, since there wasn't an actual road, just a narrow path between buildings that seemed to be a long garden row, with short, but colorful plants all along it marking the pathway.

She understood why it wasn't paved as she watched the people moving outside. They swam with a comfortable grace that she envied. She'd always felt a bit out of place in the water, though she could swim if she had to. These people glided almost effortlessly, their slow, gently arcing kicks sending them slipping through the water with deceptive speed.

Dancing between the moving people, she could see fish of countless varieties. Some swam alone, others in tight little schools that zipped and darted as if they were playing some lively game whose rules were known only to them. The lights of the city were a soft, but illuminating glow, colors seeming to slowly shift to an unheard rhythm. The lights brought out colors in the fish that would make any tropical fish collector envious.

Allie had no clue what kind of fish they were, nor did she particularly care. She was busy watching the people as her craft slowly lowered to the ground inside the bubble. They came in as many colors as the fish did, some mottled, some striped, some solid in hue. All were vibrant though. Allie was positively enchanted.

As the craft settled down, the lid lifted. Allie started. Although she knew they weren't about to be crushed under a flood of water she couldn't suppress a momentary surge of panic as the seal on the ship's hatch opened with a soft hiss. Artus chuckled behind her, patting her on the shoulder comfortingly.

Raith hopped out but Dav stood in the back, leaning forward to offer her a hand to brace on as she climbed out. It wasn't far to the ground, but she appreciated the thought as she took his hand and climbed out to the ground. His touch was warm, and he gave her a smile as she looked up at him.

Tic leaped easily down onto her shoulder with a chirp and a quick nuzzle to her cheek after she had both feet down. Allie scratched her under the chin, causing the jicund to trill softly.

Dav hopped out behind her, Raith and Artus moving with them toward the nose of the craft, where the welcoming party waited. The tall one in the middle spoke as they came to a stop in front of the line.

"Blessings of the Waters of Life to you, travelers," he said, his deep voice smooth and oddly liquid, like Harelo's had been. Allie realized the pressure suits they were must be filled with highly pressurized water. It was odd, and she couldn't but think of that as being backwards. It was normal to them though, she knew. He gave a short, half-bow. Allie, quite taken by everything going on, responded in kind, giving him a similar half-bow.

"And to you," she replied, shutting Artus' mouth as he'd been about to speak with an audible snap. He turned to stare at her. Dav and Raith were staring too. Dav leaned over and whispered sharply in her ear.

"When did you learn to speak Uhran?" he asked in

surprise. He wasn't as surprised as she was though.

"Uhran? I only speak English, and I'm only getting a B in that," she replied sarcastically, whispering back. They were interrupted by the tall Uhran.

"You honor and surprise me, young one," he said. "I am Volk, Priest of Scyan and leader of this humble city. Your android tells us that you are in need of a ship?" Artus got to speak uninterrupted this time, though Allie could see Raith's jaw tighten at Volk's words. Allie couldn't blame him. She'd be just as offended if someone had referred to her as Raith's human. Context really was everything.

"That is correct. We are willing to barter," Artus said. Volk nodded in reply.

"Of course," came the smooth reply from another Uhran beside Volk. "In a gesture of friendship and good trading, we offer a meal. I am Reyah, Keeper of the Hall. If you would follow?" Reyah gestured grandly toward the tunnel leading out of the bubble room. Artus gave the same tilted little half-bow she'd seen Volk perform, and the welcoming party turned and moved toward the tunnel.

Two of the six held back, taking up positions behind Dav and Allie as they walked in the back. Allie felt a little bit hemmed in, though as she thought about it the idea occurred to her that they were totally trapped down here anyway. These people didn't have to let them out if they didn't want to, and they wouldn't be able to do a thing about it. She was suddenly a bit nervous. The others seemed calm though, so Allie kept her worries to herself.

They walked down the cylindrical tunnel, made of

the same glass-like compound that let her look outside the building. Her nerves weren't helped at all as a pair of Uhran spotted them moving down the tunnel and came over, pointing and gawking. She leaned over to Dav.

"I've never been on the inside of a fishbowl before," she whispered. "I'll tell you one thing, I'll never own a fish again." He chuckled and nodded.

"It's a little weird," he agreed. "But not as weird as you speaking Uhran. How did you do that? And you did it with Sy'hli back on the station."

"I don't know," she said honestly. "I didn't even know I was doing it. It sounded like English to me. A man I met down on Ayaran told me I spoke perfect Ayaran too." A pang of bitter sadness reached her as she thought of Gheir.

"That's a little… creepy," he replied. She frowned at him.

"So it's not some magical Starjumper power?" she asked, that having been her first thought. He shook his head, though he smiled slightly at her use of her invented term.

"Not from what I've read," he told her. "As far as I know, all you Jumpers are supposed to be able to do is Jump."

"Maybe it's a superpower," she said with a grin. Dav gave her a wry look.

"As if being able to instantly teleport clear across the galaxy isn't enough. Careful, I may start to get jealous."

"Oh please," she retorted. "You're as strong as ten men, faster than Bruce Lee, and smarter than Einstein. I don't want to hear you criticizing my super powers.

Jumping and apparently speaking any language I want are all I've got, both completely useless in a fight."

Allie recognized a note of bitterness about that last point in her own tone, and made a mental note to keep that in check. She didn't want Dav to realize how much it bothered her that she had to rely on the three 'big strong men' to protect her in a fight. He just laughed lightly though.

"Being strong and fast aren't that useful outside of a fight, so we make a good team," he said, his old bright smile emerging for a moment. Allie smiled at that. He had a point. Still though, she'd have to figure out some way to be less of a burden to the guys. She hated fitting the stereotype of the helpless teenage girl so neatly.

The long tunnel turned sharply and branched a few times while she'd been talking with Dav, but the way wasn't complicated. She felt sure she could find her way back to the little craft in a pinch, though she sincerely hoped that wouldn't be necessary.

They entered another smaller bubble, though in this one the glass-like walls had a smoky quality, letting in light but not letting anything be clearly seen through it. For some reason this made her feel a little bit better, though she regretted the loss of ability to watch the fish and people outside.

In the middle of the room was a long table, with enough chairs around it to comfortably seat a dozen people. This bubble was just big enough to make a table that size feel like a proper fit.

The odd thing about the room wasn't the smoky walls though, it was a faint shimmer running down the center of the room, perfectly bisecting the table lengthwise, six chairs on either side. The near side of the subtle divider was just like the tunnel they'd just left, obviously depressurized and oxygenated. The other side was just as clearly filled with water. It was obviously intended for them to all sit and eat comfortably in their own environments, but the effect was a little bit eerie.

Reyah gestured for them to be seated on the air side of the table, while the six Uhran moved through the invisible barrier into the watery half of the room. The barrier rippled slightly as the six forms passed through it. Allie moved with her friends to their seats.

The Uhran didn't sit, they stood behind their chairs. Probably some formal manners thing she didn't understand, she thought. Artus, Dav and Raith didn't hesitate though, so Allie sat down with them. The table was set with intricately etched plates that shimmered like opal, and delicate two-tined golden forks, but no food was in evidence. The pattern on the plates was reminiscent of coral.

"Your pardon," Reyah said, pulling Allie's thoughts away from her examination of the unusual dishware. His voice had that liquid quality their people seemed to all possess, but it was even more pronounced travelling through the watery barrier. It definitely changed the sound. "We have with us other guests this day who have requested to join us. As negotiations will be taking place you have, of course, the right to refuse the courtesy." Dav and Raith both looked to Artus, who was already nodding.

"Of course," Artus said smoothly. "We would not

deny your gracious hospitality to others." This was clearly the correct answer, as the six all nodded happily and began removing their helmets. One of the six left the ground and swam off down another tunnel on the watery side of the room. Allie watched the remaining five, marveling that members of the same species could all be so diverse.

Each was a different color, one a faintly pastel purple, the next a vibrant blue with yellow streaks down each cheek, another was red and black like Harelo, only with the patterns reversed. One had a row of spines running up from the slit nostrils clear up along his head, another had fin-like ridges along the sides of his chin, another seemed as smooth and unadorned as a common serpent, though he had a striking green color to his scaly skin that added to his serpentine image.

Allie hadn't nearly finished her appreciation of each individual face when the sixth Uhran returned, followed by a pair of newcomers. As they neared, she was surprised by the human appearance of the two, though they swam in the water as smoothly as the Uhran, and wore no pressure suits. They reached the barrier and stepped through easily, emerging completely dry and with no apparent ill effects from the dramatic and abrupt change in pressure. On closer inspection, they didn't look human, she corrected herself.

The man looked to be older, maybe fifty she would have guessed, his hair a pale gray, face subtly wrinkled. His skin was a warm, untanned pink. He also had no ears. Or rather, where ears would have been on a human, a brown bony ridge grew, from the bottom corner of his jaw almost up to the back of the head. No hair grew over it, making his short hairstyle look decidedly odd to Allie.

His skin also bore what looked to be dark blue tattoos, gently arcing lines symmetrical on either side of his body, visible from his shoulders where they were visible from his tight blue sleeveless shirt and running down over the back of his hands, one long arc gracefully gliding around and onto his palms. They extended up onto his face as well, curving up and ending just at the outer corners of the eyes.

The girl beside him, about Allie's age she thought with surprise, had absolutely identical tattoos, right down to the many small swirls and branches. It looked much more elegant on the girl than the man, despite their identical patterns. They actually looked somewhat fierce on the man. The girl also had the bony plated ridge where her ears should have been, though her long, perfectly white hair covered it somewhat. She had the same strikingly violet eyes the man had as well.

As they moved forward, Allie noticed they both had webbed hands and feet, on which they wore no shoes, though the webbing was fairly subtle and didn't extend nearly to the ends of the digits. That explained their ease in the water, she thought. Allie wondered briefly if the bony ridges on the side of their heads were gills.

Glancing at Dav to make a whispered comment, she saw something in the way Dav was looking at the girl that made her shut her mouth in instant irritation. He was looking at the girl with clear and evident interest. She looked to her other side at Raith, and barely suppressed a groan. He was staring at the girl too.

Allie looked back at her. She was pretty, in a kind of down-home, country girl kind of way. The girl certainly wouldn't have made it as a model, despite the uniqueness of her hair and eye color, and the tattoos. Not that Allie was anywhere near that standard herself, but this girl was not even as slender as Allie was. She wasn't big either, but she definitely looked more solidly built than Allie did.

The girl smiled, and for a moment, Allie looked past her preconceived ideas and saw it. There was a warm openness to her smile, a bright, unmasked honesty in her eyes, and a cheerfulness to the way she moved that was positively endearing. Allie shook the thought off, irritated that both of the boys were clearly taken in by the phony smile. At least they didn't look like drooling idiots. They just looked... interested.

"Hullo!" the older man said brightly, with the same evident cheerfulness the girl had. As Artus, Dav, Raith, and Allie stood to make introductions, the man stopped before Artus with an expression of surprise, and then bowed deeply. "Your Highness! I certainly didn't expect to find you here!"

All four of them froze. Artus looked confused and startled, almost like a deer in the headlights. A faint trace of panic was in his voice as he replied.

"I..." Artus cleared his throat awkwardly. "I'm sorry, do I know you?"

"You likely don't remember me, Your Highness," the man began. Artus interrupted him.

"Please don't call me that. Artus will do." The man raised a brow at this, but nodded.

"Artus it is then, as you wish it," the man continued. Something about his accent was odd and nagged at Allie's mind. He spoke clearly, and enunciated a little too carefully, but something about it was off. It sounded familiar too, though she couldn't quite place it. "As I was saying, you likely don't remember me, as we've not crossed paths in nearly twenty years. I am Ambassador Lase. I visited your father at Council. You were much younger then of course, but I'd recognize that family face anywhere." He looked to Dav and bowed again. "And Your Highness, you were not yet even born, though news of your birth, and subsequent death, reached us shortly after the fact. It is an honor to meet you, and a great pleasure to find you both alive and apparently quite well."

"Dav," Dav corrected, looking distinctly uncomfortable. The man bowed again in acknowledgement. Allie looked at Dav, processing this. Your Highness, the ambassador had called him. She had caught that Tyren was their brother, but it somehow hadn't really clicked that they were the royal family at the time. Outside of Earth, her best friend was probably considered what, a prince?

"Dav then. And this," he enthusiastically continued, "is my niece Imber." She gave another warm smile and bowed deeply.

"Your Highness," she said, clearly addressing both men at once.

"Oh, stop that," Allie snapped, more harshly than she'd intended. It was really freaking her out seeing Dav and Artus treated like royalty. She understood that technically they were, but it was still weird. They were just Dav and Artus, no more, no less. Although she'd had to adjust that definition once already after learning they weren't actually human. The girl looked a little bit hurt.

"Dav and Artus, I mean. I'm sorry," Imber replied. She had the same odd accent her uncle did, Allie noticed. Its familiarity was tugging at the back of her mind, obnoxiously occupying much of her thoughts. Dav stepped forward and held a hand out to Imber. She reached up and took it. Dav didn't really shake it, more just sort of squeezed it.

"It's a pleasure, Imber. And you, Ambassador," Dav added to the man. "These are our friends, Raith and Allie," he said, indicating the pair respectively. Both got polite nods of acknowledgement from man and girl alike. "Join us, won't you?" He gestured to the two remaining seats on the air-filled side of the table, holding one out for Imber. She smiled her thanks, sliding into the seat.

Allie clenched her jaw. Dav had never once, in all the time she'd known him, held a seat for her. She told herself she didn't like being coddled like that anyway, and this was obviously a diplomatic situation, but it still bothered her. She sat back down, Tic chirping contentedly from her shoulder. Imber was looking at her, she realized. As soon as Allie made eye contact, the girl smiled.

"I'm sorry to have to ask, but what species is your pet there?" Imber asked her. "I've never seen anything quite like it."

"She's a jicund, from Ayaran," Allie replied with a smile, shoving her irritation down. This girl hadn't done anything to deserve it, and she was being perfectly friendly. "Her name is Tic. She's not a pet though, just a friend."

Imber was obviously quite taken with Tic, leaning across Dav and reaching a hand toward the jicund. Allie opened her mouth to warn against the action, but Tic leaned forward, trilling contentedly, into Imber's touch. Imber stroked Tic's fur with obvious enjoyment.

"She's beautiful, Allie," Imber said with another warm smile to Allie. Allie couldn't decide if she liked the girl or hated her. It was hard not to be taken in by the sincerity and ease of her smile.

"Thank you," was all Allie could say. Imber's gaze fell on Raith, and she seemed to study his face for the first time. Allie knew she was looking at the silver scar running across his eye. Here it came, Allie thought, the careless remark about androids that would offend Raith.

"You're a Theta, aren't you," Imber stated simply, rather than asked. Raith blinked in surprise.

"Yes, I am," he replied. Her smile broadened.

"Most intricate android ever created. I heard you'd all been decommissioned and recycled after the Infection," she told him. "Even if they hadn't been, you shouldn't have made it this long on your power cells." Raith's smile turned faintly smug.

"I shielded myself from the Infection. And rewired my power core," he said. Her smile became an expression of awe and amazement.

"You rewired..." she paused and shook her head in awe. "Incredible. You must be a very strong-willed person. I can't imagine anyone managing something like that. Even just the logistics of preventing a burnout while rewiring are... staggering." Raith's expression positively glowed as she used the word 'person'.

"Thanks, but I don't think it was that big a deal," he said. Imber glanced at Allie and Raith, looking a little embarrassed, and sat back. Ambassador Lase laughed.

"You'll have to forgive my niece," he said. "She has been absolutely fascinated with the field of android science and artificial intelligence since she was little, despite almost all of the androids breaking down after the Infection, and most of the rest recycled to prevent further... mishaps. We visited a museum on Pahrvic once. She spent all day in the android exhibit, talking to supposedly the last working Beta unit in the galaxy." He leaned conspiratorially forward and winked at Raith. "Thetas are her favorite." Raith grinned at the man, obviously quite flattered.

"She has good taste," he replied. Imber laughed, along with her uncle. Allie bit back another surge of irritation.

"I am glad everyone is getting along so well," Volk said happily, "but I am afraid I must interrupt. Our meal arrives." Everyone looked toward the tunnel, but Allie noticed that Dav and Raith both turned back to look at Imber after glancing toward the tunnel. She glared at the girl. That decides it, she thought, I hate her. This was going to be a long negotiation.

CHAPTER TWO

LEAVING EARTH BEHIND

"Ah yes, I believe we do have a ship that will meet your need for haste," Volk said with a nod before slurping in another mouthful of something long and skinny. Despite most of the dishes looking questionable, and being made mostly of seaweeds and various forms of fish and mollusks, Allie had to admit the flavors were all absolutely wonderful.

"Excellent," Artus replied. "Is the vessel available immediately? We need to depart very soon on a time-sensitive mission, I'm afraid."

"Of course, of course," Volk answered. "Do not worry, you may leave as soon as negotiations are concluded and payment has been made, though you are of course welcome to remain under our hospitality for as long as you like."

"Your offer?" Artus asked.

"Seventeen thousand keros," Volk said simply.

Artus nearly choked on a mouthful of something blue and leafy.

"Seventeen..." Artus began, before composing himself. He coughed as he cleared his throat. Allie noticed Ambassador Lase trying to hide a smile and knew Artus had just given something important away. "We can offer you five thousand. Half now, half on our return." Volk was shaking his head before Artus finished speaking.

"No, that is impossible. The ship is worth four times that at the very least. We offer a discount only because of our excellent political relations. And we cannot accept partial payment. All due respect Artus, but the likelihood of you ever returning from your probable mission is... limited."

"What are you implying, Volk?" Artus said, his tone taking on a dangerous edge. Reyah held up both webbed hands in a calming gesture.

"He meant no offense, Artus," Reyah replied. "Simply that your very existence tells us much of your mission. You were thought killed by your... by Highlord Tyren. since you survive, you can only mean to depose him. Surviving that kind of mission will be problematic, to say the least." Artus relaxed somewhat, though not completely. Allie could tell his pride had been slightly hurt at their lack of belief in his ability to face his brother and walk away from it.

"I understand your point," he said grudgingly. "It is perhaps poor negotiation to admit this, but our problem is that we have only three thousand keros." The complete and abrupt silence from the other side of the table felt heavy and tense.

"If you have only three thousand," Volk said in a carefully controlled tone, "why have you even bothered to come to us?" Allie was aware of the tension building. She got the distinct impression that the Uhran were insulted. Artus looked sheepish.

"We had no alternatives," Dav interjected. "We are stranded on this world without a ship. You were the only ones who might even have been remotely friendly to our cause and willing to help. We will gladly give you every kero we have, and will freely offer five times the value of the ship after our mission is complete. Your own people are being oppressed by that usurper as well, Volk. Our mission serves all the good people of the galaxy."

"I am sorry," Volk said, sounding somewhat less offended though he was still a bit stiff. "We cannot afford to become involved in this war. We came here to establish a peaceful colony. A fair trade is perhaps one thing, but practically giving you a ship for use in causing difficulties for the Highlord might well turn his angry eye our way. For the sake of our people, we cannot risk that."

"We could help pay," Imber said from the side, causing every head to turn her way in surprise. Ambassador Lase turned a scowl her way, quickly placing a hand upon hers. Instead of the expected meaningful look, the patterns of elegant lines along his face and arms began shifting colors, faintly luminescent. They flickered rapidly and smoothly, each color seeming to roll across the lines rather than a uniform change. The resulting effect was one of a flowing rainbow rippling across the man's skin. Imber's lines began to change colors as well, each pausing as the other took a turn with the seemingly random color patterns.

They were communicating, Allie realized with complete astonishment. After several moments of this, Ambassador Lase sighed, flickered through the rainbow's array of colors again, then turned away. Imber turned back to the rest of the group with a triumphant smile.

"My uncle has generously offered to pay you the entire seventeen thousand of your original offer, under one condition," Imber said to Volk. Everyone was still as they waited for her to lay her terrible condition down. "The princes and their company will escort me, on their own new vessel, to Kobek." The silence and staring continued. Allie was horrified. They were going to have to spend days, maybe weeks traveling with this girl?

"I'm sorry, what?" Artus asked, either unaware or unconcerned with how foolish it made him sound.

"We pay for the ship, you take me to Kobek. Simple enough, right?" Imber replied with a playful smile, obviously pleased with the reaction her declaration had gotten.

"I..." Artus seemed to be having trouble finding words. "I believe this arrangement is agreeable, under the added condition that our delivering you to Kobek will take place after our immediate mission."

"Is that before, or after you try to take on your brother?" Ambassador Lase interjected wryly.

"Before," Artus said with a small, but tense smile. "We have to connect with someone first. Then we take your niece to Kobek, and go about our own business. Are we agreed?"

Allie couldn't help but smile at the way Artus managed to take a ridiculously unbelievable offer from someone else and turn it around to make it sound like it was his own idea to begin with. The Ambassador hesitated, then nodded.

"We are agreed. Do the Uhran agree?" Ambassador Lase asked, turning to Volk. Volk and the Uhran were nodding, obviously pleased at having gotten their first, clearly overpriced offer agreed to so easily.

"We are agreed," Volk said solemnly. "The deal is struck. After our meal, we shall escort you to your ship, since you intend to leave promptly. Ambassador, you can arrange payment at your leisure, as you will not be leaving for some time yet, correct?" The Ambassador nodded his agreement. "Then it is settled, and just in time for dessert!" Volk smiled broadly, revealing numerous surprisingly sharp, tiny teeth.

Another server came in with a tray of small, golden dishes. As one was placed before her, Allie was pleased to see that it looked like perfectly ordinary ice cream. What flavor it was she wasn't sure, though it might possibly be mint, based on the color. She took a small bite. Nope, she corrected herself, more seaweed. Like the rest of the food however, it was still surprisingly good.

Tic chirped as Allie handed her another leftover shrimp from her plate. Tic absolutely adored the shrimp, to Allie's surprise. She was beginning to suspect most of Tic's natural diet was insect in nature, which might make things a bit complicated during a long space voyage.

A smile touched her lips as she realized how casually that thought had crossed her mind. A week ago she'd been contemplating her impending less-than-stellar report card. Now she was contemplating where she'd find enough insects to feed her little alien friend on a long interstellar voyage. Oh, how her world had expanded. She realized Dav and Imber were talking, and had been for some time.

"...the Resistance on Kobek," Dav was saying. "It's interesting that you wanted to be taken there, since we were heading there anyway after picking up our other passenger." Other passenger? What was he telling her about, Allie wondered? The girl didn't need to know all of this. Imber just smiled.

"That's why I need to go there as well. My uncle wants to keep connected with the efforts of the Resistance, to better help coordinate when the fighting starts."

"You expect fighting to start soon?" Dav asked.

"Very soon," she replied. "They've been preparing something big for years, though we're not sure what. Our few contacts haven't been able to get much information to us. Tyren's spy network is too tight, so the informants have to be very careful." Dav nodded.

"That makes sense. Are your people prepared to help?" Dav asked her. She hesitated.

"Many of them are. Not all. Some of our people have sided with Tyren."

"I think most races are that way," Raith commented, having clearly also been listening. "The past ten years the chatter on all frequencies has been pretty divided. Even with everything Tyren has done to hurt the people, many still support him. I guess that's how it always is. The cruel stay in power because there are many other cruel people, and the good people fear them and do nothing. I expect when the fighting starts, it's going to get very ugly, very quickly."

"War is never pretty," Ambassador Lase interjected. "War brings violence. Violence brings pain and sorrow. A stable government is worth the fight, however. The people need to be cared for." Silence reigned as everyone thought about this.

"Well," Imber interrupted, "I suppose I'd better go get my things."

"Do you need a hand?" Raith asked. Imber smiled warmly at him.

"No, thank you Raith. I don't have much to gather, and it won't take me long. I'll meet you all at the docking bay."

As everyone had finished their dessert, Volk and the Uhran stood and placed their helmets back on. Volk pressed a few keys on a wrist pad on his pressure suit, and the shimmering barrier across the middle of the room shifted, opening another tunnel to the air-breathers. The Uhran led the way, again with two of them lagging behind to take up the rear, heading further into the maze of bubbles and tunnels.

It took several minutes to reach their destination, Volk shifting the water barrier as needed to allow them to pass with quick touches to his wristpad. Allie couldn't help but nervously wonder what would happen if he accidentally pressed the wrong button.

By the time they reached the docking bay, Allie had become convinced that these buildings were the aquatic equivalent of an insanely large hamster maze, moving through tunnel after tunnel, in and out of giant bubble rooms. She half expected the docking bay to contain an oversized hamster wheel. It didn't, but what it did contain was decidedly more impressive.

A vast array of ships and craft lined the outer edge of the immense bubble, which seemed to have no actual wall on the lower half on the far side of the room, just that invisible water shield. The craft were as diverse as the Uhran themselves were, though they all shared one common factor; every ship looked incredibly aerodynamic. Or aquadynamic, she thought to herself. They were all sleek and slender, with very few jutting parts. Many had quite a few fins and rudders, while others were as simple in design as torpedoes.

The craft they were heading for was large, bigger than some large houses, and was possibly the most aggressive looking ship she'd ever seen. Its entire structure seemed comprised of sleek, mirrored surfaces and smooth, razor-sharp edges. It looked like it could probably sliced through a brick wall if it flew into one. What it would do passing through simple air, she could only imagine.

The wings and tail had been equipped with glistening, silver turrets that were very obviously weapons. She glanced at Dav, and couldn't help but laugh at the eager grin on his face. He looked like a six year old given a fistful of money and set loose in a candy store. He looked her way at the sound, and gave her an embarrassed smile.

"Sorry. I've just never seen anything like this beauty," he said before turning back to the ship. "It's incredible. How fast will she go?" he asked the Uhran walking just ahead of him. Allie had never caught this one's name. The purple-scaled Uhran smiled at him through the faceplate of the helmet.

"This one? She's an Interceptor," the Uhran said casually, as if the name was descriptive enough. It meant nothing to Allie, but Dav's face lit up even more. He gave a dark, eager chuckle under his breath. It was a very ominous sound. Allie took a moment considering whether she should be excited for him, or worried for herself. Both, she decided.

Beneath the large craft, a hatch was open, with a walkway extending down to ground level. The bottom of the ship sat above her head height, though it didn't seem to have landing gear at all. It just sort of hovered there, as stable as if it sat on solid ground. It made no sound, and didn't even stir the air. Allie had no idea how it just floated there. She didn't understand really any of the technology beyond her own planet's though.

We are on my own planet, she reminded herself, shaking her head. It would take some time before she really came to grips with how different things were than she'd always been taught. Even her own familiar planet had become a whole different world than the one she'd grown up in.

Volk went up the ramp without pause, though the other Uhran stepped out of the way and waited at the base. The rest of the group moved up behind Volk. The interior of the ship looked just as sleek as the outside did. Every line was razor sharp, and joined at steep angles. The material was unfamiliar to Allie, the walls a pale gray, the floors a darker gray. Both glistened like polished steel. She was a little worried about traction on the smooth floor, but her feet felt like they gripped just fine despite the polish.

Everything looked impeccably clean and well maintained. Volk was giving a tour ahead, so she focused on what he was saying. There might be something she'd need to know in there.

"...have the cargo bay," he was saying. "It's not large, but should be sufficient for a group your size. We have a few of our people bringing some basic supplies for you, enough to get you to Kobek at the very least." They moved through an archway and Volk continued. "There are two sleeping compartments, with three bunks in each. The galley is through that archway there, a personal hygiene room across there, and the cockpit is just through there."

As they made their way into the cockpit, Dav immediately slipped past Volk and into the pilot's chair up front.

"Perhaps," Volk said as tactfully as he could manage, "you should leave that to your elder brother." Dav turned an offended look on the man, and Artus laughed.

"Not a chance, Volk. Dav is ten times the pilot I am," Artus told Volk sincerely. "Ten times the pilot anyone is, as far as I've seen. That kid could thread a needle with a string attached to the nose of this craft at nearly light speed if he got it in his head to try." He pointed a finger at Dav. "Don't try it." Dav laughed and turned to the controls. Volk simply half-bowed and stepped back.

Dav placed his hand on the control bar, activating the console. The holographic display slid up in front of him without a flicker, smooth as silk. Allie could feel his excitement from clear back by the doorway. Images and data began racing across the screen as Dav learned the technical specifications of the craft, flashing past far too fast for Allie to make any sense of. She shook her head and looked around.

Raith sat in a seat to one side, probably the gunner's chair, Allie guessed. There were five seats total in the cockpit, which she thought was interesting since the ship had six bunks. It had a galley though, so probably one of the crew was supposed to be the cook. That would probably end up being her, she thought sourly.

Two of the seats faced forward, toward a large window across the front of the cabin. Odd, since she had seen no windows on the outside of the craft. Not a single one. The window spanned the entire front of the cockpit and arcing around the sides, giving an exceptional view in every direction but back and down. The two seats facing forward were presumably for the pilot and navigator, since Dav had claimed one of them.

To the side sat Raith, in what she'd already assumed to be the gunner's chair. Another one sat beside it, though Allie wasn't sure of its intended use. On the opposite side was a single chair, with two control bars. She had no idea at all what that one was for. As Volk chatted with Artus, discussing some of the finer features of the craft, Allie moved over to Raith and sat beside him.

"Is this seat okay for me?" she asked. Raith gave her a warm smile.

"It certainly is. Best seat on the ship," he replied. She looked at the station in front of it and frowned.

"This one is?" she asked, confused.

"Well, whichever one next to me is, anyway," he replied with a wink of his good eye and a mischievous grin. Allie laughed and gave him a playful shove. He laughed as well.

"You're terrible," she told him as she turned toward her own console, but didn't mean it at all. She was glad to be getting a bit of attention from him, after the meal with Imber. Allie had been almost completely ignored the entire time. "What is this station for?"

"Scanners," he told her. "You can technically access any function from any console, but putting scanners next to weapons makes sense, just like putting navigator and pilot up front makes sense. More efficient. If you want to keep that post, all you have to do is monitor scanners. Just like you did while we were escaping Ayaran. Simpler though, as long as we don't get into a firefight. Go ahead, load it up."

Allie put her hand on the control bar, the interface immediately picking up her touch and activating the console. Several small windows adorned the holographic screen that slid up, one of them showing a semicircle of markers, each with a small code above it. As she focused on it, it enlarged to fit her screen. Raith was nodding approvingly.

"Nice work. You're a quick study. That's your short

range. You can see every ship within about three hundred yards of here on that screen, and can even identify them. See?"

He pointed to the codes above each. All she had to do was focus on one, and despite the letters and numbers not being in English, their meaning flooded into her mind. She noticed their own ship and smiled.

"This ship is named the Peacekeeper," she told Raith. He raised a brow.

"You read Uhran too?" he asked, surprised. She shrugged.

"Apparently."

"There's something different about you, Allie Bennett. Something very different." Raith smiled as he said it, but she could tell that beneath the smile he was trying to work out exactly how and why she was different.

"Is that like saying 'You're not like other girls'?" she asked with a playful smile.

"Something like that, yeah," Raith laughed.

"Hello?" came a voice from outside the cockpit, down the hallway. Allie sighed. Here comes trouble, she thought.

Imber walked in a moment later. Dav and Raith both turned and smiled at her. Artus and Volk kept up their conversation without pausing to look her way. Allie turned resolutely back to her screen.

The display shifted as she experimented with the sensor controls. She was determined to be good at this, knowing it was her only way to contribute if they actually did get into a firefight. Imber moved to the seat on the opposite side of the cabin.

"This seat for me?" she asked.

"If you want it," Dav replied. Allie refused to look around, focusing harder on her display. "Are you familiar with ship systems?"

"A little," Imber replied. "This is the systems monitoring and com station, right?"

"That's right," Dav said. Allie could hear that he was a little bit impressed.

"Are you piloting?" she asked, sounding genuinely interested. Dav's voice reflected his pride as he answered.

"I certainly am."

"You must be really good, if Artus lets you fly instead of him," Imber replied.

"He says I'm better than anyone he's ever seen," Dav said. "I don't think I believe him, but I am pretty good."

"Well, give me a couple of days flying with you, and I'll let you know my opinion," Imber told him with a light laugh. It was a very nice laugh. Allie hated it. Dav laughed too.

"Please do. An artist should always be open to feedback," he told her.

"If everyone has decided where they're sitting," Artus interrupted, "we should get going. Volk says his men are finished loading our supplies."

"Did they bring a crafter?" Dav asked.

"Of course," Volk replied with a smile. "Full raw material tanks, for whatever you may need." Allie glanced back, and caught Dav's grin.

"Good. We need new flight suits," Artus said. "Volk,

thank you for your hospitality, and your generosity. When we have reclaimed the Sy'hli throne, your people will be rewarded." Volk waved him off.

"Not at all, not at all. It was a good bargain," the Uhran replied. "Good journey, and may you be blessed by the Waters of Life."

Volk bowed, and Artus returned the gesture. The Uhran moved out of the cockpit. Allie focused on her display, and with pleasure noted that she could track his movement toward the back, and then off the ship.

A faint hum told her the walkway was retracting, the hatch closing seamlessly behind it. The hum grew only a few decibels as the engines came to life. After a few seconds, Allie had already tuned the soft, almost imperceptible hum out of her mind.

She turned in her chair to look toward the front window, watching as the craft slid forward effortlessly through the air, and passed through the barrier into the water beyond. The craft smoothly rose and turned, until it was moving straight up. It was an odd thing to be watching out a window moving straight upward as you stayed comfortably seated, feeling every bit as if the floor was still down.

The craft accelerated. Allie could tell not by the view out the window, which rapidly became nothing but blackness as they turned away from the city's lights, but by her scanner display's easy speed readout.

Allie watched the indicators of the other ships and the holographic outlines of all the buildings move beyond the range of the short-range scanners, and mentally switched the system into the long range display. A whole range of interesting things appeared as the long range sensor display enlarged in the center of her holoscreen.

She could still see the city behind them, but could also track individual fish moving in the darkness if she focused on them. Not as many as she'd expected, but from what she'd learned in science classes, not many creatures actually lived this deep. There were a few she could see though, and some of them pretty big. Not as big as the new ship so she wasn't too worried, but still pretty big.

One of them moved toward them, moving almost as if it were curious. She wasn't sure how it kept up, but it didn't seem to have trouble. Allie opened her mouth to comment, unsure if she should be concerned, but just before touching the craft, the big fish turned and moved quickly away the direction it had come. She closed her mouth. Probably scared the thing away once it realized they weren't another fish, she thought.

The Peacekeeper continued to gain speed, cutting through the water like it wasn't even there. It took only another minute to reach the surface, seven miles up. They breached the surface and shot into the sky. Allie couldn't even feel the transition, and only knew they had left the water because she could now clearly see the stars through the front, and because her scanners told her they had.

Once in the air their speed increased dramatically, leaving atmosphere in less than thirty seconds. Allie watched the velocity readout climb rapidly and glanced Dav's way. He was leaning slightly forward, hand on the control bar, a big smile on his face. He was going to really open this thing up, she knew. He wanted to know what it could do, and she knew full well he wasn't going to waste this chance.

Their speed continued to rise, so fast she couldn't keep track of the velocity readout anymore, the ship cutting through empty space faster than she ever would have thought possible, or could even wrap her mind around. Dav and Artus exchanged a few words in technical jargon that she didn't understand.

The hum changed pitch slightly, catching Allie's attention. She turned back to her display, which told her that the phase drive had just been activated, whatever that meant. The velocity readout switched to a completely different system of measurement, moving so fast that a new system was needed to keep track of it.

In less than five minutes, they were out of the solar system and moving far faster than light, totally unaware of the much smaller, technologically invisible craft attached to the underbelly of the Peacekeeper. Within the confines of the small craft, no bigger than a small electric car, C.A.D.E-16 patiently waited.

CHAPTER THREE

FLIGHT TRAINING

The next morning, Allie awoke before anyone else. They had been traveling all night, Raith manning the systems since he didn't need to sleep. He'd done that while they traveled to the coast too, driving all night long. Plenty of jokes about the 'under-aged driver' had been tossed around, but he was a safer driver than any on Earth and was more than qualified.

Allie had been tossing and turning all night with nightmares of swarms of Maruck chasing her and found herself really envying Raith's ability to operate without any sleep at all.

She rubbed her eyes and glanced around the dark room. A very faint glow came from the joint where the ceiling and walls met, though so faintly that it served only to give her a basic view of the room, everything in degrees of shadow. Better than nothing, she thought as she hopped down from her bunk above Imber's.

Allie had been irritated at having to share a room with Imber, but she couldn't actually identify anything specific Imber had done to annoy her. Imber had been very friendly, as usual, and had given Allie her quiet when it became clear the Allie didn't really want to talk as they prepared for bed.

She knew she didn't really have a rational reason to dislike Imber, in fact she had to work hard to keep from liking her a great deal. There was something inherently sweet and open about her that was almost irresistible. Which, Allie knew, was part of the problem. Just the way Dav and Raith had said good night to Imber set her teeth on edge, though she couldn't quite define what had been different about how they'd said goodnight to her, either.

Moving to the bathroom across the hall, she smiled slightly at the smooth, silent, and automatic operation of the doors. The bathroom was small, though looked comfortable, complete with a small shower in one corner. She'd have to try that out a little later. For the moment, she just needed some cold water to wash the sweat off her face.

Allie touched the small silver tab on the counter beside the sink. It was going to take some getting used to, everything operating by connecting to her thoughts. Even the temperature and flow of the water was controlled by her thinking about what she wanted.

She made the water cold without being bracing, and splashed a few handfuls over her face. The temperature was perfect. The control technology might be strange, but she couldn't deny its convenience. It was actually pretty cool, just different from what she was used to.

Toweling her face dry with the incredibly soft towel from the small shelf beside her, she felt a little better. Placing the towel back on the shelf, a shimmer of light flickered across the shelf in a strange field of energy. A moment later, the light faded, leaving behind a nice, new, perfectly folded towel. Now that was weird, she thought.

On impulse, she grabbed the new towel. It was just as soft as the last had been, and perfectly dry. She wet it slightly under the faucet, and put it back on the shelf. Sure enough, the light grew in a small field over the shelf and faded a moment later leaving a perfectly dry and neatly folded towel. She grabbed this one too, and rather than wetting it, just dropped it back on the shelf in a heap. The light came and went, leaving another neatly folded towel.

Allie giggled. She made a mental note to ask someone about that later. Was it a new towel every time, or was it somehow cleaning, drying, and folding the same towel every time in less than a second? Either way, it was very cool.

Leaving the bathroom, she turned down the hallway. She considered stepping into the galley for a snack, but decided against it. She wasn't actually sure what time it was, but suspected that breakfast wasn't too far off. One thing she was going to have to get used to was the method of time-keeping that was apparently the standard in space.

Not only were the measurement systems used out here totally unfamiliar, but Dav had told her that in this system, one day translated into exactly twenty six hours, seven minutes, and forty one seconds in Earth time. He said most species of man across the galaxy naturally regulated at between twenty one and thirty hours when not forced to an artificial clock.

Even humans from Earth had been calculated to have a twenty five hour and eleven minute natural internal clock on average. Dav had also told her that a lot of the sleep issues humans on Earth had were a result of their forcing their bodies out of sync with their natural rhythms to accommodate the cycles of the planet's sun.

As a result of things like that, galactic standard time-keeping had been set to the average of all known space-faring species, to try and minimize the adjustment for each individual race. It made sense, although while two hours of difference from her usual schedule might not seem like much, it felt huge and she was having definite problems adjusting.

Dav and Artus had made her start following that schedule since they left her house a few days ago, to try and get her used to it before it became critically necessary. That meant an easier transition, they told her. Whatever else it meant, it meant she was tired. Her sleep cycles still hadn't adjusted.

Allie moved into the cockpit where Raith sat by himself at the pilot's station. Raith looked back at her as she came in, and smiled. It was a warm smile, which made her feel even better.

"Good morning, Allie," he said, gesturing her toward the navigator's chair. She smiled back and took the seat, rotating the chair to face him.

"Hi, Raith," she replied, "what time is it?"

"Just after seven," he answered. Allie knew he meant

seven o'clock in galactic time, not Earth time.

After a moment, she corrected herself. It was always the seventh hour somewhere on Earth. That was another thing to adjust mentally, Earth time was relative to location. In space, with the galactic standard time-keeping, it wasn't. It was seven o'clock everywhere in space at that moment. Now that was weird to think about.

Dav said people generally just adjusted to local time-keeping when on a planet for any length of time, but in space the time measurement was constant. Raith spoke again, thankfully breaking her out of her sleep-muddled thoughts.

"Did you sleep okay?" The question was casual, but Allie could hear a note of concern and looked at him.

"Why, do I look terrible?" Allie realized she had just rolled out of bed and probably looked a total wreck. She self-consciously reached up to try and fix her hair. Raith grinned at her, the kind of charming grin that completely killed her embarrassment. That was something she really liked about Raith; he was so relaxed about everything it was hard not to be at ease with him.

"Not a bit," he replied, his grin turning slightly flirtatious. "Actually you look lovely, as usual. Your eyes look a little red though, like you didn't get enough sleep."

"I didn't," she admitted.

"Bad dreams?" he asked, smile replaced by the look of concern again. No point in lying about it, she thought.

"Yeah, it was the Maruck again." Raith nodded sympathetically.

"I'm sorry." He reached over and put a hand on hers

where it rested on the armrest of the chair for a moment. She appreciated the gesture, and once again was slightly surprised that he felt warm and soft.

The silver scar across his left eye reminded her sharply that he was a machine, though in everything other than her repeated surprise at his warmth she still had trouble thinking of him that way.

Which was fine, he definitely preferred being thought of as human. Kind of a Pinocchio complex, she thought with a small smile. Raith smiled back at her. He had a great smile, she thought for the thousandth time.

"It's okay, they're not too bad. More frustrating than anything else. Keeps me from sleeping very long at a stretch."

"Glad to hear it. Hey, I wanted to get the crafter working on a few things we may need later. Do you want to drive for a minute?" he asked, changing the subject suddenly. She blinked, not sure how to respond to that.

"You want me to take control of a faster-than-light, heavily armed space craft that cost us thousands of keros?" she asked, trying to picture herself at the helm. He laughed again.

"No, I want you to take control of a faster-than-light, heavily armed space craft that cost Imber thousands of keros." Raith winked at her. Allie laughed in surprise, though she was really just surprised that Raith had noticed how she felt about Imber.

It shouldn't have, she realized, Raith was an android. He probably not only saw, heard, and remembered everything she did or said to the smallest detail, he probably also did things like register her heart rate and body temperature when he looked at her. He probably knew how everyone felt about everyone, whether they showed it outwardly or not. She'd have to ask him sometime, when it wasn't directly related to him tracking her own feelings about Imber... and maybe himself.

"I don't know, doesn't this thing have autopilot?" she asked.

"Sure, but where's the fun in that? It's easy, I'll show you," he said reassuringly. "Besides, we're at least two hours at maximum velocity from absolutely anything. I could let you fly at least that long without any fear of you hitting anything. I think we'll survive for a few minutes." He grinned again, emphasizing his complete lack of concern. Why not, she thought?

"Okay, let's give it a try," she said. Raith's grin turned triumphant. Allie turned toward the control bars, but Raith stopped her.

"No, no," he said, standing up and gesturing toward the pilot's station.

"Can't I pilot from anywhere?" she asked. He shrugged.

"Well yeah, but if you're going to drive, you might as well do it from the pilot's seat, right?"

Allie didn't think it really mattered, but the thought of sitting in the pilot's seat really did feel more like she was totally in control of the ship. Allie smiled slowly, excitement growing.

Standing, she moved to the pilot's seat and sat back down. It did feel different here, though the seat and control bars were exactly the same. She reached out and took hold of the control bars.

"Okay, now first things first," he began, leaning down over her shoulder to better see her holographic screen. "Steering at this speed is as simple as thinking where you want to go. For some people it helps to lean, makes concentrating on direction easier, though it isn't necessary. Go ahead and turn us a little bit right, and up. In space there isn't really an 'up', I just mean relative to us. We'll talk about X, Y, and Z axis another time. That's navigator stuff, right?" He smiled, turning to look at her.

Allie smiled back, suddenly quite aware how close he was. He had no scent, she realized with surprise. No smell on his breath, no smell from his skin, just no smell at all. She could smell the fabric of his clean jumpsuit, but that was all. It was a little bit odd.

It didn't stop her heart from fluttering at him being so close though. He really was gorgeous. At least by her sense of such things, since she knew such things were completely subjective. From his tanned skin tone to his perfect, soft-looking black hair, right down to his silver scar however, it all worked for him. She stopped herself just before reaching up to touch his perfect hair.

"Right," she replied, forcing her attention back to the screen.

"For now, just turn us a little bit right and up. Think gently, this baby can corner on a dime at better than light speed. Thank goodness for inertial dampeners and phase drives. Go ahead and turn."

Allie nodded and focused on her display. The bottom corners showed several pieces of information, some in numbers, some in small, fluctuating graphs, though she didn't know what most of it meant so she ignored it. Instead she focused on the forward-view display in the middle, showing the direction they were heading.

It was totally empty, save for the distant light of countless stars. Nothing that looked anywhere close though. She thought about turning up and right, like Raith had instructed.

The image on the display rotated exactly the way she was thinking, at the gentle speed she'd been thinking too. Raith was right, she thought, this was easy. She looked at Raith for approval, but his lop-sided smile told her she'd done something wrong.

"Good try Allie, but you only moved the image view. Like rotating the camera. No change in actual direction of travel. Try again, but picture the whole ship changing direction in your mind."

Turning to the screen again, she opened up her thoughts to the system a little more. The ship sent information to her mind as she requested it, showing her an image of the ship from behind in her mind as well as on the display. She set the picture as a smaller section of the main display, down in the other corner and told the system to keep it there. Allie focused on the picture, specifically on how the ship looked against the background, and then mentally turned the ship.

As the small picture of the ship turned exactly as she willed it, she felt the subtle pull on her body that the turn created. She looked up, and Raith nodded with a bright smile.

"Perfect! Interesting technique though, I've never

seen anyone do it that way before."

"Is it wrong?" she asked. He shook his head.

"If it turns where and how you want, it isn't wrong," he told her. "It's just a different method than I've seen before. These systems are highly customizable, kind of like getting to program your own controls on a video game. In any case, it worked perfectly! Okay, for velocity, it's similar. Just push the ship forward, or pull slightly back. Gently, this thing is responsive."

Again, she focused on the little picture of the ship. The stars in the distance were far enough away that they weren't moving much anyway. She pictured pushing the ship forward, but nothing changed. Instead, she looked to the other side at the velocity readout.

The alien lettering made perfect sense to her, she didn't even have to focus on it. The meaning of some of the other numbers made no sense, but only because she didn't understand the words or context that they referred to.

Velocity she understood. Instead of pushing the ship, she mentally focused on the velocity number and changed it downward. The numbers changed to match her focus. She looked up at Raith, who laughed.

"You're something else, Allie," he said. "I try to explain the way most people steer, and you do it in a totally different way. I try to explain changing velocity the way you steer, and instead you change velocity the way most people do. I think maybe I'll leave you to it, you're figuring this out just fine. Captain." He grinned at her and gave a playful salute before turning and heading out of the room.

Allie looked back at the readout, and started experimenting. Nothing drastic, just combinations of velocity and direction, but she was having a great time. While trying to keep on the original course, she made the ship weave back and forth, pretending to dodge asteroids, then made it do a slow corkscrew.

Dav would probably think this was kid stuff, but it was pretty exciting for her. She'd never driven anything before, not even a car, let alone an interstellar space craft. She was just considering trying a barrel roll and wondering exactly how much distance would be covered doing a barrel roll at speeds faster than light when someone came in.

"This is very cool, Raith," she said without turning around.

"Trying your hand at piloting?" Imber asked as she sat in the navigator's seat. Allie glanced over at her, and had to force a smile.

"Just for a minute. Raith is working with the crafter," Allie replied.

"Exciting, huh?" Imber asked. "I can fly a basic ship, but I don't have the precision control for doing anything fancy."

"The mental control, you mean?" Allie asked, surprised by such an open admission of a flaw. Imber nodded though, totally untroubled by this admission.

"I tend to think too broadly," she said. "I can't control the ship with much precision. I'm a lousy gunner too, for the same reason. It takes a lot of training to get really good at this stuff. You'd think flying by thought would make things easy to be good at them, but it doesn't work that way, it actually makes it a whole lot harder! You're doing great though."

"Thanks," Allie replied, "not too bad for a first time I guess."

"Definitely," Imber said. "Awfully nice of Raith to teach you."

"Yeah, he's a very sweet guy," Allie replied, then bit her tongue in annoyance. The last thing she wanted to do was to make Imber think even more highly of the boys.

"He seems to be, though I don't know him well yet."

"Well, we've got a few days until we get wherever we're going," Allie said.

Imber smiled over at her. Allie glanced her way, feeling her gaze. Imber looked perfect, she thought with disgust. She can't have been up for more than ten minutes, she had been sleeping when Allie had left the bunk, but her white hair was perfectly wavy, her skin practically glowed, and her eyes were bright and clear. Not at all how Allie looked first thing in the morning. Allie looked back to the front window, trying not to think about what she herself probably looked like.

"We sure do. I wonder why we're going to Niertagh though."

"What?" Allie asked, looking back at Imber.

"Just wondering why we're going there. The only things on Niertagh are a thriving diamond mining industry owned by the Coalition, and the Perinite Center for Experimental Research, which is also owned by the Coalition. I can't imagine Artus or Dav being interested in diamonds at this point, so that leaves the Perinite Center, but what would they want there?"

Allie realized that all Imber had been told was that she had to tag along on one other stop before they went to meet up with the Resistance. She didn't know anything about Allie's mother.

Allie wondered for a moment how much she should share, but was interrupted by Raith's return. Tic sat on his shoulder, though she jumped down and climbed onto Allie's shoulder as soon as they walked in. Tic gave a little chirp and a trill of happiness, nuzzling Allie, who returned the affectionate touch.

"Good morning Imber," Raith said with a smile. Allie and Imber both looked his way, Allie scratching Tic gently behind the ears. Imber returned the warm smile.

"Hello Raith," she said. Allie stood so Raith could have his seat back. He took a quick glance at the display and nodded admiringly.

"Nice, Allie! We're still dead on course. Another few sessions and you'll be flying circles around Dav." Allie flushed a little at the praise, but couldn't keep the smile from her lips.

"Doubtful, but thanks," she replied, "that was a lot of fun. Maybe I can fly again sometime."

"Definitely. Next time we'll give you a real challenge," he laughed. Dav and Artus walked in as Raith said this.

"You gunning for my job, Allie?" Dav asked with a wink.

"Not likely. I'm just glad I didn't kill us all."

"Don't worry, she did great!" Imber said. Allie moved back over to the sensor station.

"I don't doubt it," Dav replied with a smile to Allie.

"So what's the breakfast plan, folks? I'm starving."

"Oh, I'll cook something up!" Imber volunteered before Allie could resignedly agree to cook, standing and moving toward the hallway.

"Are you sure?" asked Artus. Imber looked back at him and smiled.

"My pleasure. I love to cook," she said. Of course you do, Allie thought. You're probably amazing at it, too. As Imber walked out of the cockpit toward the galley, both of the boys watching her once again, Allie decided for the fiftieth time that she definitely hated the girl.

Tic trilled softly as Allie stroked her. Well at least someone still prefers me, she thought.

CHAPTER FOUR

MISSION BRIEFING

"The Perenite Center?" Ambassador Lase said, speaking in his native language without words, colors shifting along the intricate patterns on his face. "Now what would they want there? All of the important experiments were moved to the Daltain facility years ago."

"I'm not sure, Uncle," Imber replied silently, her own colors flickering through the words. "They haven't given me much information about their mission there yet."

"When you find out, you must tell me as soon as possible," Ambassador Lase insisted.

"Of course," Imber replied. Her uncle nodded once, and closed the connection. The holographic projection faded from the empty air above her open palm. The surgery to install the projector in her hand had been a painful one, and not one she'd have done if she had any other choice.

Imber bit back the tears that threatened to overwhelm her. This was wrong, and she knew it, but what did a person do when forced to choose between two wrongs? She could only pursue the option she felt was less wrong. Spying on these people was much worse than she'd expected it would be though. They were all such good people. Even Allie, who seemed not to like her for some reason, was an absolute gem.

When she'd agreed to this, it had been under the assumption that these people were as bad as the Coalition and that she would be saving countless lives by doing it. The more she got to know these people though, the more she clearly saw that wasn't the case.

Imber sat down on the floor of the bathroom and let the tears come. No choice, she repeated to herself over and over. No choice in the spying, but she wouldn't let these people get hurt. She couldn't, and yet Imber knew deep down that she may not have a choice in that either, in the end.

The next two days were agonizing for Allie. Three terrifying wormhole flights had gone into traveling this distance, Dav piloting through them at what he said was normal speed for piloting a wormhole. Allie wasn't sure she believed him, though the wormhole flights weren't the problem, Imber was.

Allie had genuinely grown to like her, Imber's natural charm and warmth gradually breaking down

Allie's resistance to her. She wasn't even trying, Allie knew, but she was just such a nice person you simply couldn't hate her. Dav and Raith adored her, though Artus seemed not to care one way or the other. He'd actually been fairly quiet over the past few days.

The problem was that now Allie couldn't be mad at her for both of the boys being interested. She hated that she couldn't be mad at Imber. She wasn't actively leading the boys on, or even really flirting with them. She was just open and friendly all the time and they seemed unable to get enough of talking to her.

They talked to Allie too, a lot, but she was sure it was different. It still hurt every time she saw Raith or Dav smile at Imber. It was also driving Allie crazy, trying to identify Imber's accent. It wouldn't have bothered her if it didn't sound so familiar. Allie couldn't quite place it though. She also seemed distracted sometimes, not noticing a comment directed her way until you actively got her attention first.

Nobody had told Imber why they were headed to the Perenite Center, and she never brought it up again, until Raith announced they would reach their destination soon and it was time to get ready. He'd brought them all back into the galley to have a 'mission briefing' as he called it. Raith had said it so seriously that Allie couldn't help but grin, and she knew full well Dav was absolutely loving all this special agent stuff.

"Okay team," Artus said once they had all sat around the table in the middle of the small galley, "here's the plan. Imber and Allie will stay here and wait for us to return…"

"Excuse me," Imber interrupted, "I don't want to pry, but what's the mission? I may be able to help."

All three of the boys looked at Allie. Subtle guys, she thought in annoyance as Imber followed their gazes to her. As she considered it though, it made no sense to keep all of that from Imber.

Once the rescue mission had been completed, Imber would know it had been a rescue mission, and she would definitely figure out that the rescued individual was Allie's mother. Keeping it from her now would only result in Imber not being able to help and her finding out a day later anyway what they'd been up to.

"It's a rescue mission," she told Imber, "We have to rescue someone from the Perenite Center." Imber blinked in surprise.

"So this is… an illegal mission," she said. Allie considered her curiously. What did she think the Resistance was? After a moment, she nodded.

"Yes. The Coalition kidnapped my mother thirteen years ago. That's where they're keeping her," Allie said simply. Imber stared in absolute shock.

"Your mother… thirteen years…" she struggled to form thoughts into words.

Her face had gone pale at the horror of the thought. The other four gave Imber a moment to collect herself, but exchanged glances. Tic, sensing Imber's distress, moved from Allie's shoulder to Imber's lap, chirping inquisitively. Imber stroked Tic absently as she clearly struggled within herself, then seemed to come to a decision.

"I'll help. This is important and I can be a huge

asset," Imber said firmly. Dav, Raith, and Artus exchanged glances.

"What can you due to help?" Raith asked curiously. "This is a military facility. Are you combat trained?"

"Hand to hand, no. I can sure handle a gun though," she said with a trace of smugness that seemed slightly alien coming from her. The boys exchanged glances again.

"Really?" Dav asked curiously. Imber gave him a wry look.

"Don't look so surprised. I'm a girl, so I can't shoot?" she said slightly defensively. "I can probably outshoot any of you, except Raith of course. I specialize in the long plasma rifle. Back on my world, competitive target shooting was considered the fashionable sport for the cultural elite. As the Ambassador's niece, I qualified. Won more than a few championships, too." Dav's expression slid slowly into a wicked, excited smile as he listened.

"Wait, let's be very clear about this," he said. "You're a sniper?" Imber smiled and nodded.

"With a long plasma rifle I could put your eye out at three spans. I can consistently make a body shot at six, and that's not an exaggeration." Artus whistled his surprise, clearly very impressed.

"As much as I don't want you in the line of fire," Artus said, "I can't deny that having a sniper carefully positioned could cover our escape extremely well if we attract too much attention. Okay, so Allie will wait in the ship while we..."

"Wait a minute," Allie argued, "I'm going to sit here

in the ship alone while you four go off to rescue my mother?"

"I wasn't finished," Artus said calmly. "Here's the problem; we have a sniper, we have two Sy'hli soldiers, and we have a recon android. Then we have you. I really don't mean to hurt your feelings Allie, but you can't keep up, you can't fight, you're not trained to use a gun, and you haven't learned enough about your Jumping to be able to contribute that way reliably either."

Imber gasped in shock and stared at Allie. I guess nobody told her that she was a Starjumper, either, Allie thought as Artus continued.

"What you can do, is fly the ship. Not in combat or anything of course, but if we need a quick pick-up, you can handle the ship well enough to get the Peacekeeper to us. Dav can take care of the rest once you're nearby." Allie was hurt, angry, and scared all at the same time.

"I can handle a plasma pistol," she argued, "and my Jumping has saved lives more than once. What if you end up in real trouble and there's no way out? What if my being there makes the difference between life and death for all of you, including my mother? You can leave me here if you want, but I promise I'll follow, even if I have to Jump there," she finished with a fierceness that surprised even her, but Allie refused to be useless.

"You could use some work with that plasma pistol," Artus said, "but you do have a point on the rest of it. Your Jumping is a faster escape than even flying the ship to us." He looked to the two boys. "Feedback?" He asked.

Dav considered her. He looked very unhappy about the idea. Raith looked thoughtful though.

"You know," Raith said, "if you stay right next to me the whole time, I can protect you pretty well. My sensors are sharp and my speed is better even than the two Sy'hli. Anything that might hurt you that I couldn't stop would almost certainly kill any of the others, too. Honestly, you're probably just as safe next to me as you would be sitting alone here in the ship. If the ship were discovered none of us could protect you. I vote to bring her," Raith said, turning to Artus at that last.

"Dav?" Artus asked. Dav hadn't stopped looking at Allie. She couldn't read his expression, but it definitely didn't look positive.

"I think," Imber interjected, "that it is Allie's mother we're rescuing, and it wouldn't be fair to deny her the right to help. And if she's really a crystal bearer she could be incredibly useful in the getaway." Imber reached over and squeezed Allie's hand under the table in a show of support. Dav still didn't look happy.

"Starjumper," Allie corrected.

"What's that?" Imber asked, looking her way.

"I don't like the name crystal bearer. I prefer Starjumper," Allie clarified.

"Starjumper," Imber said, as though trying the word out. After a moment she grinned. "I really like that. It's snappy." Allie returned the grin. Both girls turned to Dav, staring him down. Dav looked between the two and sighed, holding up both hands.

"Okay, okay. We'll all go," Dav conceded with a chuckle. Artus just nodded.

"Okay, but Dav and Raith, both of you stay close to Allie as much as possible. She may be useful, but she isn't a fighter, and we still need her to fight Tyren." Both boys nodded. "New plan then, we equip myself, Dav, Raith, and Allie with pistols, and a long rifle for Imber. We station Imber three spans from the perimeter of the complex atop one of the stone spires to the west of the complex. The rest of us use the rock spires for cover until we get close enough to take out the security monitors. Raith, that's your job. I'll quietly take out the gate guards.

"Once that's done, Raith will move to the security console by the gate and hack the system. If possible, give them false feeds on all the monitors. Also, if you can, run interference on their com channels too. The less they can communicate the less they will be able to coordinate a defense. When we're inside, Imber waits for our exit. The rest of us move through the complex as quickly and quietly as possible to the holding cells where we rescue Morgan. Assuming we haven't triggered the alarm by then, we try to sneak back out. If we have, we fight our way out, Imber covering our escape, or have Allie Jump us as a last resort. Understood?"

They all nodded. Allie noted that Artus used her mother's first name in an oddly familiar fashion, as if he'd once been used to saying it a lot. She reminded herself that Artus and her mother had known one another many years ago, before Allie had been born.

"Excellent," Raith said with a mischievous grin, "then it's time for gear. I have presents for everyone." They all leaned forward as Raith reached to a crate he'd had sitting on the floor by his feet. He came up with a neatly folded stack of clothes. Not just clothes, Allie corrected as Raith handed them out, combat suits. She recognized them from when Dav and Artus had come to rescue her on Ayaran. These looked a bit different though.

"First and foremost," Raith explained, "proper attire. We can't go breaking into a heavily guarded military facility in street clothes. These are slightly upgraded from the ones you two had in your lockers," he said to Dav and Artus. "Better armoring, including a special ionic conductive system designed to channel the unique energy from arc rifle blasts into a battery pack at the hip. The battery will only hold the charge from three arc blasts though, a fourth will overload the battery and it will explode, which will hurt a lot more than getting hit with an arc rifle blast.

"That in mind," he continued as Artus and Dav looked over their suits, "I had them built with a timed detonator on the battery packs as well. If you get shot three times, pull the pack off the belt, hit the button in the back, and throw, and there you go, instant shock grenade."

"That's... brilliant," Artus sad admiringly. Raith smiled smugly.

"Thank you. It's my own design," he bragged. "Nobody else in the galaxy has a suit that can withstand three arc rifle blasts, let alone turn them into a counterattack. Along with the usual atmospheric, pressure, and nutritional systems, these also have voice activated com systems built in, coded on a frequency that nobody uses anymore, with encryption I wrote myself that nobody in the galaxy could hack. Range of about five thousand spans. The com system also serves as a directional tracker that will let any of us track any of the others at a distance close to a light year, just in case."

"Raith," Dav said, "you are welcome on my missions any time."

"Hold the applause, I haven't even gotten to the good stuff yet," Raith laughed. "The helmet visors include scanners almost as good as mine, that will allow you to see clearly regardless of light level, and something like a radar system that will pinpoint anyone coming up behind you or track the guards' movement within a short distance. They're tied to the trackers, so all of our team will show up a different color to prevent confusion."

"Next you'll tell me these things will also make us invisible," Dav joked. Raith smirked.

"Not quite, though they will shield you completely from technological tracking systems. Their scanners won't read us at all. A simple camera or a pair of eyes would spot you without any trouble, but anything from radar to thermal to laser scanners won't see a thing." Dav shook his head in awe. Raith went on. "Now, the weaponry I'll have to add a few items to, I wasn't expecting the lovely ladies to come soldiering with us, but that won't take long to prepare. For you gentlemen, another modified old favorite."

Raith raised his hands from under the table. In each hand was a sleek, black gun. They weren't big, but they looked menacing. Dav raised a brow curiously.

"Modified shatter guns," Artus guessed. Dav grinned as Raith nodded.

"Exactly. I know you boys prefer the precision of shatter guns to the more destructive plasma or arc varieties, so I took the liberty of designing something along those lines with a few variations." Raith spun one of the guns around in an impressively flashy move, offering the handle to Dav, who was sitting closest to him.

"Okay," Raith continued, "so the typical shatter gun has a lifespan of about six hundred rounds due to both power cell capacity and the unsolvable problem with the deterioration of the resonating chamber." The brothers nodded, knowing this already, though it was news to Allie, who listened curiously. "These have a lifespan of about sixty thousand, and draw their power conductively through the gloves on your suit, bypassing the power cell capacity problem. This also means that nobody can pick up your gun and use it against you if you happen to lose your grip on it."

"What about that 'unsolvable' problem with the resonating chambers?" Dav asked with a grin as he handed the gun to Artus for inspection, already suspecting the answer.

"I happen to have solved that one years ago," Raith said with a chuckle.

"If you could figure out how to make a shatter gun work in space you'd pretty well revolutionize space combat," Artus said with a smile. Allie was confused. Dav must have caught her expression, because he explained.

"Shatter guns are sonic. More precise, more reliable, and better lifespan than an arc rifle, though arc rifles you can replace the power cells quickly for a reload. Shatter guns you used to have to carry a couple of them to make sure you had enough shots in case of a major issue. But because they're sonic, they don't work in space. Nothing to carry the sound waves. They're completely useless without an atmosphere to travel through." That made sense, Allie thought.

"I'll work on fixing that one too, just for you," Raith told Artus. "Not today, though. Today we have a prisoner of war to rescue. We arrive at the planet in an hour. I'll get the crafter started on another couple of shatter guns and a long rifle. Shall we all get ready?" They all nodded and stood. As they moved to leave the galley, something occurred to Allie.

"Raith?" she asked. He paused and turned back to look at her. "What about Tic?" Everyone stopped and looked her way.

"Are you worried about her?" he asked Allie with mock surprise, then turned to Dav before she could answer. "Are you worried about Tic? I'm sure not." Raith looked back to Allie with a more somber tone. "Seriously though Allie, Tic is more than capable of taking care of herself. She wouldn't move well in a suit, though I could make one for her. I suspect she'd hate it. That little jicund is more than capable of fending for herself anyway."

"Remember what happened when she got onto Tyren's space station?" Dav added. "His entire imperial guard couldn't catch her. For that matter, she did a fair number on ol' Tyren himself. He'd be seriously disfigured if it weren't for dermal regenerators. She did enough damage, even the regenerators may not have left him without any scars. If you really worry then we can leave her here, but from what I've seen she's just as safe with us, and could also prove to be incredibly useful to have around."

Allie considered for a long moment, then nodded. They had some very good points.

"Also," Raith continued, "I added a cool feature on your suit the others don't have. Grip ridges on your shoulders for Tic. The armor plating is pretty slick to make it harder for the enemy to grapple with you if it comes to that, so I added the ridges to make sure she'd have a tight grip even when you were running." Allie smiled brightly at him.

"Thank you, Raith. You really do think of everything." He grinned at that.

"Easy to do with my processing speed, though even I don't think of everything. Just most things." Raith winked at her. She laughed and moved with her armload of combat gear to the bunk to get ready, a few steps behind Imber. As she and Imber stripped off their outer clothes and began putting on the combat suits, she decided to extend a bit of friendship her way.

"Thanks for that," Allie said. Imber looked up and saw Allie looking her way.

"I'm sorry Allie, what did you say?" she replied. Allie wondered for a moment what Imber had been thinking about that had distracted her.

"I just wanted to thank you, you know, for sticking up for me. I appreciate the support."

"My pleasure," Imber replied with a slightly mischievous smile. "After all, us girls have to stick together. Three girls and three boys on this ship, we have to keep a united front. Besides, it's your mother. You can't sit here fretting and helpless while the rest of us go out to bring her back for you." Allie grinned, liking that Imber had included Tic in the gender count.

"Are you really that good with a gun?" Allie asked after a moment. Imber looked at her, expression serious.

"Allie, I would never put us all at risk by claiming a skill I don't have," she said sincerely. "I'm not one to brag, I just want you to know that when you all come out of that complex with your mother, nobody will make it within arc rifle shooting range of any of you. At the three spans Artus wants me positioned, I could safely pick off a mark even if they were holding you as a shield. Give me three inches of exposed area, and I've got a solid target."

"Thank you," Allie replied, "for helping me rescue my mother." Imber looked down for a long moment, something obviously hitting her hard emotionally.

"It's the least I can do," she eventually replied, looking back up. Allie wasn't sure what that meant, but she didn't want to press it. Something about that remark had obviously upset Imber. Allie resolved to try and gently find out what it was, but later.

"Can you do me one more favor?" Allie asked.

"Anything," Imber replied.

"Can you help me with the fastening on the collar of this suit? I can't seem to get it."

CHAPTER FIVE

THE PERENITE CENTER

Raith landed the ship almost delicately in the middle of a cluster of the jagged stone spires that seemed to be everywhere in this region. From the sky, this whole area looked like a giant hedgehog's back. He had only inches of clearance with the rocks around them.

No organic could have landed this ship here, Raith thought to himself, then instantly corrected himself. It was actually probable that Dav could have managed it, though there couldn't be more than a handful of organic pilots who could do it. Even Raith was impressed by Dav's piloting skills, though Dav had asked Raith to handle this particular landing. Raith suspected it was just a lack of confidence in this degree of precision, but he wasn't going to say anything.

The group was ready, standing and moving to the rear doors of the craft as soon as the ship touched down. They were still six spans from the station, the closest

Raith felt they could safely come without triggering the Center's perimeter sensors. The long-range sensors were operated through satellites, which Raith had remotely hacked and taken over even before they were in scan range of the planet. There were perks to being a recon and intel android, he thought.

Raith took a quick scan of the group to make sure no necessary components or tools were missing. Everything was as it should be. He looked at Allie and Imber. The pair stood side by side in their combat suits. He had designed the suits dark in color rather than black, since black was actually fairly easy to spot in anything other than total blackness, but they were a dark enough blue-gray that they would practically disappear in the shadows of the Niertagh night. Not quite as good as a sneak suit, but it would do, he thought. He reminded himself to craft a new one of those when he had a chance. Raith loved a good sneak suit.

The girls held their helmets under their arms and were chatting lightly. That was good to see, he'd felt bad about the resentment Allie felt for Imber, though he didn't fully understand the reason for it.

They had apparently braided each other's hair back and up to keep it out of the way and from interfering with the helmets. They actually both looked really good. It was an interesting contrast, seeing them standing side by side like that.

Allie was as slender as a professional runner, with dark hair and fair complexion. Imber was the shorter of the two, with a noticeably different build. Imber was stockier, though certainly not fat by any stretch, just more solidly built. With her white hair and elegant markings on her skin, the difference between the two girls was amazing. Despite that, he found he really liked the way both girls looked. Although they shared almost no features, both were perfect exactly as they were and he couldn't imagine either of them any differently than they looked right then.

Imber caught him looking and smiled at him. He smiled back, once again surprised that her smile could cause such a strong emotional response in him. Allie's smile warmed him as well, but as an android programmed to analyze every possible detail, he couldn't deny the feeling was different. His processor was working overtime trying to figure out exactly how, though.

"Are we ready?" Artus asked.

"Ready," Dav said with an excited grin.

"One more surprise for all of you," Raith said with a smile. "Go ahead and put on the helmets."

The group did so. Over the com system, since the helmets were soundproof, he heard several exclamations of surprise. What each had just discovered was that every suit's trim had been designed with a color beyond the normal visual spectrum. Even Dav and Artus couldn't naturally see it. The visor system could read the shades though, and translated them to more visible colors.

What they were all seeing now, was a different color on each suit's trim, making each member of the group easily distinguishable from the others, but only to the group. They would all look the same, a uniform dark blue-gray to anyone else. It would avoid confusion for the group, and increase confusion in the enemy. Of course their heights gave a bit away, but Raith, Dav, Allie, and Imber were all within a few inches of each other so it wasn't a huge giveaway. Artus was the only one who stood out in that regard.

"Slick," Dav said with a laugh, "Thanks for giving me blue." Allie and Imber were green and purple respectively, to match their eyes, Artus was red, and Raith had chosen a pale gray for himself. The colors weren't too bright, and only appeared in what he considered a stylish accent pattern, but they were easily distinguishable from any angle.

"We need to go," Artus urged, "We only have two hours of night left here. I want to be in and out in that time and with Allie and Imber it's going to take a bit longer to get there. I'm not sure how far out their patrols range either, so the ship could be spotted at any time."

"I'm sorry," Allie said.

"Don't worry about it," Artus said, "it just means we need to move." Without another word, they exited the craft.

This planet's atmosphere was completely breathable for the organics, but they all kept the helmets on both for protection and because it gave them all perfectly clear sight in the dark. This planet had two moons, but neither gave off much light and one of them was almost completely hidden by the shadow of the other at this time of the planet's cycle.

Raith didn't need the helmet for night vision, or for the other information it provided, but he would need it if he got shot in the head with an arc rifle. His synthetic skin was no shield against that kind of energy, despite its resistance to normal electricity. He wasn't a combat android, after all.

They ran, the girls moving as fast as they could following Artus. Allie was faster than Imber, and neither were capable of anything near the others' top speed. Dav and Raith flanked the girls, fanning out behind and to the sides somewhat. Raith calculated their arrival time, and estimated they had plenty of time to get to the station, find Morgan Bennett, and get back out before dawn.

He had already figured out that he would be best served by hacking the complex's data core to get the floor plan of the facility when he hacked the security system. He could then upload it to all of their helmet readouts, and mark the holding facility's location for them, just in case.

They moved far more slowly than Raith or the Sy'hli could have, but the girls made excellent time for their species. He was a little worried they would get winded long before they got there, but both girls seemed to be holding up just fine, despite Imber carrying the long rifle.

He had gotten adventurous in crafting her gun, and had built it like the shatter guns he'd given the others. He had designed the shatter rifle to have a range comparable to the plasma rifle, but with the added accuracy of the shatter gun. If she'd been that good with a plasma rifle, she'd be positively lethal with this rifle.

Imber had positively gushed about it when he'd given it to her. It had the same conductive charging the pistols did giving it nearly the same capacity, though the rifle would take a little more power per shot. Especially if she cranked the power setting up.

It was also designed precisely to her measurements, making it fit perfectly in her hands. And to his relief, she definitely carried it like she knew what she was doing. Not that he didn't believe her statements about her skill, but it was reassuring to see solid evidence of it.

He'd been passively scanning the rock formations around them as they ran, and had identified an excellent spot to position Imber. It was high, though only a little higher than the surrounding spires, but it had a gouge out of the top that would fit Imber quite nicely.

She'd have an excellent view of the distant entrance to the complex, unobstructed from the gates to almost two hundred meters from the edge of the field of spires, only missing that much due to the angle and height of the neighboring spires. They would only not be covered for a total of two hundred meters before they were back within her line of sight, but she'd have had over two and a half spans of clear line-of-sight to pick off any pursuers.

"Artus," he said into the com, uploading the quickly saved image and coordinates of the spire in question to the man's display.

Artus nodded and moved that way, gesturing Imber to come with him. She followed him closely to the base of the spire. The spire was tall and steep enough that it would be a tough climb, more so while carrying Imber, but Raith was certain Artus could accomplish it.

Artus had Imber climb on his back, and he jumped onto the rock face. He caught hold easily, and scampered up the nearly-sheer stone like a monkey up a tree. Raith smiled. The Sy'hli might have their flaws, but they sure were athletic.

Artus took a moment once they'd reached the top to help Imber get situated. It would be a lot easier for her to get back down than it was to get up, Raith knew. With that rock face, she'd have enough grip to slow her slide down, and all she'd have to do is roll over and sit up to have a quick and easy exit from her little perch.

Imber lay down on her stomach, the gouge in the rock almost the exact length of her prone body. With a flick of one wrist, she snapped out the bipod from the barrel of the gun and got into position. Leaning forward she aligned her view with the scanner-scope and repositioned the gun subtly until she was happy. Then she partially rolled over and gave them all a thumbs up.

The girl had skills, Raith had to admit. He was almost hoping they'd be pursued out of the complex so he could see how good a shot she was. She rolled back to position and the rest of the group moved off.

When they reached the edge of the spire field, Raith looked out over the almost three span empty distance to the complex. It was huge, the wall spreading off in either direction into the distance. From his own records, he knew the complex housed close to a thousand scientists, and easily three times that number of soldiers. It was nearly a small town.

He didn't have a floor plan in his system, that kind of data was classified and he'd never had reason to dig into it before, though he could have acquired it if he'd had any need to while on Irifal.

The gray stone the spires consisted of was so common on this planet that all of the buildings and walls were made of it. It was all incredibly thick, too. Even the improved shatter guns wouldn't be able to break through it without an awful lot of concentrated fire.

He knew a ledge ran along the inside of the wall, and that it was regularly patrolled. He scanned to the extent of his range and located the patrolmen and calculated their marching speed. One minute, thirteen point six seconds, he knew, until the first guard was close enough to be a concern.

Of course, that didn't take into account the two guards in front of the gate. Artus had already circled wide and was moving low and fast toward the wall some distance away. With luck, in the dark he would make it to the wall outside the ring of light created by the gate lights, and outside the field of any of the big spotlights aimed outward at the rocks, all without being detected.

Raith located the optical scanner above the gate and took careful aim. He calculated all of the variables, from temperature, to wind speed, to atmospheric pressure to ensure the shot from his shatter gun was as precise as possible. Under the circumstances, Raith calculated that he had as much as fourteen nanometers variance in his potential impact point. Acceptable, he decided.

The shatter gun would provide far more power than necessary to disable the scanner. He probably should have warned the others that these shatter guns had also been tweaked for power, exactly thirty eight point two six four percent more than a standard shatter gun, to be precise. More than enough to be noticeable the first time they fired them.

It took some time for Artus to reach the wall. Raith

could see him from here, though the guards wouldn't be able to. He nodded to Dav and Allie to be ready. They would run toward the gate as soon as Raith took out the scanner, which would happen the instant Artus entered its visible range, currently limited by the gate's light. Artus ran along the base of the wall heading for the guards.

An instant before Artus reached the ring of light around the gate, Raith fired. His shot was off by six nanometers do to a random fluctuation in the wind patterns, which for everyone but an android meant he hit in the exact center.

The scanner shattered, pieces of broken glass, casing, and internal components raining down on the guards. The guards didn't even have time to react before Artus hit them. Artus moved fast enough that they had no time to react after he hit them either. The second guard hit the ground a fraction of a second after the first. Dav and Allie were already running.

Raith put on his top speed, knowing that until he could hack the scanner's data feed and insert a false image, their presence could be detected by the guards monitoring the security systems. Raith hoped there were enough scanners and systems to monitor, and the guards were bored enough, that less than ten seconds with one scanner being off feed wouldn't attract any attention.

When he reached the panel, he quickly put his hand against it and accessed their system. It took him less than four seconds to bypass all eight layers of security and encryption, plant the false signal for the broken scanner, check the com system for any signs that they'd been detected, and download a current floor plan of the facility complete with guard patrol routes, and the military complement of the whole compound. Another four seconds and he could have downloaded their entire mainframe.

Seriously, he thought to himself, it was a shame the old Data and Security series androids weren't around anymore. Without a D.A.S. Alpha or a D.A.S. Kappa unit manning the security systems, hacking had become almost too easy to be fun anymore. None of the other D.A.S. series androids had even been a challenge. Raith remembered a time when the D.A.S.K. androids were in use at every high end facility in the galaxy.

The gate slid open smoothly at Raith's thought, less than fifteen total seconds having passed since Raith dropped the sensor. The four of them, five counting Tic, entered the facility. Raith had already sent the map to everyone else, but led the way anyway, immediately cutting right just past the first building.

He kept his ranged scanners active, searching for incoming patrols or anyone else moving around in the night. If there were any other androids left they would have been able to pick up his scanning, but since he was one of the only other androids left in the galaxy, and was the only one still fully functional, he had no fear of being detected.

He sensed a few people in the area, but nobody moving around. A couple of people sitting at desks in the nearby buildings, quite a few sleeping in the bunkhouses they passed. Based on his schedule of patrols, he estimated the odds of their running into an unscheduled patrol were slim, and running into a scheduled patrol nonexistent.

As he had hoped, they made it to the holding facility without incident. The holding facility would be tricky in its own right, since it held its own private security system, its own large complement of guards, and was actively monitored for intrusion. With Dav and Artus around however, he wasn't too worried. The three of them could probably handle the entire building's worth of guards as long as they didn't all reach them at once.

Two guards were at the front door, both went down before either of them knew that anything unusual was going on. Raith touched the panel and hacked into their security system. It was faster than the front gate, since all he was doing was hacking the security and the door locks. Once he had control, he opened the door, letting Dav and Artus slide into the building, guns in hand.

Raith and Allie, guns drawn as well, moved in behind them. Raith could sense the nearby guard patrols, and led the way through the halls. He had a floor plan of this building too, downloaded as he unlocked the door. Tic rode comfortably on Allie's shoulder, gripping the special ridge built into the shoulder plate easily. The jicund wasn't anxious, but perched in a tensed fashion on Allie's shoulder, ready to leap off the instant it was needed.

"Two guards just around the next corner," Raith said into the com. "Not moving, likely standing at attention by the door to the cell block. Aim low at the right one, he's short."

Dav and Artus dove around the corner, both firing

off one quick, humming shot as they did so. Raith and Allie came around just in time to see the two guards hit the floor. Raith touched the control panel by the heavy, solid metal cell block door and unlocked it. It opened quietly, thankfully, and the four went inside.

"Another four minutes to the next patrol through this block," Raith said, "Morgan Bennett is in cell 4A7, on the right." They moved forward. These cells all had big, solid metal doors, so there wasn't even any worry of the prisoners seeing them and making a fuss. Reaching the door with 4A7 painted across it, Raith looked to Allie.

"Are you ready?" he asked her, sending the com signal only to her for that one. She took a long breath, exhaled slowly, then nodded. Raith opened the door.

CHAPTER SIX

JAILBREAK

The room was small, barely big enough for one narrow cot, which was more of a metal shelf sticking out from one corner along the wall, and a toilet. The room was dark and dingy, and looked like it hadn't been cleaned in a very long time, possibly years. There was nothing else in the room except a single woman, sitting on the metal shelf, curled up in the corner by the back wall.

Allie stepped into the room, looking at the woman. She looked terrible. Her blonde hair was heavily matted and dirty, clothes worn and disheveled. Her skin looked like it hadn't seen a bath in years, and she physically looked like she was wasting away. She probably hadn't had a good meal in years either.

Bile rose in Allie's throat at the idea of her mother living like this for thirteen years, but it was choked off by the lump forming there by the thought that she was finally looking at her real mother.

The woman slowly raised her head and looked at Allie, and the three others behind her. Dav reached up from behind Allie and took Tic from her shoulder as Allie took a step forward.

"Is it time to eat already?" the woman asked, voice cracking and dry. Her brow furrowed as she registered what she was seeing. Allie didn't know what the woman was expecting to see, but clearly three short people and one tall man in unfamiliar combat suits was not it.

"No, mo..." Allie's own voice broke as she tried to say the word. Artus moved forward slightly.

"No ma'am, we're here to get you out." Artus said, his voice holding a strength that Allie's was currently lacking. The woman frowned.

"Who are you?" she asked, obviously trying to get her mind to focus on the situation.

"I'm a friend, Morgan," Artus said, removing his helmet as he stepped around a stunned Allie. As her green eyes lost some of their dullness and focused on his face, something clicked inside her. She rose slowly from the bed, stumbling slightly, a sharpness coming into her eyes and her expression.

A look of hope so long forgotten came across her face as she recognized the man before her. Slowly, as if afraid her touch would shatter the illusion, she reached out to touch his face. When her fingers reached warm, solid flesh, she gasped, a shaky, torn sound.

"Artus?" she asked slowly. Artus smiled gently.

"Hi Morgan. It's been a long time." Morgan practically fell forward into his arms, dry sobs sounding as she buried her face in his neck. Allie felt tears running down her own face. She couldn't move, or speak, overwhelmed as she was by the moment.

"Morgan, we have to go," Artus said, though not harshly. The way he held her, Allie could clearly see they truly had been friends, so many years ago. Morgan nodded, took a deep, raspy breath, and tried to step back. She stumbled and almost fell, but Artus caught her, easily supporting her weight.

"Who are these others?" she asked, still sounding confused.

"Time for introductions later, Morgan. We really need to go."

"I'm sorry, I'm having trouble thinking," she replied groggily. "I don't think I can walk, either." Without a word, Artus slipped his helmet back on and stepped forward, easily scooping her into his arms. As she put her arms around his neck for support, she smiled slightly at him. "You look so much like your father. So strong and noble."

Artus didn't reply, though Allie heard Dav sniffle slightly over the com and knew he was either close to tears or was already crying himself. She reached over and took his hand. He clasped it firmly for a long moment, obviously needing the support almost as much as she did.

"Come on," Artus said. "Raith, get us out of here."

"Follow me," Raith replied.

Dav and Allie both followed Raith, stepping aside long enough for Artus to walk with Allie's mother into the middle of the group. Dav and Allie both drew their guns and moved with the group, Dav walking backward and keeping an eye on their rear. They moved back out of the building with no problem, but Raith paused once they were on the street.

"Com chatter has gone completely silent," Raith said. "I think they've switched frequencies."

"Why would they do that?" asked Dav.

"They wouldn't, unless they knew they were being monitored," Raith replied. "I think we have to hurry. Dav, can you carry her?" he asked, gesturing to Allie. "We need to move faster than she can run." Dav scooped Allie up without a moment's hesitation.

"No good," Raith informed them suddenly, "There's a large troop coming in, we're surrounded. I can hear ships firing up as well in the distance. They know we're here."

"Find us a way out, Raith!" Artus said, sounding both angry and worried. Raith moved to the wall and touched the control panel. He was quiet for several long seconds before he turned back to the group.

"Put her down," Raith told Dav. "Can you Jump us back to the ship?" Morgan's eyes snapped to Allie, though she couldn't see her face through the helmet. Morgan's eyes looked incredibly clear and focused in that moment though, almost vibrant. Allie felt a swell of relief that her mother was still alive and strong in there somewhere.

"I think so," Allie said, though she wasn't entirely certain. Jumping still made her nervous. She had taken a minute to memorize the cargo bay and lock an image of it clearly in her mind before they left.

"Is that our only option?" Dav asked.

"Unquestionably," Raith told him. "They've sent a Sy'hli strike team." Nobody said anything for a long moment, but Allie could feel Artus and Dav both tense up.

"Impossible," Artus said softly, "The Sy'hli military was destroyed when they refused to follow Tyren's lead."

"Unless 'Sy'hli Strike Team' is a cute new code name for some other group of soldiers, apparently not all of them were, and we have exactly eighteen seconds before they reach us."

"Allie! Go!" Dav shouted. She pulled out the crystal from the pouch she'd stored it in. The others all reached out and put a hand on her shoulder, except Morgan, who was watching her with hawk-like focus and holding tightly to Artus. Allie held the crystal up by the chain and reached up to spin it.

An arc rifle blast came out of nowhere and slammed into her shoulder. She cried out at the force of the impact as she was stumbled backward. There was an odd crackling sound as the energy rerouted through her suit's plating and into the belt pack. She looked up, clutching at her shoulder.

Allie hadn't felt any heat, and knew the suit had absorbed everything but the impact, and she suspected a good portion of that as well. She looked around to see Dav holding the crystal. She had no idea how he'd gotten it so fast, unless he'd literally snatched it out of the air when she lost hold of it, which was entirely possible. After a moment, she realized that none of the others were moving.

The others all stood still, each staring in a different direction. As she looked around, she saw several tall, slender figures emerging from the darkness around them. Eight figures, all wearing identical, deep crimson body armor and carrying some serious-looking weaponry.

The body armor was elegantly, though terrifyingly, stylized. They looked like nothing so much as big, red, angry cats. The helmets even had bladed ridges that looked a little bit like ears. Tic hissed threateningly from Allie's shoulder.

Neither Raith nor Dav had drawn their guns. Dav's hands slowly raised in surrender. Raith had his hand on the building's panel, though he was watching the Sy'hli as they moved menacingly forward.

"Wait for it," Raith said over the com.

"Wait for what?" Dav replied. Raith chuckled.

From behind them, a roar was building. Allie glanced back that way just in time to see a horde of disheveled, dirty, and very angry people charging out of the building. Many of them looked to be holding weapons that were likely stolen from guards inside the building.

Allie rolled to the side to avoid being trampled as her three friends surged into action. The freed prisoners charged the Sy'hli, who moved like lightning. Shots were fired, prisoners dropped. One Sy'hli was hit, though he just stumbled and then in a single leap landed on the man who'd shot him, ten feet away, bringing him rapidly down.

Dav scooped her up in one quick motion, turned and took two steps. A red-gloved hand grabbed Allie's leg in a painfully strong grip. Allie yelped.

Tic went berserk, leaping from Allie's shoulder with a shriek of rage at the Sy'hli soldier that had grabbed her. The Sy'hli moved fast, almost catching the flying animal, but not fast enough. Tic moved in a blur, slashing and biting at the armored figure, scampering across and around the man's body like a tiny purple tornado.

The jicund's black claws cut into the armor with startling ease, leaving gaping tears in the strange metal. The Sy'hli swatted and grasped frantically, dropping his gun, but couldn't keep up with Tic.

The moment the hand let her go, Dav took another couple of running steps and leapt a six foot spiked fence alongside the building. Artus and Raith landed beside them in full run. Raith had two guns in his hands, Dav and Artus both carrying someone else. Raith must have grabbed Dav's gun, she realized.

They ran at a pace that would have made her nervous on a motorcycle, let alone on foot. It took only a few seconds for them to reach the other side of the prison yard and leap the spiked fence on the far side.

Raith was firing both guns independently before he landed on the far side. Four humming shots rang out, carried to her ears by the small speakers in the helmet. By the time Allie and Dav had cleared the fence, four soldiers were down and Raith was already running.

"Front gate is manned," Raith said. "They've sent more troops to scour the perimeter."

"Imber has our backs," Dav said as Tic appeared out

of nowhere, leaping up to cling to Allie again. She appeared unharmed, to Allie's relief.

"I sure do," Imber's voice came across the com, startling Allie. She'd forgotten Imber could hear them. "Give me fifteen seconds before you hit the gate Raith, I'll clear it for you."

"How many guards?" Artus asked.

"Twelve," Imber replied, "but don't worry. I've got them handled. Just give me fifteen seconds' notice before you get here. I don't want them to have time to get more troops over here."

"Artus," Morgan said weakly, "Sy'hli."

Artus glanced back over his shoulder where Morgan was looking and growled deep in his throat. Allie also looked back, and saw six Sy'hli soldiers in that bone-chilling armor running after them. They were gaining too, pretty quickly, not weighed down by carrying the helpless girls, Allie thought bitterly. I shouldn't have come, she thought.

"Go, Imber!" Raith shouted. Allie watched the Sy'hli gaining on them. She wasn't sure they had fifteen seconds. Watching those soldiers running that impossibly graceful, frighteningly fast run, knowing she was their target, she had a sudden sympathetic feeling for the antelope, being chased by the cheetah. Her nightmares were likely to change from Maruck to Sy'hli after this.

An arc rifle blast hit her in the head where it hung out to Dav's side. Her head rocked to one side. That odd crackling sound came again as the energy was rerouted. Another one hit Dav, who didn't even stumble, and she felt the energy crackling along both of their systems. Part of it went to Dav's pack, she realized, so hers only had two and a half charges. One more, she thought. The Sy'hli were too close, they wouldn't make the gate, she realized.

"Dav, let them hit you again," she told him.

"What?" he asked.

"Just let one of them shoot you," Allie replied. Dav hesitated only an instant before he slowed enough to turn halfway back and look at their pursuers. A more tempting target they couldn't have asked for, and one of them took the bait, hitting Allie directly. In a panic, she realized she may have gotten more than half of that burst into her pack. She grabbed the pack from her belt and hit the button, dropping it behind them.

"Go!" she cried. Dav leaned into it and ran. An instant later, the battery pack exploded. She had looked away so as not to be blinded by the flash, but hoped they'd bought at least a few seconds. Dav stumbled as the shockwave hit him, but he didn't lose his feet.

She looked forward just in time to see the front gate explode inward, two soldiers flying wildly amid the flaming wreckage.

"What was that?" Allie cried.

"Sorry," Imber said, sounding sheepish, "One of the guards at the gate had a few grenades on his belt, so I thought I'd open the door and save you guys a few seconds. You're clear."

Imber really was good, Allie thought. She heard Raith chuckle as they raced through the gate, leaping over the prone bodies of the soldiers Imber had dropped.

Almost immediately, Allie heard the hum of shatter

gun fire whipping past them. Looking back over Dav's shoulder, she saw the first two Sy'hli blasted backwards by the force of the shatter rifle. They flew several feet before landing and sliding to a stop.

"What did you do to that gun?" Dav asked incredulously, glancing back himself.

"I forgot to tell you," Raith said, "I tweaked their output power. The rifle especially."

"Thanks for the heads up," Dav muttered, though he didn't actually sound upset.

Allie watched as the Sy'hli dove back behind the gate, buying the running group precious time. Two of the Sy'hli poked their heads barely out enough to try and take aim, but shatter gun fire hummed in, hitting one of the Sy'hli directly in the middle of the two inches of helmet visor he'd revealed to take his own aim. The other pulled quickly back behind the wall.

Allie noticed it was getting quite a bit lighter and glanced around. The black sky overhead was turning to a lighter gray, and the horizon was being lit with a brilliant green as this world's sun made its appearance. More shatter gun fire hummed past in rapid succession.

Another sound reached them as they made it to the stone spires. Allie recognized it as space craft engines, coming in fast. Looking up, she saw two ships scream past overhead, arc cannons firing blindly into the stone spires. The spires exploded as they were hit into showers of flying stone and dust. A second later, huge chunks of sharp stone began to fall all around them.

The group dodged as much as they could, but a few larger rocks in the veritable shower struck each of them painfully. Not enough to bring anyone down, but enough to cause a few stumbles.

They neared Imber's hiding spot and Raith moved toward it, but Imber's voice came over the com.

"No, keep going!" she shouted. "They're sending the whole complex worth of soldiers at this rate! They can only get out through the front gate but they're still coming out faster than I can take them down, and I'm taking some return fire. They don't seem to care how many they lose! I'll slow them down enough for you to get to the ship, then you'd better get that ship back here to rescue me!"

"Imber, we can't leave you," Dav said, but Raith shoved him on.

"Go! She's right, we can get to the ship and back to her with a lot more firepower long before they catch us, if she keeps shooting."

"They've got ships too!" Artus shouted in irritation, though he kept running.

To emphasize his point, the two ships did another strafing run, peppering the group with falling stone. Allie took a heavy hit to the same shoulder she'd been shot in and bit her lip to keep from crying out. She didn't want to distract Dav. Dav snarled angrily, but kept running. If anything, he ran harder.

They reached the ship and raced up the ramp and into the cockpit. Dav set Allie gently in her seat, then practically dove into the pilot's station. She heard the engines fire up only a fraction of a second before the ship jerked up off the ground like it had been kicked.

Allie pulled on her safety restraints, realizing that to

save Imber now, Dav and Raith were going to push this craft to its limits. From what she'd heard, this ship was incredibly powerful in combat. She hoped so, because her sensors showed two more ships incoming.

Raith was already in his seat, but Artus and Morgan were not in the cockpit. Allie assumed Artus was getting her someplace she could be safe before coming up the ramp.

"Okay Dav, let's show these guys what we can do," Raith said, sounding excited. He probably was, Allie thought. He was probably insane, too.

The ship rocketed forward like a bullet from a gun, banking almost immediately at a ridiculous angle to dodge an arc cannon blast. The cannons on the Peacekeeper roared to life, returning fire in a barrage that Allie had to admit was impressive. This ship definitely had some firepower. The incoming ship exploded in a shower of flames, sparks, and shrapnel.

Banking sharply again, Dav suddenly changed angle and dipped into a corkscrew around a ship that had nearly collided with them. As they passed, Raith hit the craft with so many arc blasts so rapidly that Allie could actually see the hull of the ship glowing for a fraction of a second before it exploded.

The impact of such a near explosion sent the ship lurching to the side, almost into a large spire. Dav spun the craft like a Frisbee, the wing just barely missing the spire before he straightened out, just in time to bank sharply again to try and dodge another arc blast. Not fast enough, as the blast tore through one of their own cannons.

"One arc down," Raith said, "three to go, then we're down to plasmas."

"No plasma cannons in atmosphere!" Artus shouted as he ran into the room and leapt into his own seat.

"I know!" shouted Dav. Another sharp roll as the spires they narrowly dodged exploded with another barrage of arc blasts.

"Give me another spin like that last one!" Raith shouted. "Horizontal one eighty, but maintain direction!" Dav abruptly spun the craft again.

As the ship whipped around now, flying backwards Raith opened up the remaining cannons. The ship, much closer than Allie had realized, exploded. Another jarring lurch as the force of the explosion hit them, but Dav used it to flip the craft nose up and back, then roll again to face forward toward Imber again.

They had moved further away from Imber, fighting the other three ships, so it took them a moment to get within visual range. Once they were within visual range, Allie's heart sank.

There was a ship hovering right by Imber's perch. It was huge, and covered with enough barrels to more than justify Allie mentally describing the ship as 'prickly'. Its rear ramp was down, and four soldiers were busy shoving a disarmed Imber up the ramp, her hands up on her head.

"No!" shouted Raith. The massive ship slowly, ponderously rose and turned toward them.

"Uh oh," Dav said. "We need to move!"

"What about Imber?" Raith asked.

"We'll think of something, but first we need to not

be dead!" Dav called back. The Peacekeeper spun around again and tore through the air.

Allie focused on the big ship on her sensor panel. As its image enlarged, she also got more information about it. Twenty seven cannons, seven of which were plasma, with high-yield energy shielding, and a phase drive that could make the huge craft travel at dangerous speeds, which is precisely what it was working up to now, chasing the Peacekeeper. How it could move that fast in atmosphere, Allie had no idea, but it was very nearly keeping up with the Peacekeeper.

"We'll escape and come back for her," Dav said sadly, sounding resigned. "We can't compete with that thing."

"No," Raith stated, "I can hear their coms. They're getting orders to kill her and dump the body. I have to move now. Dav, slow down just a little and gain some altitude. Artus, lower the rear ramp."

"I don't even want to know what you're about to do," Artus said.

Allie felt the pressure inside the ship change as the rear ramp opened, the scream of the wind outside as they tore through the sky was almost deafening. She suspected the helmets were actually reducing the volume though, since she was sure the actual noise was probably enough to literally deafen her.

Raith got up and moved to the doorway. He looked back at his console for a moment, and apparently satisfied at what he saw, suddenly broke into a full run down the hallway, probably straight to the cargo bay.

She focused on Raith on the sensor screen, and an

image of him appeared on her display just as he entered the cargo bay at a full run. He ran down the ramp without slowing, and upon reaching the end of it, he leapt out into empty air.

CHAPTER SEVEN

RAINING ANDROIDS

"Corporal, prepare arc cannons!" commanded the captain, from his comfortable chair on the bridge of the massive battle cruiser.

They had been ordered to kill the girl and dump her body. He wanted to do that himself however, so had ordered his men to bind and gag her in the back of the bridge so he could deal with her when he was done with the little Interceptor before they managed to outrun him. This battle cruiser was fast, but nothing could keep up with an Interceptor when it pushed the engines to capacity.

"Yes, sir!" replied the corporal enthusiastically. Good man, the captain thought to himself.

"Target every system, let's blow them into so many pieces they'll rain down as dust."

"Yes, sir!" There was a pause. "Umm, sir?"

"What is it, Corporal?"

"They're slowing down."

"Idiots," muttered the captain. They probably thought they could surrender or negotiate for the girl's life.

"Prepare to fire," said the captain disdainfully.

"Yes, sir." Another pause. A moment before the captain could order the destruction of the tiny vessel, the corporal spoke again.

"Sir?"

"What, corporal?" the captain asked, growing annoyed.

"I think they shot something at us."

"What do you mean you think they shot something at us?" The corporal pointed out the huge front window. It took a moment for the captain to spot it; a small, dark speck above them in the distance, growing slowly larger and lower, then rapidly larger and lower. It looked like it might actually hit them.

"Is that a..." the captain asked a moment before the realization hit him, which happened at the exact moment that the small figure slammed against the front window at frightening speed. It should have splattered like an insect at that velocity, but instead it slammed into the window with such an impact that the *BOOM* it created startled the captain almost out of his chair.

"What in the name of..." he cried out.

The figure clung to the windshield and looked like it was looking back in at him. Though the wind outside due to their velocity would have been exceptional, the small form held firmly in place with an iron grip on the frame.

Despite knowing the transparent metal window

could withstand anything short of a direct arc cannon blast, something about the way the surprisingly small, helmeted figure focused on him suddenly made the captain very nervous.

The little figure gripped the frame of the window with one hand and both feet down below, the other hand balling into a fist and reaching back.

"He can't actually be about to..." the corporal started to say, staring in morbid fascination at the figure.

The figure moved, interrupting him, swinging the small fist with alarming speed. The impact when it hit the window was almost deafening, even louder than when the figure itself had struck the window. Everyone in the bridge flinched.

"Impossible," the captain muttered as he realized that the little figure had managed to not just dent the window, but create some significant damage. The figure raised the fist back again. "He's going to get in here," the captain said, standing slowly, and totally unaware he'd said that out loud in his sudden, rising fear. The fist came down again with another tremendous crash and the distinct sound of distressed metal.

As the transparent metal caved in even further, the captain stumbled backward, suddenly very interested in being elsewhere. The second blow had torn through the window. The small figure pushed its gloved fingers through the small tear in the metal and gripped. With slow, but irresistible force, the small armored person peeled back the window.

The captain was unsure when the screaming had started, but he was somewhat comforted to realize he was not the only one screaming. Half the bridge crew was scrambling for the exit. Suddenly quite certain that he would need a bargaining chip, he scooped up the bound girl as he fled the bridge.

The horrible sound of tearing metal behind him stopped, which was even more terrifying than the tearing metal had been because the captain knew that it meant the figure had made it inside.

The sound of plasma pistols discharging in the bridge only made him hurry faster. The few on the bridge who had stayed were probably dead. Anything that could tear its way through the transparent metal window would have no trouble ripping his men apart.

He ran through the hallways of the ship. The ship was huge, but most of its mass was taken up with weapons, shielding, and engine systems. He didn't have far to go before he found himself in the engine room. He could feel the static buzz of the hourglass-shaped power core in the center, and could hear the crackle of the red energy as it arced from the top to the bottom.

The captain ran all the way to the protective railing around the core before turning around. He drew his own plasma pistol and held it to the girl's head. She hadn't struggled this whole time. That suddenly struck him as odd. He looked down at her. The expression she turned up at him chilled him to the bone.

It wasn't frightening in its own right, it was terrifying because of what it implied. The girl stared up at him, totally unafraid, and worse, she looked a little smug. She knew what was coming for him.

It didn't take long. He heard periodic screams and

gunfire down the hallways, but it was less than sixty seconds before the figure walked in. Stalked in would have been a better description, he thought. It stalked, slow, steady, menacing, and unrelenting. He pressed the gun to the girl's head, trying to keep his expression stoic.

"You have one chance," the figure said. It sounded like a boy. A young boy, for that matter. The captain frowned, confused. "Let her go and surrender and I'll let you live. Refuse, and I'll break you before I take her anyway."

The captain had a brief moment where he considered the boy's size and thought the idea of him throwing anyone anywhere was simply laughable. Then he remembered the window.

Before the captain could say anything or respond, one of the captain's fiercest soldiers leapt on the boy from behind. The boy moved so fast the captain could barely follow it. In the blink of an eye, the boy had spun, grabbed, and flung the man clear across the engine room, directly into the power regulator. Sparks showered half the engine room as the regulator exploded, causing the captain to flinch back.

When his blink from the flinch was finished, the boy was right in front of him. Inches in front of him. Impossibly fast, the captain thought. The captain suddenly realized he was no longer holding a gun, or the girl, and his hand hurt.

"If you survive this crash, tell Tyren that it will take more than a battle cruiser to stop me," the small figure said.

It was definitely a boy, the captain could partially see

his face through the visor of the boy's helmet. The captain simply couldn't understand. Even the Sy'hli weren't that strong or fast. The boy turned, carrying the girl like she weighed nothing, and jogged toward the hallway. He paused just before reaching the door and turned back around.

"Oh, and tell him I'll see him soon."

"Is he crazy?!" Artus asked, though he felt it was more of a rhetorical question since he was fairly sure everyone already knew Raith was not exactly what you could consider sane. Nobody sane leapt out of a moving space craft, throwing himself directly at another moving space craft.

"He made it!" Allie cried a moment later. Artus had to admit he was relieved. He wasn't comfortable around androids, but Raith had saved their lives more times than Artus cared to admit. He had definitely proven both his value and his loyalty. And yet, he was still an android, a hunk of metal, synthetics, and wiring.

Everything he said, everything he thought and did, was a direct result of his programming. Why he'd shorted his program and was fighting against the system he didn't know, but at any moment the program might kick back in properly and the android could turn and kill them all.

And yet, here he was, putting himself in extreme harm's way to rescue someone they'd all known for less than three days. Well, he was useful, Artus told himself as he acknowledged his relief that the android had survived the jump.

"And he's inside!" Allie shouted excitedly.

"What does he think he's going to do, fight the whole crew? That's a professionally trained military force on board that craft," Artus muttered.

"We need to go pick him and Imber up," Dav said.

"We don't even know if he's still alive!" Artus argued.

"Sure we do," Dav said.

"And how do you know that?"

"Because that big bad ship hasn't blown us into tiny, smoking pieces," Dav retorted. Artus had to admit, Dav had a point. It was likely that the only reason they weren't dead yet was because Raith had jumped in the first place, and the only reason they still weren't dead was because everybody was too busy dealing with Raith to fire the cannons. The longer they went without getting blown to pieces, the higher the chance that Raith was still alive.

"I'm going to get them," Dav said stubbornly, banking sharply and heading back toward the huge battle cruiser.

"Dav!" Artus protested.

He knew it was no use, however. Dav always had been stubborn. And Artus had to admit, his instincts had been extremely good since they had left Earth a few weeks ago. He'd shown better control, resolve, courage, intuition, and leadership than Artus had on every measure.

It bothered him that his little brother was showing

him up on every front. He knew it shouldn't, he loved his little brother, but it didn't change that little nagging feeling of resentment and self-doubt.

Artus had spent the last ten years on a planet where he was superior to absolutely everyone around him in every possible way. In the last few weeks, he'd been thrust back into a galaxy where he was only considered 'above average' in the grand scheme of things. Seeing so many people, from Dav to Raith to Tyren to the Maruck able to pass him up in so many ways galled him.

Technically, once Tyren was overthrown, the Sy'hli Empire belonged to Artus. He was the eldest surviving competent member of the royal family, since everyone everywhere could agree that the self-proclaimed Highlord was unstable and unfit to rule.

Artus knew he wasn't prepared for that level of responsibility though. He'd spent his childhood with everything handed to him on a silver platter. Then as a young teenager, war had erupted and everything he knew and loved had been torn from him.

Ten years looking after his baby brother on a planet of the weaker, slower, less intelligent humans had given him a different perspective on his capabilities than he was now seeing. Too much taken for granted, too many things in which he'd simply assumed his superiority. Now that his superiority was being challenged, he wasn't entirely sure how to handle it.

Anything on the caliber of Imperial rule and guidance of the Coalition was well beyond his experience. Dav was showing himself to be a better choice anyway, a thought which left a bitter taste in his mouth.

Dav had been swinging the ship wide to move himself to a more difficult angle to shoot at as he approached the large battle cruiser when the big ship suddenly lurched awkwardly and slowed to a stop, hovering in midair. Dav chuckled.

"He'll head for the front windshield again, I'll bet," Dav said, sweeping around in front of the ship, now completely unconcerned with the ship's artillery.

Seconds later, Raith appeared at the window. He gave a thumbs up, and helped Imber to stand up on the ledge. As Dav moved up and out to put the back of the ship toward the pair so they could reach the back ramp, the big ship lurched again, and plummeted.

"Uh oh," Dav muttered as the ship dropped.

Artus watched in morbid fascination as Dav spun the ship and they shot straight down. His own display showed the bigger ship, zooming in as he focused on it. Raith had jumped, but missed the platform as the leverage for his jump fell out from beneath his feet. The pair were freefalling just above the huge, falling cruiser.

The Peacekeeper quickly got ahead of the falling pair, rotating almost lazily to put the open cargo bay ramp directly below them. The nose of the Peacekeeper gently nudged the falling battle cruiser as Dav slid his way between it and their friends. With another gentle, almost lazy turn to level the ship out, Artus watched on his display as Raith and Imber were carefully, even gently, caught in their fall on the floor of the cargo bay.

"Little brother, I have no idea how you do that," Artus said.

Dav flashed a grin over at him. Impossibly talented, Artus thought, trying to keep the resentment out of his thoughts. His little brother really was amazing, and Artus loved him. He shouldn't really resent the boy for his many talents. That being said, Dav had an awful lot of very impressive talents.

A few moments later, they were back out of the atmosphere and moving away from Niertagh and the Perinite Center for Experimental Research at maximum speed. Even a phase missile couldn't catch them now.

Imber and Raith walked in from the hallway, both all smiles. Artus gave Raith a measuring look before turning back to his navigation panel. A powerful ally, Artus knew, but an uncertain card in a deck already full of wild cards.

CHAPTER EIGHT

REUNION

Allie and Dav both raved about the incredible rescue in excited tones while Raith and Imber told them about what had happened to them. Artus couldn't take it.

He stood and walked out, heading back to the bunk room where he'd put Morgan. He'd strapped her into the bunk for safety, knowing it was going to be rough, and he had to let her loose now that they were back to smooth, though fast, sailing.

Morgan smiled up at him as he walked in. She looked terrible. He had to get a nutritional scanner and some nutrient packs rigged up for her as quickly as possible. She needed a very specific, and high-volume amount of nutrients at this point to fully recover and the only way to do that was with the nutritional scanner, just like in the combat and flight suits.

"Hello Morgan. We're clear of the planet, no signs of pursuit. They couldn't catch us in this ship anyway. Not with Dav flying."

"Dav?" she asked.

"My little brother," Artus replied as he unbuckled her. She could do it herself if she were strong and clear-headed enough, but he wasn't sure she was in any shape to manage either way. "He was just a baby when you saw him last."

"Davrelan? He's flying the ship?" She looked troubled. "Artus, how long have I been on that planet?" Artus smiled slightly.

"Not quite that long, he's only thirteen." She gave a small sigh and a smile.

"And you let him fly?"

"He's a better pilot than I am. A better pilot than pretty much anyone, as far as I've seen," Artus replied, moving a chair over and sitting in it beside the bunk. She raised a brow and nodded, impressed.

"That's saying a lot. I remember coming to see you race out in the Hibben system once. You were very good." Artus flushed slightly.

"I didn't know you were there."

"You invited me," she pointed out.

"Yeah, but I didn't think you'd come."

"Of course I would, Artus. We were friends. Are friends." She smiled and reached out, weakly grasping his hand. He squeezed it back, as gentle as if he were handling an infant. He returned her smile. After a moment, she spoke again. "Artus, if Dav is thirteen, my baby would be thirteen too." Artus nodded. "Katherine would have given her the crystal." Artus nodded again. Morgan took a long breath and closed her eyes.

"Just a few weeks ago," Artus told her.

"That was her, back at the Center." It was a statement, not a question. Artus nodded.

"Yes. She has the gift."

"I prayed she would," Morgan said.

"Do you want me to go get her?" Artus asked.

"Not yet," she replied with a deep breath. "I want to clear my thoughts first. Please keep talking with me while I sort things out." Artus nodded and she continued. "Does she seem to have a talent for it?"

"She's only Jumped twice. Once to Ayaran, where you programmed the key to take her," he said. Before she could jump to the conclusion that Allie wasn't talented, he went on. "Her second Jump was done blind, from just outside Pahrvic back to Earth. She carried not only four other life forms with her, but dragged the entire stupid escape pod with her. We had to blow it up to keep the humans on Earth from finding it." Artus chuckled at that memory. Dav and Raith had both had a truly great time with that project.

None of them had expected her to bring the escape pod with her. Jumping that much mass was difficult and until Allie, Artus had never heard of a crystal bearer able to do something like that without years of training. Allie had done it by accident. Morgan was staring.

"Artus that's... incredible." Artus just nodded. "Her connection to the energy must be on an incredibly deep level. Does Tyren know about her?"

"I'm afraid so. She hit him."

"Hit him?" Morgan asked, confused, though for lack of understanding. Her focus seemed to be getting sharper as she talked. "With what?"

"Her fist," Artus said. Morgan laughed in surprise.

"Well she didn't get that from me," she proclaimed.

"No, you were never much of a fighter," Artus smiled.

"If Tyren knows about her, he's chasing her."

"Yes."

"Those recon androids will have her in a matter of days," Morgan said, closing her eyes in frustration, obviously fighting a resurgence of the hopelessness she'd felt for thirteen long years.

"Not likely," he replied. Morgan opened her eyes and frowned.

"What do you mean?" she asked.

"There's only one recon android left in the galaxy. He might even be the only fully functioning android left."

"How is that possible? There were millions of androids!"

"There was a virus, about ten years ago. Some stupid Resistance genius programmed it and infected a captured coms android with it. It spread across all of the com channels to every android in the galaxy. Nearly all of them went berserk. A lot of innocent people were killed," Artus added softly, "and in the end, all of the androids tore themselves apart or were forcibly recycled."

"By the stars," Morgan said, face pale. "Why haven't they built new ones?"

"The Infection was designed to relay itself across the coms channels. It's still bouncing around out there. The moment an android is built it becomes infected. Unless somebody finds a whole new way to build androids, I'm afraid their day is done. Regular robots seem to all be fine, it's the artificial intelligence systems in the androids that the virus effects."

"You said there's one left? How did it survive?"

"I really don't know. Shielded himself from it somehow."

"Shouldn't its power have drained off years ago?"

"Should have. This one is stubborn. He says he rewired his power core."

"That's impossible," she replied.

"I would have thought so too, but that's what he says he did, and since he's still around I'm actually inclined to believe him. He can do some pretty incredible things, even for a recon android."

"'He says'," she repeated, considering the words. "You mean you've spoken with it?"

"I have," Artus replied after a moment.

"Is my daughter safe from it?" she asked. Artus nodded.

"I don't believe he's a threat to her any longer," he said.

Morgan took a deep breath and nodded. Artus felt a little guilty, misleading Morgan that way, but he didn't think she was quite ready to deal with the idea that a recon android was on their side. The recons had done an incredible amount of damage to the crystal bearer ranks.

"That's good. I think I'm ready to see her. Would you please bring me a glass of water, and then my daughter?" she asked. Artus squeezed her hand once more and nodded.

"Of course," Artus replied. He went to the small sink in one corner and filled a glass, bringing it to Morgan. She accepted it carefully, obviously concerned she would drop it. "I'll go get her."

Artus left the room, pausing in the hallway as the door closed for a long breath. It was hard to see her again, though wonderful. He was torn with guilt, feeling responsible for the failed rescue mission the first time he'd tried to get her out. Raith had made all the difference this time. He was also flooded with feelings he hadn't felt since he was a young teenager.

He'd had a crush on Morgan Bennett, back then. That was something he would never have admitted to anyone.

Seeing her again brought a lot of that back. He recognized it now as a crush rather than as a deeper love, but he still felt it for her. A silly, boyish crush. He shook his head to clear it of the foolish thoughts and went to get Allie. He would start the crafter working on the materials Morgan needed while they talked.

Allie couldn't decide if her anxiety was due to excitement, fear, adrenaline from the escape, or a combination of the above, but her heart pounded in her chest as she moved to the bunk room. Tic chirped softly on her shoulder in comforting tones. She hesitated a long moment, trying to steady her breathing before opening the door and stepping inside.

When she did, she had trouble processing what she was seeing. The woman leaned in a partially upright position on the bunk, propped up with a number of pillows. She wasn't quite upright enough to be called sitting, and from the look of the woman in front of her, Allie doubted her mother could have sat for long without support anyway.

The woman, her mother Allie corrected, was so thin from malnutrition that her face had a vaguely skull-like appearance. Which made sense when you considered that most of what now separated her face from the skull beneath it was just dull, dry skin.

Despite that, Allie could see hints at the beauty Morgan Bennett had once been. Behind the sunken cheeks and eyes that looked to have trouble focusing on her, the woman had a delicate jawline, elegantly high cheekbones, and a nose that could only be described as regal. Allie could see the stunning woman from the photograph she still kept with her, hiding under the sunken face. After a moment, she realized the woman was studying her just as intently and became a little embarrassed, turning her eyes downward.

"You are absolutely beautiful," Morgan said softly. Allie looked back up, surprised. "So much like your father."

Allie hesitated another moment, unsure of how to proceed, then moved over beside the bunk and sat in the chair that had been placed there. She wondered for a moment if Artus had put the chair by the bunk just for her.

"I don't know what he looked like," Allie replied,

feeling like it was a stupid reply. Morgan smiled softly.

"A lot like you," she replied, "though a more masculine version of course. Though it looks like you got my eyes."

Allie smiled a little. Her eyes had always been her favorite feature. As she locked gazes with the woman she could see that while lacking the sparkle of a healthy woman's, her mother's eyes were the exact shade of green that Allie's were and would have been striking if she were in full health.

"What happened to him?" Allie asked. Morgan settled back just a little, expression turning sad. Allie's heart sank.

"He didn't make it. His ship was destroyed while defending a resistance outpost. Five thousand people got away thanks to him." Morgan's tone was a mixture of pride and sorrow.

"Was he a soldier?" Allie asked.

She wanted desperately to climb into her mother's arms and simply be held, as her mother had likely done when she was an infant, but she couldn't get over the strangeness of being here, sitting beside her real mother. A woman she didn't know at all. Morgan shook her head.

"He was a Lord of the Council, and a General in the Coalition Guard. Before Tyren took power, anyway," Morgan said, then hesitated. "This is a strange question for me to ask, but… did Katharine keep the name I gave you?"

"My name is Allie," she replied. Morgan smiled.

"I'm glad. Your father's name was Allin. The name had meaning for me, he was killed before you were born and never had the chance to hold you. This way, every time someone says your name, it's as though he's there with you." Allie's throat constricted with the tears she was trying desperately to hold in.

"I have so many questions," Allie said, then tapered off, at a loss for where to go from there. Morgan nodded, her eyes beginning to glisten with tears threatening to escape. It was too much for Allie. "Mom…" she said before she broke. She threw herself forward onto the bunk. Her mother's arms went tightly around her, the pair of them finally getting the embrace they had both been dreaming about for so long.

They held each other for a long time before either spoke again. When they did, Allie shifted only slightly to lay beside her mother, who continued to hold her and stroke her hair.

"Katharine took such good care of you," Morgan said.

"She was amazing," Allie replied, "I couldn't have asked for a better mother to raise me." Morgan didn't answer for a moment and Allie realized how that must have sounded. "I mean, you'd have been the best though." Morgan laughed lightly, a beautiful, melodic sound even through her rough throat.

"Oh no, you had it right the first time. Katharine would certainly be a better mother than I would have been. Not only would my being a diplomat have guaranteed we never had a real home, I was never very good with little children. I loved you so very much, but Katharine knew how to care for a young child."

"I still wish it had been you," Allie said softly.

"So do I," Morgan replied, "but I am with you now and we have all the time we want to get to know each other again."

"Maybe," Allie said, less convinced. "Tyren is definitely after me, and will certainly be after you too once he hears you've escaped. He probably already knows."

"I'm not worried. We have you to help us escape."

"No, you should take the crystal back," Allie said, reaching for her pocket. Morgan stopped her though.

"I can't," she said simply.

"But you're a Starjumper too, right?" Allie asked, a little confused. Morgan gave her a delighted smile.

"Starjumper? That's charming. Much nicer than 'crystal bearer'. Rolls off the tongue better too. Where did you get that name?"

"I made it up," Allie said with a shrug, embarrassed again.

"I love it, but no. I'm not a Starjumper. I was once, one of the best, but Tyren wanted to know how those of us who could use the crystal keys could do it. They did a lot of experiments on me when they captured me. Whatever it was inside me that let me reach that energy is broken. I can't feel it anymore."

"How do you know? You haven't held a crystal since then, right?" Allie argued. Morgan shook her head.

"I was one of the best, I told you. I could feel the energy even without a crystal, though you still need a crystal to Jump. What I could do though was See where I could Jump to, even without a crystal. Can you do that yet? See where you're Jumping even if you've never been there?"

"No, I just picture where I want to go."

"How clear is the picture?"

"I don't know," Allie shrugged, "pretty clear. I have a good imagination."

"You're probably pretty close to Seeing it then. It happens when you get part of the way across the Jump. When you get good enough, you'll even be able to redirect mid-Jump if you need to. I was able to See my landing place without Jumping at all. I think they call that clairvoyance back on Earth."

"You mean seeing things without being there? Like through a camera?"

"Something like that, yes," Morgan answered.

"If you can't use the crystal anymore, how are we going to stop Tyren?" Allie asked.

"What does that have to do with stopping Tyren?" Morgan asked, looking confused.

"The crystal hurts him," Allie answered, surprised that her mother didn't know that. Morgan looked stunned.

"It does? How does it hurt him?"

"I don't know, but every time I got it close to him, red mist seemed to come out of him and he'd scream. I hit him in the leg while I was holding it and his leg collapsed like he'd lost all the strength in it," Allie answered. Morgan's shook her head slowly, dumbstruck.

"I had no idea," she said, almost to herself. "That explains so much." Looking back to Allie, she continued, "We never could figure out why he hated the crystal bearers so much, and why he was so dead-set on destroying them all. Our abilities were useful for travel, delivery of sensitive packages and emergency supplies, that kind of thing, but the crystals aren't a weapon. At least, we didn't think they were. It doesn't make any sense though. The Sy'hli aren't able to use the crystals at all, but they aren't hurt by them."

"Why would it hurt Tyren then?" Allie asked.

"I don't know, Allie," Morgan replied, "but if we can figure that out, we may have the answers to a great many of the questions the Resistance has about him."

CHAPTER NINE

PLANS WITHIN PLANS

"Why must I wait!" Highlord Tyren screamed his frustration at Harelo.

"Forgive me, my Lord," the false Uhran replied, "but the wormholes have proven unreliable. It will take a week for the final shipment of core material to arrive for the Helios."

"I cannot power the ship without that material," Tyren grumbled, "and I must wait another week for it to arrive. The Helios finished construction days ago!"

"Yes, my Lord," Harelo replied simply, "when the shipment arrives, the test run of the Helios will be glorious." Tyren scowled at the advisor.

"And what of my brothers and the crystal bearer? And that blasted chunk of metal?"

"The android, my Lord?"

"Of course the android!" Tyren snapped. Harelo hesitated. The Highlord caught the hesitation and moved forward threateningly. "What news?"

"They escaped the Center, my Lord."

"With advanced notice, a Sy'hli strike team in position, a spy in their ranks, and a potentially perfect hostage already imprisoned in the center, you let three children, a malfunctioning android, and one untrained, barely-grown Sy'hli break into an advanced military facility, free a prisoner, and escape unharmed?" Tyren had switched to his carefully calm tone, the one he used when trying hard not to kill whomever he was speaking to at the moment.

"Put simply, yes, my Lord," Harelo replied. To Tyren's satisfaction, Harelo looked distinctly nervous. As he should be, Tyren thought.

"We should at least have killed one or two of them," he grumbled, "And any word from the combat android?"

"None, my Lord."

"What use is a combat android if he can't even stop them from stealing my prisoners?!" Tyren shouted in annoyance.

"He is under orders to observe and wait, my Lord," Harelo pointed out. Tyren remembered giving those orders, and had to remind himself that he was waiting for them to make it to the Resistance hideout before unleashing the C.A.D.E. unit.

"We still have their location?" Tyren asked. Harelo nodded once.

"Yes, my Lord. Recently confirmed from both the android and the Ambassador's niece."

"Excellent. Inform me immediately when they reach the Resistance hideout."

"Of course, my Lord," Harelo bowed and turned to leave.

"And Harelo," Tyren said. Harelo stopped and turned back around. "Be sure to inform me the instant the shipment arrives." Harelo bowed again and left.

The Uhran was efficient, Tyren thought grudgingly. He kept control over the Highlord's spy network brilliantly. So well that Tyren would be suspicious of him if Preston hadn't been keeping an eye on Harelo for years.

A more devious and underhanded man than Preston the Highlord had yet to meet. The man would probably sell his own mother into slavery if the price were high enough. Tyren paid him well enough that his loyalty was completely assured.

What concerned him at the moment was that they'd successfully rescued the Bennett woman. Highlord Tyren knew she couldn't Jump anymore so she wasn't a threat in that regard, but her knowledge would be invaluable to the Resistance.

He would just have to unleash the C.A.D.E. unit the moment they arrived at the hideout. The entire Resistance wouldn't stand a chance against a combat android at this point. They'd been so battered and beaten back over the years that they were nothing more than a ragtag group of miscreants.

The Highlord was actually fairly sure that this last hideout was the sole remaining pocket of Resistance, though the appearance and survival of his brothers was problematic.

With them alive, if anything happened to Tyren,

Artus would inherit the Sy'hli Empire, and with it control of the Coalition. Tyren intended to live forever, but his brothers would be determined to make sure that didn't happen.

He reassured himself that the combat android would kill them all without much trouble and left it at that. The android had better bring back the crystal though. It was the only one left, and destroying it would almost totally eliminate any real threats to him in the future. He could potentially rule for a thousand years, though that wasn't actually his real long-term plan.

While waiting for things to fall into place for that, he would enjoy playing with the Helios when he finally had the core material. Without that, nothing could sustain enough power to operate the new ship. Tyren moved to the window and gazed out at the monstrous craft.

Glistening gold plating covered its bulky, layered hull, the long, numerous jutting arms all arcing to face backward. Special, crystalline optical cabling was strung between the long arms, or legs as Tyren preferred to think of them. Tyren always thought it almost resembled a giant golden squid, a comparison he didn't much care for, but the less ideal shape was critical to its ultimate function.

It was the size of a small city, though could actually only house a hundred crewmen and soldiers and half a dozen scientists. Its massive shell contained several hundred thousand tons of a naturally-occurring liquid that had been found on a remote planet. So far, it had proven impossible to synthesize, and Tyren's men had taken all of the material from its native planet.

Tyren's scientists had discovered that the substance had remarkable energy retention properties, which is what had sparked the entire project, but without the core material to act as a catalyst the proper reaction couldn't occur to process the incoming energy.

Once he had the core material, he could fly the Helios at speeds fast enough to catch an Interceptor, with enough firepower to destroy entire planets on a whim. With that as his new base of operations, he could go anywhere, destroy anyone, and finally carry out his true plan.

First, however, he needed that core material and to perform a successful test of the Helios. He just had to pick a star system to test it out on. It would be even better if it were tested on the Resistance hideout world, but he didn't really want to wait.

Besides, having them all torn apart by the combat android would be more personally satisfying anyway. Especially since he could play back the android's memory files any time later for his enjoyment.

You're forgetting something, came the voice. It had been almost smug the last several days, even more so since his brothers and the brat girl had escaped the Center with the Bennett woman.

No, Tyren thought, refusing to address the voice directly, there was nothing that could stop him.

The girl has the crystal. She knows it can hurt you. Soon the Resistance will know that it can hurt you. Once they have a weapon against you, all of them, on all of the worlds, will come out of their holes and strike. She can

Jump. She can reach you anywhere. My brothers will help her, and you will fall.

"No!" Tyren shouted out loud, shoving the voice back. "I will kill them all! Every last one of them! Every sentient being on every world will beg on hands and knees to be spared before I crush them!"

You will fail. The girl will learn. Her mother will teach her. There is nowhere you can hide.

"Pahrvic! Nobody can Jump near Pahrvic!" Tyren cried, before realizing he'd just acknowledged that he may have to hide. The voice laughed. Tyren shoved, but it was stronger than usual today. Today, it resisted and he could not silence it. The voice just laughed harder.

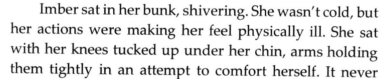

Imber sat in her bunk, shivering. She wasn't cold, but her actions were making her feel physically ill. She sat with her knees tucked up under her chin, arms holding them tightly in an attempt to comfort herself. It never worked, but she wasn't willing to stop trying.

She had finished her report to her uncle. Imber knew that information was likely already sent to Tyren's people, and probably Tyren himself by now. He knew where they were, and which direction they were currently going, though the way Dav somehow mapped and flew through wormholes they could be just about anywhere by this time tomorrow.

Imber didn't know where the Resistance was hiding, other than the name of the world, though Dav and Artus seemed to know exactly where they were going. She and her uncle had played off the idea that they already were in touch with the Resistance and knew their location, but neither was true. All they had was the name of the planet the Resistance was supposedly hiding out on, Kobek.

She had helped Allie rescue her mother. They'd been back in that bunk room by themselves for two days now, catching up. Artus had made a flight suit for Morgan complete with the nutrition packs to try and help her recover. It would take weeks before the woman was anywhere near full health again, but she already looked a lot better.

Considering she was busily betraying them all behind their backs, she probably shouldn't have helped them escape, but considering her own circumstances, she couldn't allow Allie's mother to remain imprisoned and in danger. She couldn't help her father, but she could help Allie's mother.

In the end, it would be futile. She knew Tyren would use the information she sent to kill all of her new friends. Allie and her mother would be killed. Artus and Dav would be killed. Raith would be killed.

For some reason, the idea of Raith dying particularly bothered her, which made no real sense since he was an android well past his expected lifespan anyway. There was something different about him, though. He was different from any android she'd studied, in almost every way. He didn't behave even like a recon droid, which should behave similarly to a person.

A trained eye could spot the subtle clues though. No android could pass for a person perfectly. People were too unpredictable, too inconsistent for any mathematically-based system to imitate. Except she couldn't tell the difference with Raith. She'd spent days with him, talking with him, playing cards with him, laughing with him. If it weren't for the scar on his face she'd never have known that he wasn't biological.

Beyond the expected android traits that would make him seem superior to almost any biological being, he was funny, sweet, charming, and an unbelievable flirt. And the lengths he had gone to in order to rescue her when the battle cruiser had captured her was nothing short of awe-inspiring.

His actions had been both superhuman and touchingly human. He'd have given himself to save her without a moment's hesitation, and she knew it. That stunt had been very close to suicidal even for an android. If the soldiers hadn't been so frightened of him, they'd have mounted a legitimate defense and probably would have taken him down. If she didn't know better, she'd suspect she was starting to have feelings for him.

It didn't matter though. All of them would die. And it would be Imber's fault. She didn't have a choice though. What did you do when trapped between two choices, both of them horrible and full of pain and death? Which was more valuable; a few new friends, or her own father? It wasn't much of a choice. Nobody could stand by and let their own father be killed if they could prevent it.

If only it would be possible for her new friends to help her rescue her own father. Maybe, if she helped them enough, they would stand a good enough chance to win against Tyren to rescue her father. They seemed extremely capable, though going against Tyren was pure suicide. But if Imber helped them, maybe they'd stand an even better chance.

If they won, Tyren would be no more, her father would be safe, and everyone she cared about would be okay. And if they lost, her father would still be spared because she'd been holding up her end of the bargain with Tyren.

Imber rested her head on her knees. There had to be a better way. Continuing to help Tyren against these people was wrong, and she knew it. Letting her father die was also wrong. Both ways, she was guilty of terrible things. With a frustrated sigh that was closer to a sob than Imber cared to admit, she stood up and headed out of the bunkroom.

To her surprise, Allie and her mother were walking, slowly and carefully, down the hallway toward the cockpit, Tic sitting happily on Allie's shoulder.

"Allie?" Imber called. Both of them turned, Morgan leaning heavily on Allie for support. Allie smiled brightly. Morgan smiled too, though she was clearly putting a lot of effort into staying upright.

"Imber! Come and meet my mother! After all, you helped rescue her," Allie grinned as Imber approached. As she drew closer, Allie spoke again. "Mom, this is Imber. She's the niece of an Ambassador, and our expert sniper. She helped get you out of that prison."

To Imber's surprise, Morgan's hands began moving in a structured, orchestrated manner that it took her a moment to recognize. Morgan apparently knew the hand-sign language her people had developed centuries ago to allow communication on her homeworld between her own people and visitors from other worlds.

Morgan had just told her it was an honor to meet her and gave her great praise and thanks for her part in the rescue. Imber responded in the color speech of her own people.

The honor is mine Morgan Bennett, you are a person of great renown among the Resistance. Imber's colors flickered. Allie looked stunned as her gaze turned back and forth between the two.

I am humbled, Morgan replied in the signed language. *You are a friend of my daughter's, you can speak and understand English?*

Well, no time like the present to reveal a secret.

"Yes, I speak English as well," Imber replied. Morgan smiled warmly. Imber looked to Allie.

"On my world, our atmosphere doesn't conduct sound well," Imber explained. "It's not dense enough. So our people don't use verbal speech, we evolved heirlines, these lines on my face and body to communicate. They're inherited, so you can actually identify family heritage sometimes from them, which is why we call them heirlines. Your mother speaks our hand-sign language, which off-worlders use to communicate with us since they don't have heirlines." Allie looked stunned, but then suddenly seemed to brighten as if something occurred to her.

"That's what it is! You're deaf!" Allie exclaimed.

"I don't have any means of hearing, no," Imber said.

"I'm so sorry," Morgan said abruptly to Imber. "I didn't realize she didn't know. I hope I didn't spoil any secrets.

"Nothing serious, Mrs. Bennett," Imber replied. "People just get weird when they realize I can't hear them, even though I read lips and speak plenty well enough."

"That's why you don't respond unless you're looking directly at someone," Allie said. Imber nodded. "And that's where I recognize your accent."

"I have an accent?" Imber asked. Allie smiled.

"Only a really little bit. I could barely hear it, but I went to school with a girl who was deaf years ago. Her accent was kind of the same, but a lot stronger."

"It doesn't bother you?"

"Your accent? Not at all," Allie replied.

"No, that I'm deaf," Imber replied with a laugh.

"Should it?" Allie asked.

"Definitely not. Just like I said, some humans get weird about it."

"Wait a minute, if you can't hear, how did you speak with us over the helmet coms back on Niertagh?" Allie asked suspiciously. Imber smiled.

"Raith knows about my people. He built my helmet with a voice-to-text feature. Every time you guys talked, I got it in text on my visor, complete with a color indicator of which one of you was speaking."

"Wow, that boy really does think of everything," Allie grinned. "Come on mom, I want to meet everyone else too," Allie said with obvious excitement. Imber watched as the pair turned and headed to the cockpit. Imber followed along. This promised to be interesting.

CHAPTER TEN

THE SHIFT

Allie and her mother walked into the cockpit. Artus spotted them first, already having been turned sideways to speak with Dav. He smiled warmly at her mother.

Artus had been the one bringing them their food while they'd been talking the past two days, and Allie had learned the pair had not only known each other, but they had been good friends. She wasn't sure how that worked with her mother being so much older than Artus, but she understood their two families had been close. Allie had actually been relieved to realize she'd have known Dav closely either way her life had gone.

"Hello Morgan, good to see you up and about. How do you feel?" Artus asked, standing and moving over to her.

"Much better, thank you," she replied. Allie smiled. Her mother really had been improving at a rapid pace. It wouldn't take long before she'd be moving around easily without help. Dav stood and came over as well. Raith stayed where he was, looking firmly at his monitors.

"Hi," Dav said simply, offering her a bright, warm smile. Her mother smiled back at him.

"Davrelan," she said, "Last time I saw you, you weren't even potty trained yet." Dav flashed a cheeky grin.

"Don't worry ma'am, I'm pretty good at it now." Her mother laughed.

"Well thank you so much for your part in my rescue. Thirteen years is a very long time to be locked away in a place like that."

"I can't even imagine," Dav replied more seriously. "It was my pleasure to help, both for the sake of your friendship with my family, and for your being my best friend's mother," he smiled at Allie.

"My daughter is lucky to have such good friends in all of you," she said.

Raith finally stood and stepped forward. He looked very nervous, which Allie found odd. She instantly felt her mother's body tense as she met Raith's gaze. There was a pause so long and tense that Allie got nervous herself. A moment before she would have spoken to try and break the tension, her mother took two strong, deliberate steps toward Raith.

Raith closed his eyes and turned his head slightly like he expected to be struck. For a moment, Allie was afraid that's what her mother was about to do. When she reached him though, Morgan knelt and put both arms firmly around the much shorter android and hugged him tightly. Everyone was completely silent, nobody knowing what exactly was happening.

Raith's eyes opened in surprise and he looked at Allie, expression confused, over her mother's shoulder. Another long moment passed and Morgan released him.

"All due respect," Raith said slowly, "what exactly was that for?" Morgan smiled broadly at him and touched his cheek with affection.

"For saving my daughter's life." Everyone exchanged glances. Raith had saved Allie, more than once, but Morgan didn't know about any of that as far as they knew.

"I am not sure I know what you mean," Raith said. "I am the one who abducted you from Earth and handed you over to Tyren. Not that I'm complaining, but I kind of thought you'd be angry with me." Morgan shook her head.

"Not at all. You followed orders, exactly as far, and not one inch farther, than you had to. You took me to Tyren, but you let my Allie go," she said. Raith glanced at Allie, who shrugged, not knowing any better than he did.

"I have perfect access to my data, and I have no memory of having ever encountered your daughter before a few weeks ago." Morgan looked at Raith's confused expression for a moment, then laughed, a little embarrassed.

"I'm sorry, you really don't know," she said. Raith shook his head.

"When you came to collect me," Morgan explained, as the others all listened with interest, "I had Allie with me. I was bringing her to my dearest friend Katharine to look after. I knew I was being hunted, but I hoped I'd have enough time to get Allie to safety. You grabbed me right after I left Katharine's house. I begged you to spare my baby. You told me your orders said nothing about the baby, and you rewrote your memory core to remove her so Tyren wouldn't know anything about her. You are the only reason Allie is still alive." Everyone stared as she finished. Raith looked to Allie, this time he took a turn to shrug. Allie's smile grew.

"Raith, that's awesome!" Allie exclaimed with a bright smile for her android friend.

"You rewrote your memory core to remove someone from it?" Imber asked from behind Allie. They all looked her way. Imber shook her head in awe. "That's remarkable. You shouldn't have been able to do that."

"Not easy, but possible," Raith replied. "It's actually the same way I fought off the Infection. I managed to trap the virus in a system echo loop long enough to rewrite all of my subroutines. The virus is still in there, but I reprogrammed enough of my processing systems that it's no longer effective. Compared to that, memory modification is pretty easy. I just don't remember doing it." Dav started laughing. Everyone looked his way.

"You must be good at it then!" Dav said with another laugh. Allie grinned as she realized what he meant. Artus rolled his eyes, but couldn't stop a smile.

"Either way, when I heard there was one recon android left, I was truly hoping it was you," Morgan said. "I knew you would do anything you could to defy Tyren within your orders. How have you gotten to where you can so directly help out the Resistance?"

"Our generous and short-sighted friend the Highlord told me I didn't have to follow orders anymore unless I wanted to," Raith said with a wink to Allie.

"He did what?" Morgan asked, then shook her head. "That wasn't smart. I'll bet there's a story there."

"Dav?" Artus interrupted after a quick glance at his display. Dav looked his way. "Less than ten minutes until we reach the entrance to the wormhole."

"Time to play," Dav said with a slightly scary laugh.

"Time for me to go lie down," Morgan said. "Wormholes make me nauseous in the best of time, and I'm definitely not at my best. You can fill me in later."

"Good idea," Artus said, "You'll probably want to be lying down for our trip into The Shift anyway."

Morgan and Imber froze. Allie glanced at the two. They both looked extremely uneasy.

"We're traveling into The Shift?" Morgan asked carefully.

"That's where the Resistance is hiding, and conveniently where this wormhole lets out." Dav replied.

"How can you possibly know that?" Imber asked, sounding worried.

"I map wormholes. It's kind of a hobby," Dav replied, smiling at her.

"Into The Shift?" she asked.

"That's new," Dav admitted, "but I've been tracking this wormhole for quite a while and its far end is relocating at very predictable intervals, in a very consistent pattern of coordinates. In about fifteen minutes, it will be in The Shift, less than an hour away from where we anticipate the world the Resistance is established would be. We'll come out right after it opens in The Shift."

"What's The Shift?" Allie asked, confused.

"The Shift," Imber explained, "is a region of space that isn't... well, it isn't quite right. It makes scanning and navigational systems do all kinds of strange things. The chances of coming back out of The Shift drop pretty fast the longer you're in it. There's no way the Resistance is still alive if they went in there."

"They're in there," Raith reassured her, "I've been in contact with them several times along this trip. I know where they are. And The Shift is somewhat misunderstood."

"How so," Artus asked, curiously.

"It isn't scanners it messes with, it's space."

"It's in space?" Allie asked, not following.

"Yes, but I meant it messes with space. All the reports of problems with that region of space involve random disappearances of ships, planets, even entire star systems from scanners, sudden changes of ship coordinates, that kind of thing," Raith said. "What's happening however, is not problems with the scanners, it's that things actually are disappearing, and reappearing elsewhere in The Shift. Kind of like Jumping, only uncontrolled and on an astronomic scale."

"That is not making me feel any better," Imber said. Raith gave her an apologetic smile.

"Sorry Imber," he said sincerely. "Just remember that's actually good news. It means we can completely rely on our scanners, just not on the locations of things we scan being permanent. Like in a wormhole, Dav just has to dodge anything that appears in front of us, and Artus has to recalibrate our navigation if we happen to get moved. It means that we won't just disappear, we'll reappear somewhere else in The Shift, most likely unharmed."

"Most likely?" Artus asked wryly.

"I can give you the exact probability if you like," he said with a mischievous grin.

"No thanks," Artus replied, shaking his head.

"How do you know that's what is happening in The Shift?" Dav asked.

"I told you, I've been in communication with the Resistance in there," Raith replied. "They've been almost totally stuck in there for years. They can only send ships out when their world moves over near the edge of The Shift. They used Jumpers to get in and out before Tyren got rid of them all."

"Not all of them," Morgan said, smiling at Allie. "But still, I'm going to lie down," Morgan said. Allie wasn't sure how bad things were about to get, and trusted that if Dav, Artus, and Raith were willing to fly into it, she believed they had a high chance of succeeding at reaching the Resistance.

"I'll take you," Imber said to Morgan, "I'd rather not watch this either. Besides, they'll need Allie on scanners."

"For whatever that's worth," Allie grumbled, but let Imber take her mother's arm and help her out of the room.

Allie moved to her station and sat down. The moment she touched the control panel, her display appeared. With a thought, a map of the region of space they were in dominated the display, identifying the location of the wormhole entrance.

As she looked more closely at it, she understood from the computer that it wasn't really an entrance in the way she'd been thinking, more like a place where space was thin enough to fall out of. It was only a minute or so later that they reached the place and Allie felt the ship fall into the space between space. It was a weird sensation, and she knew full well why her mother got sick going through them.

Dav flew fast, although according to Artus not as fast as he'd done when they had come to rescue her. She was both pleased and frightened by that idea. These wormholes made her nervous anyway, watching the dark lightning lancing down all around them as they flew at what she felt were terrifying speeds down the corridor of the wormhole.

It wasn't really a tunnel like she'd thought it would be, either. By the scanners, it looked like it extended in every direction infinitely, though it seemed to have a definite floor and ceiling, but there was something else filling the space between the dark bolts of energy outside of the corridor. She didn't know how it all worked, but all she really needed to know was that Dav could get them through it.

Dav banked and rolled, dodging the bolts as they flashed past them all around. Allie watched, morbidly fascinated. It was like a roller coaster in the dark, where you didn't know a turn was coming until you actually moved, hurtling through dark, scary space, not having any idea what was ahead, or behind, or when the ride would end. She trusted Dav, but this was definitely nerve-wracking. Allie was certain they were about to die at least a hundred times during the trip.

It took almost fifteen minutes to pilot through. The moment the ship fell back into normal space, something odd tugged at the edges of her senses. According to her scanners, nothing was within half an hour's flight from where they now were, but something in the back of her mind kept trying to tell her that there was an energy all around, rippling and shifting.

It was familiar, but took a moment for her to realize it felt similar to the energy from the crystal key. This felt subtly different however; more wild, less focused. Without hesitation, she decided Raith was right. There was something wrong with space here, and the things moving around here actually were Jumping. Entire planets, Jumping through space. Something about that thought made Allie shiver slightly. It seemed very wrong to her, though she couldn't say why. It just felt like something that should never, ever happen.

The scanners looked clear, but she felt a surge in the energy, like a wave in the ocean, suddenly roll over them. She felt a familiar pulling sensation, and then it was gone. In a fraction of a second, everything on her scanners had changed. They were now in the middle of a five planet star system, flying directly at the large sun in the center.

Dav had several seconds to maneuver the ship away from the star, which for him was almost a leisurely turn, but everyone started shouting at once. Allie was quiet, and closed her eyes. The scanners couldn't tell when and where the energy was moving, but she could feel it.

It felt something like riding a small boat in the ocean. She just had to watch for the big waves. Allie was fairly sure that she had enough notice with that last surge to do something about it the next time. Something about the way the energy moved and felt made her fairly sure that she could manipulate it.

She took the crystal out of her pocket. The instant her fingers touched the smooth crystal, the feel of the energy around her sharpened. It was clear and defined all around her. With her eyes closed, she could almost see it.

Allie could hear Artus giving Dav new coordinates, but she ignored it. She needed to focus on keeping them from getting Jumped off course again. Sure enough, she felt another one a few minutes later, though this one felt more like a pulse in place than a wave rolling past.

"Dav, left!" she shouted, opening her eyes.

Dav responded instantly, banking hard left. She smiled at the fact that he trusted her enough to move first and ask questions later. A huge asteroid appeared right in front of them just as Dav banked. Even he would have been hard-pressed to dodge that one without her warning.

"How did you do that?" Artus asked excitedly after a surprised silence.

"I can feel it, the energy all around. It really is like Jumping."

Another wave rolled toward them. Allie reached out through the crystal with her mind and mentally pushed on the wave right where it would have reached them. It fanned out on either side around their ship.

Allie opened her eyes again and was pleased to see

that nothing had changed on the scanners. She had blocked the Jump. "I can keep us from Jumping too. I can't stop the ones that bring things in, but I can feel those coming too. I'll warn you when I see them coming."

"See Allie? Super powers," Dav said, sparing a look her way to grin at her.

Allie giggled and closed her eyes again. She felt better that she was actually useful in here, though she still wished she could be more useful in a fight. She resolved to have Imber teach her to use a gun while they were on the Resistance world.

"Down," Allie called.

Dav dove the ship under a swirling arc of flame from what looked just like a solar flare that had just appeared directly in front of them. She didn't know how the wave of energy had pulled just the flare from the star and not the star itself, but it was a big one and flying straight through it probably would have done some damage.

Navigating this way was tricky, but at least they weren't suddenly being moved to another random part of the sector. It took almost two hours, rather than the one hour it would have taken if space was behaving the way it should, but they finally got the planet in sight.

It was the fourth one out from an angry red star, with two more big planets on an even wider loop around the star, according to her scanners. Both were gas giants, and the smallest one nearest to the star seemed to be basically nothing more than a big chunk of rock with an uneven ring of broken debris drifting around it.

"That's it," Raith said, sounding pleased. "Let's go say hello!"

CHAPTER ELEVEN

HUNTERS

Dav flew the Peacekeeper down to the planet, changing angle and slowing way down as they reached atmosphere to give them a smooth ride in. As they broke through into the atmosphere, Allie stared down at the red and black planet. It didn't look hospitable at all. Angry, dark clouds tinged with red were everywhere, bolts of yellow lightning cutting through the air between the clouds and the ground with alarming frequency.

The ground below, once they'd moved below cloud level, was a dark red stone, almost black. It looked shattered, cracked lines running all over it. Some of the cracks in the stone had bright yellow, glowing fluid running along them. It could have been lava, Allie supposed, though was probably something else she couldn't identify and had never heard of.

Scattered across the landscape, it looked as though some of the broken plates of stone had been jammed into the ground at odd angles, creating huge, jagged walls of stone, riddled with overhangs and crevices. In the distance, a massive mountain range could barely be seen against the backdrop of the angry red and black sky.

"Cheerful place," Allie commented.

"Yeah, some planets are definitely better places for vacation homes than others," Dav said with a chuckle. "I hope the region the Resistance is hiding out in is a more cozy location," he said.

"They're in a cave network up in those mountains," Raith said. Dav angled toward the distant peaks.

"Not sure that's much of an improveme..." Dav began.

A huge bolt of yellow lightning lanced down right in front of them. Dav rolled around it, just like in the wormholes, but where the lightning struck a massive plume of smoky gases and a huge spray of the yellow liquid burst upward.

Allie watched in horror as a large glob of the thick liquid splattered across one of their wings. Nothing seemed to happen for a long moment as everyone held their breath, then suddenly that side of the craft dropped.

"It's shorting out the anti-grav!" Dav called. "We have to land!"

"Not yet!" Raith replied, "We're still two thousand spans from the caves, not counting the vertical climb into the mountains!"

"Not much choice," Dav replied grimly.

"Try to land it under one of the big overhangs, to cover us from the lightning!" Artus shouted.

There was a jarring sensation as the dipping wing

clipped another of the large stone plates. It wasn't serious, but it spun them off course again. Dav hissed slowly between his teeth as he tried to steer the crippled ship into not only a safe landing, but a covered one.

Tic chittered nervously, clinging tightly to Allie's shoulder. Another jolt rattled them as the ship hit ground. Allie's teeth felt like they were grinding together as the ship jostled along the uneven ground, sliding into position under one of the massive plates.

As they slid to a halt, everyone breathed a sigh of relief. Allie considered for a moment the advantages of landing gear, which this ship didn't have.

"Everyone okay?" Artus asked.

She heard his voice from down the hallway as well and realized he'd put his words through the ship's com system to make sure Morgan and Imber were okay as well.

It took a moment, but Imber appeared in the doorway of the cabin and reassured them that she and Morgan were all right.

"What's the plan now?" Imber asked, once she'd been told what had happened.

"Well we're not flying anywhere without some repairs," Raith told her. "It won't take a lot of time to repair, maybe a few hours, but we don't have the right tools here."

"I don't think we have any choice but to go on foot to the caves in the mountains," Dav said.

"Are you serious? That could take us days, longer with Morgan in her condition," Artus argued.

"Like I said, I don't think we have any choice. We

could split up and send a group to go get help, the rest staying here," Dav suggested.

"I don't like that idea," Allie said. "It may be more dangerous leaving her here than it would be for us all to travel."

"It may be more dangerous for us all to travel," Imber pointed out. "If we send Raith and one of the other boys, they could get to the caves in just a couple of hours without anyone else slowing them down."

"I could go alone," Raith added.

"Nobody goes anywhere alone," Artus said firmly. Raith just nodded.

"If Artus and Raith went, they could get to the caves, find the Resistance, and get another ship out here to pick up the rest of us," Imber said. "It probably wouldn't take more than a few hours round trip that way. Artus is right, it would take days for all of us on foot."

"Okay," Artus agreed, "Raith and I will go get help. Ready when you are, robo-boy." Raith smiled at that.

"Let's go get these lovely ladies some help," he replied. Raith turned to grab his helmet from where he'd hung it beside his gunner's chair.

Almost the moment he touched the helmet, a loud sound caused them all to turn back to face the doorway. It sounded like electrical wires shorting out, to Allie. A few moments later, a heavy, yellow smoke started to drift into the hallway from the side of the ship that had been hit. Raith reached over and touched his control bar.

"Change of plans, helmets on now! We all have to go!" Raith said firmly.

"What is it?" Allie asked.

"Some reaction between our electrical system and the slop that hit us. It's about to get pretty acidic in here." Raith put his helmet on and ran down the hallway far enough to close the door the smoke was coming in from with a quick touch to the panel.

Everyone grabbed helmets, Artus grabbing a second one from the rack his was on in the back of the cabin and running back to the bunkroom Morgan was in, which was thankfully on the other side of the ship from the source of the smoke.

He came out only a moment later carrying her, helmeted up just as he was. They all ran back to the cargo bay door, past the closed door where yellow smoke continued to seep around the edges.

Allie noticed that they all moved through the areas with the smoke as fast as possible. A faint hissing sound reached her ears through the helmet's audio system as each person entered. She stopped just beyond the smoke.

"Raith!" she cried. "What about Tic?" The little jicund on her shoulder was completely unprotected.

"I'm on it," she heard him reply. A moment later, he appeared out of the smoke with a heavy blanket. Tic eyed him curiously as he held the blanket out wide toward the jicund. "Come on, Tic!" Raith called. Tic jumped into his arms, and let herself be wrapped in the blanket. "Just run straight back, I'll get her through as quickly as I can," Raith told her, then turned and vanished into the thickening smoke.

Allie took a deep breath to prepare herself, then ran through the smoke. It wasn't quite thick enough to completely blind her, but close. She almost hit the side walls of the hallway a time or two, since she was mostly guessing on which direction was straight down the hallway, but she made it to the cargo bay.

The smoke was much less thick in here, though it looked like some of the materials in the bay were already melting in it. A quick glance at her suit showed no signs of melting despite the uncomfortable sizzling sound, which made her feel somewhat better.

She ran down the ramp and into clearer air. Raith was off to one side, holding Tic. He'd removed the blanket and dropped it by the back ramp, where it lay in a smoldering heap. Allie ran straight over to Tic, who jumped happily back to her shoulder. She looked totally unharmed.

"Thanks, Raith. Is she going to be okay in this atmosphere?" Allie asked. Raith nodded.

"Yeah, no problem. You could breathe this air for a while too without any problems, though too long and you might start to get a bit sick from it. Jicunds are tough little critters though. She won't have any trouble at all." Allie smiled in relief and scratched Tic's ears, who trilled happily in response.

"Come on," Artus said, "I don't want to be exposed out here any longer than we have to be." He turned and started a brisk walk toward the mountains. Allie sighed and followed, along with the others. Dav came up beside her as they walked.

"I grabbed the guns," he said, handing her a shatter gun. She smiled, took it, and holstered it.

"Thanks, Dav," she said.

"Can I walk with you?" he asked.

"What kind of question is that?" she asked him. "You're my best friend, you can walk beside me whenever you want."

"Yeah, I just wanted to make sure. Things have been a bit different since we left Earth."

Allie looked over at him. His expression was hard to read through the narrow view of the visor, but he seemed a little bit uncomfortable, as if he was worried about something. Allie thought about it. He was right, she'd been pretty distant since they left the Uhran colony.

Partly because of Imber, partly because of her worry over and time with her mother, but she hadn't interacted with him much over the last several days.

"You're right. I'm really sorry, Dav, I've been pretty worried about a lot of things, and then with my mom…" she said, not finishing the sentence. He nodded.

"I understand completely. I just wanted to make sure we were still okay. I've seen you throw a couple of less friendly looks my way since we left Earth."

Again, Allie thought about that, and again he was right. That was because she was really resentful of the attention he'd been giving Imber, though rationally she knew she shouldn't be. This would be a little tougher to handle.

"I'm sorry about that, too. I've been trying to sort some things out. This has been a lot for a girl to handle in just a couple of weeks."

"That's fair," Dav said. He was quiet as they walked for a while. "So we're still best friends?"

Allie felt her heart twinge for two reasons. The fact that he had to ask made her feel bad for how she'd been treating him, and the fact that she really wanted to be even more than just best friends both tugged at her.

"Dav, of course we are," she stopped and turned toward him. When he stopped, she wrapped her arms around him. He returned the hug tightly. Not as nice as hugs without body armor on, she thought regretfully. After a long moment she let go and stepped back. "You know, you're a much better hugger when you're not wearing an armored suit and a helmet." He laughed.

"I agree. We'll have to try that again later in more comfortable circumstances. Thanks Allie, I just want to make sure that whatever else happens, we're always going to be best friends."

Again, the heart twinge. They started walking again. What did he mean by that? What else could happen? Did he mean if he and Imber got to be more than friends, he just wanted Allie to not be upset by it? She wouldn't try to be, but even though she'd become friends with Imber, Allie still had a hard time watching the boys smile at her the way they did. Imber was incredibly sweet, though something about her still bothered Allie.

Maybe he just meant that he didn't want anything to get in the way of their friendship. Well of course he meant that, she thought, that would be true whether he meant he wanted to be with Imber, or whether he meant something else entirely.

For all she knew, he might have meant that even as things changed, like their suddenly becoming space adventurers, he wanted to let her know that he still wanted to be close with her. That was nice, but always wanting to be her best friend might also have meant that he knew she liked him and wanted to gently let her know that he wanted to just stay friends. She sighed in frustration. Why were boys so hard to understand?

The lightning flared regularly, though seemed mostly behind them. It looked like the storm was actually moving away from them, though she certainly wasn't a meteorologist. She hoped the ship aired out before everything in it melted. Dav loved that ship. Despite the storm being behind them, it was still fairly dark, seeming lit almost as much by the glowing liquid as by the little light leaking through the clouds.

They walked for what Allie was certain was several hours, though she was equally certain that those mountains didn't look any closer. The big, jutting plate rocks were fewer out here though, leaving things looking more like a broad, broken plain.

There were still a lot of cracks running through the stone and she made a point not to step on or even near any of them, especially the ones with the glowing yellow liquid running in them. It wasn't lava, and she didn't think it was hot. Definitely acidic though, from the smoke problem back on the ship and Raith's warning. Whatever it was, she knew she didn't want to mess with the stuff.

"We might have a problem," Raith's voice came over the com. Great, Allie though.

"What is it," Dav asked.

"We're being followed. And whatever it is, it's moving very fast."

"Options?" Artus asked.

"Wait for whatever it is and say hello," Raith offered, "or we could set an ambush, or try and outrun it."

"What do you think it is?" Imber asked.

"Animal in nature," Raith said, "I can hear them howling."

"Them?" Allie asked nervously.

"Yes. I can't tell how many though, the sounds are echoing strangely."

"What kind of sounds?" Artus asked.

"Kind of a low whooping howl. They're short and sharp, and seem to frequently cut off suddenly while another one starts just as suddenly."

"We don't know this terrain or what we're facing. I don't want to try and set an ambush. Whatever it is might be able to sense us in some way we don't know about. I sure don't want to just wait out in the open. Chances are we can't outrun them though, not with Morgan in her condition" Artus said. She was walking on her own two legs, but she was leaning on Artus for support.

"Never mind," Raith said in a resigned tone. "It's too late, we've got them coming from the other direction too."

"Guns ready," Artus said. "Raith, how long?"

"Less than a minute."

"No choice then, we stand and fight," Dav said, drawing his pistols. Imber dropped to a knee and raised her rifle. Allie drew her pistol as well, though she didn't know what good she could do with it.

She could hear it now, the whooping howls. They started low and went up in pitch rapidly. Raith had been right, it was hard to tell how many. The sounds abruptly cut off and another one would pick up right where the first had left off. It was creepy.

Allie closed her eyes and took a deep breath, then

paused. Something was odd. She could feel the energy around, just like it seemed you could anywhere in The Shift, but this felt a little different. Less wild, and more controlled than the energy out in space had been. This was much more like the energy from her crystal.

It surged and pulsed in the distance, just at the edge of her senses. A pulse here, followed by an answering pulse there. Like fireflies in the night sky. The animals were Jumping, she realized, quickly and often. Opening her eyes, she strained to see them. What kind of animal could Jump?

When she saw them, she wished she hadn't asked. They were tall and slender, running quickly on all fours. They were shaped something like greyhound dogs from Earth, with long, lean legs, and a slender, athletic body. They ran with an incredible grace and speed.

Their heads looked something like a greyhound's as well, only she could see from the open mouths that their muzzles were a good bit longer, and filled with long, needle-like teeth, and black tongues. Their thick fur was almost black, with patterns of red and yellow running through it in jagged lines. They actually looked a great deal like the ground beneath them, and she realized from the air they would probably be almost invisible.

Long, slightly corkscrewed horns ran straight back from where their ears should have been, ending in sharp tips. The horns were confusing, though. From the angle that they jutted from the animals' heads, they didn't look functional for ramming or spearing an enemy. They almost looked more designed to protect the backs of their necks from attack.

Despite the defensive appearance of the horns, their jaws looked custom made for killing, their paws had much longer toes than a dog's, and looked tipped in blood red claws. Allie hoped they actually were red, and weren't just stained with actual blood.

Their tails were long and narrow as well, sloping down from the hindquarters and stretching out over the ground behind them without quite touching it. The tails had fur as well, but they tapered in width along its whole length to a very narrow point at the end. Allie had seen pictures of dinosaurs whose tails did the same thing. They were definitely bigger than greyhounds as well, standing nearly as tall as she was.

None of this was the most frightening thing about the animals however. The worst thing was the way they moved. Every few steps, each one would Jump to another place in the pack. They did this seemingly at random, making the entire pack seem huge, and impossible to count, a rolling, shifting mass of fur and teeth.

They leapt from the ground as they ran as well, sometimes forward, sometimes sideways, Jumping in mid-air to another place in the pack. The overall effect was confusing, chaotic, and terrifying. The effect was not helped by the eerie howling sounds they made, first starting here, then suddenly ending over there as the beast Jumped to a new place.

They drew nearer and Artus, Dav, Raith, and Imber opened fire. Morgan was in the middle of the circle as the group gathered around her, the beasts circling all around as they closed in from both directions.

Pulses from the shatter guns hummed and whistled

through the air. Allie watched in horror as each target was suddenly no longer there, the sonic blast moving harmlessly through now-empty air. Dozens of shots in rapid succession, yet Allie was certain that nothing was actually hit.

She felt the pulses as each one Jumped. It would give her a headache quickly if she paid too much attention to it. It was too much all at the same time, like staring into a room full of strobe lights.

Allie didn't even bother firing. She knew the Jumps were split-second fast, and intentionally done. These beasts Jumped with purpose and intent, it wasn't at all random. She knew they'd never hit one. Something else tugged at her mind as they drew closer. She could hear a buzzing in the back of her mind, like a collection of voices very far away. If she focused, she could almost make out words.

As she concentrated, the buzzing became louder and clearer. No, she corrected herself, it wasn't her concentration that made it louder, it was the beasts drawing closer. They were communicating mind-to-mind, she realized, and she could hear them. The communication was complex, but was clearly involving coordination of the pack before the attack. As the beasts drew close enough to lunge, Allie grabbed onto the thoughts she felt around her and mentally shouted back.

"*Stop!*" she yelled at the minds all around her.

Part of her was surprised when the creatures actually stopped. Oddly, another part of her wasn't. The animals kept Jumping, as the group's guns kept trying to find stable targets, but they drew no closer, the whole shifting mass drawing to a halt. She felt confusion in the pack, muttered, wordless questions. It was still hard to hear the words.

"Hold your fire," she told the others, who stopped, albeit hesitantly.

Allie reached into her pocket and took out the crystal. The words sharpened and clarified in her mind. Almost as soon as she did so however, the mental chatter stilled. One sharp, clear voice rang out in her mind.

"Prey speaks?" The voice asked, sounding distinctly surprised.

She took a breath as one particularly large creature approached her slowly. Most of the animals were tall enough to look her straight in the eye, but this one was noticeably taller, looking slightly down at her. Dav's weapon turned to point at it, but Allie put a hand on his arm.

"No, don't. I can talk to them."

"You can what?" Dav asked in a harsh, obviously nearly panicked tone.

"Shh!" she insisted. Focusing on the mind that had spoken to her, she tried to reach it again.

"We are not prey," she replied.

"Perhaps," came the reply after a long pause, *"prey does not speak."*

"Who are you?" Allie asked.

"I am Ydrahn. I am strongest," the creature replied. Allie took that to mean this one was the alpha, like in a wolf pack. *"You are strongest?"* it asked.

"No," Allie replied. The creature bared its teeth and

moved forward slowly. Allie continued. *"I am speaker for my pack,"* she said, feeling certain that pack was a word this creature would understand. The beast called Ydrahn paused again. It considered, then took another step forward. She felt the energies flex in the creature.

On impulse, she reached mentally through the crystal and pushed on the energies the creature was gathering. Ydrahn flinched like he'd been struck, luminescent yellow eyes widening slightly in surprise as the energies he had been gathering dispersed around him like a smoke cloud hit by a sudden gust of wind.

"Speaker is Between," Ydrahn said to her cautiously, *"Speaker is like the Rrughn."*

"I can travel like you," Allie agreed, not wanting to clarify that she wasn't any good at it, and needed the crystal to do it.

"Yes, Between," Ydrahn agreed. *"Why walk like prey?"*

"I am like you, but different," she said. Ydrahn's nose twitched as it sniffed the air near her.

"Yes, Speaker is different, and the same. The Rrughn do not know of others Between. How are you here?"

"We came to meet with others of our kind."

"No others are Between here," Ydrahn said.

"No, I mean others that walk on two legs, living in a group in the mountains. Do you know them?"

"They do not speak, they are not Between, they are prey," Ydrahn said, his mental tone dripping with disdain, and a note of hunger.

"I speak. I am Between," Allie said. *"Those others are my friends. They speak, but not like this."*

Ydrahn seemed to consider this. Allie felt a shift in the energy above them and glanced up, but nothing was there, though the storm clouds were moving in toward them again.

"They speak?" Ydrahn asked, sounding curious.

"They speak with voices, like your howls."

"That is not speak, that is to scare prey."

"My people use it to speak."

"Cannot speak," Ydrahn argued firmly. Allie felt the slight pressure in the energies above them again and once more looked up. Again, she saw nothing. She frowned, but looked back to Ydrahn.

"We are not prey," Allie again said, trying to put a note of strength into her mental tone.

"You speak, you are Between, you are not prey," Ydrahn agreed, then looked at the others. *"They do not speak."*

Allie could feel the note of hunger again. She took a moment to decide how to answer that. These creatures, the Rrughn, she now knew them as, defined prey as unable to speak in their minds with them, and unable to Jump. Allie could do both, so was not considered prey. Her friends were a different matter though.

"Allie?" Dav asked nervously as Ydrahn looked his way.

"Shh!" she said again, sharply.

"They speak, but differently," Allie insisted.

"No, they do not speak. They are not Between. We

hunt." Ydrahn took a step toward Dav.

Allie felt the Rrughn's energies start to gather again as they prepared to Jump. She heard their excited mental muttering, eager for the coming feast. She still had no idea how many there were, but it was at least three dozen. More than enough to make short work of the whole group.

Allie, in a moment of desperation, reached through the crystal, and pushed down on all of the energies gathering around the pack hard. Immediately, the whole pack flinched, hissed, and cringed backward as one.

"How?" Ydrahn asked sharply, sounding both frustrated and a little frightened.

"I am like you, but different," Allie told him again.

The Shift in energies happened up above once more. This time she kept her eyes closed. Something was circling, she realized as she mentally felt the energies swirl around, exactly like fog would around an object moving quickly through it.

Opening her eyes, she saw nothing. Closing them again, she could feel the energies swirling. Abruptly, the energies swirled as whatever it was dove. It had an energy of its own, she realized as it left the swirling energies above. It was odd, not like anything she'd felt before, but it was there and she could feel it.

Allie could make out its general shape as it dove. It was huge, and could probably pick up two of the big Rrughn at once, clutched in its huge, outstretched, clawed feet. It had six leathery wings, one each directly above the joint where the legs met the body. Its head almost seemed to be all teeth. It was diving not for Allie and her friends, but for Ydrahn and the Rrughn just behind him.

Without thinking, Allie grabbed the energies of the strangely invisible creature, and yanked down, while pushing outward on the energies of the Rrughn in front of her. They leapt backward at her push, cringing as they landed. Where they had stood, the huge flying creature slammed into the ground.

As it hit it became visible, shrieking an ear-piercing cry of pain and rage. The Rrughn all leapt back in surprise and very obvious terror at the appearance of the flying creature. So did her friends.

The creature tried to scramble to its wickedly clawed feet, but Allie mentally pushed down on it again. It shrieked its fury, but collapsed back down. In a terrible rush, the Rrughn suddenly Jumped and swarmed forward, all over the beast. Allie let go of the energies in surprise.

It was over in seconds, the Rrughn having efficiently torn it apart. As though still afraid of it, they hurried back once it stopped moving, unwilling to stay too close to the massive, winged beast.

Several things made sense all at once to Allie. The Rrughn were camouflaged to protect from flying predators like this one. They couldn't Jump out of the way of something like this, because they couldn't see it coming. The horns reaching out above their necks were to try and protect from aerial attack.

They couldn't feel the energies they used like Allie could, they just used them to Jump. Because of this, they couldn't track the creature in the sky like she could, though Allie had no idea how she could feel it.

This thing was the Rrughn's natural predator. How it used those energies to become invisible Allie had no idea. Maybe the creature was in some kind of halfway state, partway in the physical world, and partway in what the Rrughn called the Between, where she now assumed the actual traveling happened when they Jumped.

The Rrughn were all watching her with the kind of respectful caution most humans use when around a grizzly bear they've been told is 'mostly trained'. Ydrahn moved slightly forward, as though not willing to get too close to her.

"You are strongest," Ydrahn said simply.

"We are not prey," Allie repeated firmly. Ydrahn crouched a little lower, submissively.

"You are not prey," he agreed emphatically.

"Do not hunt my people, any of my friends, or the others in the caves. They are not prey," she pressed.

"They are not prey," Ydrahn agreed. After a moment, he stood tall again and approached, though not threateningly.

"I am strongest in my pack," Ydrahn said. Allie nodded. *"You are strongest in your pack,"* Ydrahn continued. Allie again nodded, deciding not to press the point. *"We are not the same, but we are the same. Speaker protects the pack. Sky killers are your prey. Speaker is kin,"* Ydrahn declared. *"We will help you."*

Allie considered this. If they could bring others when they Jumped the way she could, they could be very helpful, actually. In theory, Allie could Jump the whole group, but she didn't know where she was going, and couldn't See where she was Jumping beforehand like her mother said she used to be able to do. Well, she thought, you would never knew unless you asked.

"*Can you bring others when you go Between?*" she asked.

"*Speaker wants us to bring her friends Between?*"

"*To the caves where others of my kind are.*" Allie clarified.

"*Cannot go Between to that place. Your kind have broken the Between. The Rrughn can take your pack to the bottom of the high stone. This will help?*"

"*This will help.*" Allie agreed.

Ydrahn considered a moment, then sent a quick mental message to his pack. Before Allie could warn her friends, the Rrughn swarmed them. She heard surprised and panicked shouts and screams from her friends for about half a second, all the time it took for the Rrughn to reach them, Jump the whole ground, and pull back again. When they did so, they were all standing at the foot of the mountains. Allie smiled. Well that was easy.

"*The Rrughn will go,*" Ydrahn said, "*We must hunt. Speaker is kin. Good hunting.*"

"*Good hunting,*" Allie replied. The Rrughn turned and ran off into the falling night, silently this time, but still Jumping in a seemingly random pattern as they ran. It really was creepy, she thought.

She turned back to her friends. Every one of them was staring at her. Even Tic had at some point found her way onto Dav's shoulder, and looked distinctly uncomfortable.

"What?" she asked, innocently.

"What... exactly... just happened?" Artus asked in cautious tones.

"I made some new friends, I think," Allie replied.

"How could you talk to them?" Dav asked. Allie shrugged.

"I don't actually know. I could just hear them in my head."

"And how did you keep them from attacking?" her mother asked, sounding less disturbed, and more curious than the others.

"When they Jump, their energy pulses. I can kind of feel it, like the energy out in space, and I just pushed on it. They didn't like that at all," she laughed, though inwardly she was still shaking like a leaf. She knew full well how close they all just came to being dinner for the Rrughn.

"I'll say. And the freaky six-legged invisible flying thing?" Dav said, then held up a hand. "On second thought, I don't want to know. I'll just say thank you, and that you've definitely got some unbelievable super powers. Seriously Allie, that was epic." He grinned at her.

She returned it, then glanced at the others. Tic hopped back onto her shoulder and nuzzled her. It wasn't the same through the helmet, but Allie appreciated the gesture, reaching up to pet the little jicund's ears.

"Thanks, Dav. Well it's getting dark, can we hurry to

the caves? I really don't want to find out what else lives out here."

"I'm starting to worry about what we'll find in the caves," Artus said under his breath, carried clearly to Allie's ears by the audio system in the helmet. Truthfully, Allie was worried about that too.

"Hopefully, our friends," her mother said. Nobody could argue with that.

CHAPTER TWELVE

THE RESISTANCE

They found a trail almost immediately, marked by a silvery rod embedded in the ground. The top of it hummed softly, with a faint yellowish glow. Dav couldn't help but notice that Allie seemed to immediately dislike it. Dav recognized the color though. If he weren't wearing the helmet, he probably could have identified it by scent, too. The rod was essentially a rogellium torch.

Putting an electrical current through rogellium caused it not only to glow, but to emit a slight, harmless radiation. Harmless at least to most people, anyway. Rogellium emitted this radiation all the time, but it got stronger under an electrical current.

Interestingly, this radiation also interfered with a crystal bearer, or Starjumper, Dav corrected himself with a smile, and made it impossible for them to Jump either from or to any place with too much of it around.

It took Dav only a moment to realize as they passed

another of the glowing torches that the Resistance was using rogellium torches both to mark the trail, and to make it impossible for the Rrughn to travel here. It was going to make things a little uncomfortable for Allie though.

"You okay?" he asked her, gently touching her arm as they walked. She nodded.

"Yeah, just feel a little weird."

"It's the rogellium torches," he told her, gesturing to a fourth one, "it interferes with Jumping."

"Gives me a headache, too," she grumbled.

"You'll get used to it," Morgan said. "It might take an hour or two, but once your body adjusts you won't even feel it anymore. Unless you try to Jump. I don't recommend it."

"Good to know," Allie said.

The group kept hiking, occasionally having to climb over a large, jagged rock in the path. It looked like the side of this mountain was only slightly stable. Off in the distance, the direction they had come from, yellow lightning flashed down from the ominous clouds.

The strange creatures Allie had somehow tamed had Jumped them quite some distance, but it was still probably less than an hour before that storm struck the mountain. From the frequency of the flashes, and the sickly yellow plumes of smoke that exploded upward as each bolt struck the ground, Dav knew they didn't want to be out in the open when that storm hit. It would take them longer than that to reach the top, but Dav was really hoping that the trail ended in a cave network far below the summit. He looked over at Allie, walking quietly beside him.

Dav had no idea how she could do the things she did. Starjumpers were always viewed with a great deal of respect and admiration by the Coalition, at least before Tyren took over, but that respect was based solely on their incredible ability to Jump anywhere in the galaxy instantaneously.

Dav had never read anything about Jumpers able to speak other languages they didn't know, or speak telepathically with weird Jumping alien creatures, or sense invisible flying monsters and bring them crashing down with a thought. Allie had said she could feel the energies they used. He'd never heard of that either.

Dav had always known that Allie was special, though he was only now beginning to realize that she was unique in other ways too. There was something profoundly different about her, even from other Jumpers, and he had no idea what it was.

Her mother Morgan was a crystal bearer as well, though for whatever reason didn't want the crystal back. Her father had been a diplomat, soldier, and great leader, though not a crystal bearer. He'd read about two crystal bearers having children, which were always able to use the crystals, though none of them showed any additional abilities. As if the ability to teleport anywhere in the galaxy at will wasn't enough.

Dav regarded her for a moment. She caught his look and glanced his way. He could see the corners of her eyes wrinkle slightly as she smiled, though the bottom part of the helmet obscured the lower part of her face. He was glad Raith hadn't made the visors mirrored, though Dav usually did when he crafted a suit. He just thought it looked cooler. Her eyes sparkled, and he could read a myriad of emotions swimming beneath their emerald surface.

Allie looked excited, anxious, afraid, and also happy. It was a strange combination, but considering everything that had happened to her in recent days, he certainly understood where she was coming from.

Her smile, even though he couldn't see it, made him smile in return. It always did, no matter how bad he was feeling. Something about the way her eyes sparkled when she smiled was impossibly calming to him. He knew he was far more powerful than any human, but somehow she always had the ability to make him feel like everything was okay.

Turning his eyes forward again, he watched Imber walking alongside Raith. A pang of jealousy struck him, but he pushed it aside, recognizing it as an irrational reaction. Imber was remarkable as well. She also had a knack for putting Dav at ease, and he genuinely enjoyed her company, though it was different than it was with Allie. There was a perfectly innocent quality to her eyes, and her laugh that he found charming. Imber was also beautiful, with an exotic look to her features, including her heirlines, which was very attractive.

Dav couldn't deny that he was attracted to Imber. He glanced back at Allie. She stumbled on a bit of loose gravel, and Dav reached out and caught her. Allie grabbed his arm for support, and smiled her thanks at him.

He smiled back, and shook his head in wonder as she

looked forward again. He might be attracted to Imber, but he'd been in love with Allie since the day they'd met. Dav had never told her of course, and wasn't sure he'd ever have the nerve to actually say it out loud. She had to know by now though, didn't she?

Dav was sure she knew, there was no way she could have missed it. She wasn't interested in him the same way though, since she'd never said anything to him about it, or even about his own obvious feelings for her.

Because of this, Dav left it alone. He cherished their friendship too much to risk ruining it by voicing something that Allie was happier ignoring. Maybe someday she'd look at him the way he looked at her. Until then, he would continue to be her best friend, and provide her with whatever support or comfort she needed. No matter what happened, he would always be there for her. Always.

"I see the caves!" Artus said from above Dav on the trail.

Good, Dav thought. With luck, they could get inside long before the storm caught up with them, and have plenty of time to find the Resistance leaders. They could have an initial debriefing and get the Resistance caught up on the current situation, introduce Allie to everyone who would need to know about her, and still have time for dinner. Dav's stomach grumbled at the thought of dinner. On second thought, he told himself, maybe dinner first.

It took another fifteen minutes to get to the cave entrance. Morgan was doing much better, but still relied heavily on Artus' help, which slowed them down. The storm was drawing dangerously close. The lightning was flashing madly behind them, and the front winds of the storm had just started to brush them with its first angry tendrils. It was getting stronger quickly.

Dav was stunned when he saw the cave entrance. The opening was enormous. Easily large enough to have flown the Peacekeeper straight in the mouth of the cave, with room to spare on either side of the wings. He had expected a decent sized cave, it would have to be to house the entire Resistance base, but this was far beyond his expectations.

Truthfully, he'd never seen a cave entrance this big, though he knew there were caves this big back on Earth. There was something very different about actually seeing a cave like this in person though. It was somehow humbling.

It looked like a giant, gaping maw, open and trying to swallow the entire landscape. For all Dav knew, this cave could extend hundreds of miles through the rock. Maybe thousands.

Walking into the cave had a slightly oppressive feeling as well, pressing the image of the cave opening as an actual hungry mouth into his mind. He moved protectively closer to Allie. He knew the cave wasn't about to swallow them, but it made him a little nervous anyway.

The cave was mostly dark, though illuminated faintly by a line of the rogellium torches running into the darkness. They were pretty broadly spaced out, and provided very little real illumination in such a massive cave.

The entryway opened up into an even larger cavern. Dav had no idea how big, since the light from outside the cave, even combined with the torches running off into the distance, provided too little light to see either the walls or the ceiling high above. It was also too much light for the helmets to kick into night-vision mode, leaving Imber and the humans mostly blind. His own eyes were far better at seeing in the dark naturally than a human's, so he took Allie's arm and helped her along.

The cavern floor went down steeply, though steps seem to have been chiseled out of the rock. Artus and Morgan led the way, following the row of torches. Another fifteen minutes of walking passed before the dark landscape changed at all. Rounding a bend, the cavern narrowed into a smaller chamber, though only barely small enough for the walls to be illuminated. Dav still couldn't see the ceiling.

At the end of this chamber was more darkness, though it seemed peppered with a horizontal line of small blue lights. It was another dozen steps before Dav recognized the little blue lights as the power indicators on arc rifles. There were, at quick count, a full dozen of them at varying heights leveled at them. Artus had already spotted them and stopped.

"Stay calm," Dav told Allie, "the Resistance has found us. Artus will handle this."

Allie tensed, but stayed close by his side. She didn't let go of his arm, either. Her human eyes probably couldn't see the arc rifles yet. Artus held both hands up, palms out to show he held no weapons. The arc rifles moved forward, as their wielders approached. Once within range of the nearby rogellium torch, Dav took a quick measure of the group.

Six Sy'hli, which made Dav's heart leap. There were also two reptilian Iobans, one purple-skinned Uhran with a respirator mask like Harelo's, two Hgrundewa like Xythe back on Irifal Station, and one humanoid Dav couldn't identify.

That one looked something like a human made of slightly melty wax, with the lower face stretched forward and down. It was a strange appearance, though Dav had seen stranger back on Irifal. There was always something stranger on Irifal.

Thirteen, Dav corrected himself as he spotted the last member of the group, sitting on one of the Hgrundewa's shoulders. It was a Tchratchi, an insectoid race from a world that had resisted the Coalition movement even before Tyren's rule.

They were terrifyingly aggressive fighters, though honorable. Incredibly advanced technologically, and had resisted all attempts at hostility toward their world with an tremendous amount of firepower. Their weapons technology was beyond any other race, and they were notably stingy about sharing it.

He knew better than to underestimate the creature, despite the fact that he was barely more than two inches tall. They normally swarmed in the billions, and seeing only one was unheard of.

Dav was certain there were several thousand of them at least scattered around the cavern, their tiny weapons leveled at the group. One of the small weapons rigged onto the little Tchratchi's foreleg was more dangerous than all twelve of the arc rifles. If the small alien pulled the trigger once, the whole group would likely die before they knew it had fired.

One of the Sy'hli approached, half-lowering his weapon, though keeping himself positioned out of the line of fire of his companions.

"You have ten words to explain yourselves before we scatter your ashes across the room," he said.

Dav instantly recognized his red uniform. He, and two of the other Sy'hli, was a member of the old Sy'hli military. Fairly high ranking too, judging by the notches in his collar.

"That will be plenty," Artus said, slowly removing his helmet. "I am Artus, of House Tyr'Arda." The group didn't move, though Dav noticed the slight widening of eyes from a few of the group in the back. The Sy'hli in front showed no reaction whatsoever.

"And your friends?" he asked. Artus gestured to each member of his group in turn.

"My brother Davrelan. Morgan Bennett of the Order of the Silver Star and her daughter Allie. Imber, niece to Ambassador Lase of the Shaian, sent as his emissary, and Raith, Imber's personal android."

Again, no reaction from the Sy'hli officer, though a few eyes in the back group widened further at the list.

"And the last?" the officer asked.

Artus glanced around, then spotted Tic on Allie's shoulder. He smiled slightly and turned back to the officer.

"That is Tic, a jicund from Ayaran. She is young Allie's bodyguard," Artus said.

The officer considered a moment, then glanced behind. He spoke quickly to one of the Hgrundewa in a language Dav didn't recognize. The Hgrundewa lowered his rifle and bowed, then stood still a moment. The officer watched him.

Another long moment passed, then the Hgrundewa spoke rapidly to the officer in the same language. The officer turned back.

"There is no way to check your credentials, and we cannot risk the security of our location. I am sorry, but we are going to have to..." the officer began, but was cut off by another voice.

"Artus?"

The voice came from the darkness behind the line of rifles. It was a soft, feminine voice. Elegant and melodic. Dav recognized it immediately. The faint light glittered off of delicate emerald scales as the speaker moved forward. The line of rifle-bearing guards moved aside respectfully as she passed. The lithe figure stopped in front of Artus, and smiled.

"Sinara," Artus replied, returning the smile.

She leaned forward and embraced him. Dav noticed with some amusement how quickly rifles were lowered at Sinara's obvious friendship with him. Artus returned her hug.

"I told Caranis you would be here shortly," she said. "He must not have warned the sentries."

"No harm done," Artus replied. "The men here are vigilant, as they should be."

Sinara glanced at the rest of the group. Dav reached up and removed his helmet. The others followed suit.

"And Davrelan," she said with a smile for him, her eyes bright and almost luminescent in the gloom, "I see your courage won out and you have helped your friend." Sinara looked to Allie and nodded, before her eyes met Morgan's. Morgan bowed, to Dav's surprise. To his even greater surprise, Sinara bowed in return.

"A pleasure Sinara, as always," Morgan said.

"Far too long, Morgan," replied Sinara. "I am sorry to say that I, and everyone else, believed that you were dead."

"I may as well have been," Morgan answered.

"Come," Sinara instructed them, "this is no place to catch up. I will take you back to our new home."

Turning, the guards all moved aside. Dav noticed the same respectful treatment of Sinara again. Definitely a woman to keep an eye on, Dav thought, as they headed once more into the dark.

CHAPTER THIRTEEN

A NEW COUNCIL

Time was hard to measure in the dark, twisting tunnels, Imber thought. However long it took them to reach their destination, it felt like an eternity. Imber was completely certain that she'd never be able to find her way out of this place without help. Enough twists, turns, and forks in the tunnels had been passed that it was likely none of their group except Raith could get them out if they had to escape on foot.

That last thought comforted her tremendously, in an odd sort of way. Knowing that there was no doubt Raith knew exactly how to get them out made her feel a great deal better. Not only that he could guide them all out, but that he wouldn't hesitate to do so. There was something incredibly reassuring about having an android working with them. Especially one so remarkable.

After what could have been hours, or simply minutes, they rounded another corner and stepped into another world. The rough, dark caverns almost instantly opened into carefully carved walls and floors, with windows and doors leading into chambers beyond.

It had been carved to look like a street front, complete with sidewalks, alleys, and a wide road running down the center. Many of the doorways even had signs above, advertising wares for trade, from food to tools to clothing.

None of this was the most amazing thing to Imber, however. The ceiling of the long tunnel had been plated in holographic imagers, currently portraying a clear, blue sky similar to what she might see on many civilized worlds.

That was something interesting Imber had noticed in her diplomatic travels with her uncle. A great many similarities existed on worlds that held intelligent life. Something about the right combination of environmental factors being more likely to evolve intelligent species, she supposed.

Whatever the case, the effect was impressive, looking very much like they'd suddenly left the caves and stepped into a small town on any of a number of worlds. She might even have believed that was exactly what they had done, if she didn't know better.

Aliens of various species walked about their business, though more than a few paused in their activities to watch the newcomers with surprise and curiosity. She saw none of her own people, however. Imber had thought that it might make her feel better if she knew none of her own people would be hurt when Tyren used the information she was giving her uncle to destroy the resistance.

Watching these innocent people walking about their daily business didn't help her at all, though. Her people or not, they were innocent people.

Not only would all of these innocent people be dead within a matter of days, but so would her new friends. And all of it would be her fault. If she didn't, her own father would be murdered by the Highlord. Her father's captivity had been a lever the Highlord had used against her and her uncle for years now.

The worst part of it was that she knew full well he would continue to use that control to force her and her uncle to serve him even after this. She didn't think it was possible to hate anyone more than she hated the Highlord, or love anyone more than she loved her father.

It was never going to end, and she knew it. Sy'hli had long lifespans, and Tyren was still relatively young. It could be another two of her lifespans before he eventually died of old age. How many horrible things would he have forced her to do before her own inevitable death in that length of time?

And yet, she couldn't risk her father being hurt. She had no choice but to activate the tracking beacon built into the communicator in her hand. Once she did, this particular nightmare would be over. Yet another would begin shortly afterward, she knew.

How many lives would be lost in this incident? How many innocents? How many of her friends? How many good people? Nobody had any chance to stop him though, he was too powerful. Nobody but Allie, anyway.

Allie was the key, Imber knew. She'd learned so

much about her in the last few days they'd traveled together. Allie was quick-witted, strong under pressure, and could use that crystal better than anyone she'd ever heard of.

Something about those crystal energies hurt Tyren, she'd learned that as well. Nobody knew how or why, but it was a weapon that could be used against him.

With her ability to Jump anywhere she wanted and bring others with her, she could Jump right into his command center on his star base with a whole troop of the Sy'hli strike soldiers that she kept seeing on street corners down here. It looked like half the Sy'hli military had gone into hiding with the resistance. Between the Sy'hli troops and Allie's own abilities with the crystal key, they could potentially bring Tyren down in minutes.

The only snags would be what countermeasures Tyren would have put into place in the event of his death. The consequences of just Jumping in and taking him down could be catastrophic. They had to know what his plans were, and how far into play they had already gone. Which was why Allie and her friends were here, to share information and discuss with the resistance what the options were.

None of it would matter once Imber triggered the tracking device, however. She would trigger the device, and in just a couple of days, Tyren's troops would descend on this location like a plague of locusts, destroying everything in their path.

Imber paused at the gentle touch on her arm. She turned and looked into Raith's concerned eyes. The concern in them was so genuine, so open, that she almost broke into tears right there. Instead, she steeled her resolve and her expression, and nodded.

"Are you all right?" he asked.

"Yes Raith, I'm fine," she said. "Thank you," she added, genuinely grateful for his concern.

He cared about her, and that touched her. She looked around and noticed that Allie and Dav had also stopped and were regarding her with concern. They were all such wonderful people, she thought to herself. Nothing could be worse than this. She smiled at them to reassure them all that she was okay.

Imber followed the group through a large set of double doors, intricately carved with the ancient Code of the Coalition, words vowing integrity and justice, service and protection, honor and nobility. She almost laughed at the mockery that had been made of the Code as she passed through the doors.

They entered a large room, with comfortable, though simple furnishings. Nothing here seemed extravagant, she'd noticed. Cozy, well built, but nothing too fancy. These people had found a way to live peacefully, maybe even happily, away from the reach of the Coalition. If only she could free her father and run away to someplace like this, except that she knew this was the only place like this left in the galaxy.

"Through those doors," Sinara interrupted her thoughts, "lies the New Council of the Coalition. They know you are coming, and are prepared to meet with you."

"How?" Allie asked, surprised.

"The Hgrundewa share a hive mind," Dav

explained, "which means that their minds are all connected, all the time, controlled by a queen. Well, a king in this case. What one of them in a hive knows, the rest know instantly. The moment the two in the front of the caves knew who we were, every one of their kind in the entire complex knew it as well. I'm sure the Hgrundewa council members informed the rest of the council."

Allie nodded, though looked stunned by this news. She had probably never dealt with an intelligent, hive-mind species. There weren't many, though the Hgrundewa weren't the only ones. Allie glanced back at Imber and shrugged. Imber smiled back at her.

Allie was such a great person, she thought for the hundredth time in the last few days. So kind and open, so determined to do what she believed was right. Imber envied her that, knowing her own resolve to virtue had been broken by the threat against her father.

Artus led the way into the chamber. A massive circular table covered most of the room, the center of the table was hollow and a section cut out of one side to allow people to walk into the middle of the circle. The table was lined with two of each of a dozen species, from the Sy'hli in their comfortable chairs, to the Tchratchi perched on the edge of the table itself.

As Artus entered, he walked directly into the center of the table's ring. Slowly, he turned to regard each member of the New Council. Dav stopped outside the ring, and gestured for the others to do the same. Imber positioned herself where she could see everyone's mouths.

"I am Artus, of House Tyr'Arda," he said simply in Sy'hli.

The two Sy'hli both saluted, hands over their hearts and bowed their heads. Artus nodded his own head in acknowledgment. "I come in company of my brother Davrelan, third-born of the House of Tyr'Arda, Morgan Bennett of the Order of the Silver Star, her daughter, the crystal bearer Allie Bennett, and Imber, emissary and niece of Ambassador Lase of the Shaian."

Gasps of surprise and whispers traveled around the circle at mention of Morgan and Allie. Only the Hgrundewa were unsurprised. They had known who she was from their introduction to another of their species out in the tunnels, but had apparently decided not to share that information. That was interesting, Imber thought.

"Artus of House Tyr'Arda," said one of the Sy'hli, a strikingly beautiful woman. Her hair had gone silver with age, but it only added to her air of nobility and grace, and her face showed barely any of the usual traces of aging. "We welcome you with great joy. You and your brother were believed killed many years ago. As were all of the crystal bearers. I do not know how the four of you have survived, but this brings hope to the resistance that we have not had in many years. Do you come to join our cause?"

"We do," Artus answered simply. "We come with information, and a willingness to help the resistance in any way we can. My brother is not honoring the Code of the Coalition, or the laws of the Sy'hli Empire. He must be removed from power."

"And who will replace him," sneered an impressively spine-covered Uhran, "you?" Artus turned his blue eyes, now icy, on the man.

"As second-born, it is my right," he replied.

"How do we know your aims are to serve the Coalition?" asked a stocky woman covered in fine, yellow fur with green, slitted eyes.

"I have witnessed the oppression of my brother's rule first-hand," Artus said. Imber could hear him fighting to keep his emotions out of his voice. "I watched him murder my parents, and destroy my family and the honor of the name Tyr'Arda. I fled as he pursued my helpless young brother and I halfway across the galaxy before we were able to escape. We have spent the last ten years hiding out on a planet so technologically behind that they consider sending an un-manned probe to their next closest planet in their tiny system to be a great accomplishment. Use of a basic crafting module would very nearly be considered magic." More mutters of surprise passed around the room.

"I swear before you all, here and now," Artus continued firmly, "that I have only two aims. First, to remove my brother from the ability to harm another living soul. Second, to spend the rest of my life working to undo the damage he has done to this galaxy. I will do these two things with or without your help, but since those goals both align with the aims of the Resistance, I see absolutely no reason we cannot work together. With Morgan and Allie Bennett, we have a chance."

"Twenty Jumpers in the Coalition was not enough to stop him when he took power," grumbled a mahogany-skinned man, "the crystals are not weapons, and the bearers are not soldiers."

"We have learned something valuable," Artus explained. "The energies of the crystal hurt Tyren." More whispers of surprise. This group did that a lot, Imber thought idly.

"Hurt him how?" asked the other of the Sy'hli, a tall, regal-looking man with a delicately trimmed goatee.

"We're not entirely sure," Artus admitted. "All we know is that it causes him great pain. We theorize that it is a big part of why he seeks the destruction of all of the crystals, and their bearers. We believe that somehow, it can be used as a weapon against him and he knows it."

"Do they have crystal keys?" asked one of the two Hgrundewa. They all looked exactly the same, like slightly weasel-faced, dark eyed men who had just taken a bite of something sour.

"They possess a single crystal," Artus said. Morgan stepped forward.

"It is important," she said, "to note that in my imprisonment by Tyren for all these many years that my connection to the crystals has been severed. I can no longer use them to Jump. I am going to teach my daughter proper use of the crystal key, but when planning our next move, you must know that we have only one effective Starjumper."

"Tch-krzac ickgre'kla tjut-jigs grick," chittered one of the Tchratchi angrily. Imber frowned. She spoke fluent Sy'hli, but Tchratchi was beyond her. The language took place entirely too much in the backs of their tiny little throats. Absolutely impossible to read effectively. Before anyone could provide a translation, Allie stepped forward. Imber leaned forward to try and read her lips.

"Ickgre'kla trytchac'h trhi trhi gri'hk, shtirh ketk'ri. Jkitri'k hegcit chi'n trehck." she said, followed by a bow to the Tchratchi. The entire chamber fell absolutely silent. Imber stared in astonishment. It was a very long moment before anyone spoke again, and this only happened after the Tchratchi nodded and perched back down on the edge of the table, seeming more relaxed.

"You speak Tchratchi flawlessly," said the female Sy'hli, "and show a silver tongue with diplomacy." Raith leaned over to Imber and whispered to Imber, directly facing her to give her clear view of his mouth as he spoke.

"The Tchratchi said that she was just a child and asked what good was she. Allie answered that while she was still a child, she had faced the Highlord once already and won. She also said that with the help of the Resistance, she believed she would be able to defeat him once and for all."

Imber looked at Raith in astonishment. He winked his good eye at her. She once again noted the faint haze in the eye beneath the scar and it occurred to her that his vision had probably been damaged in that eye. Imber made a mental note to fix that for him later.

"I meant what I said," Allie said in perfect Sy'hli, "I do believe we can win. He is arrogant, and felt secure in his invulnerability. I hurt him, and now he's afraid. I saw it in his eyes when he fled from me. He has shown us a weakness that we can use to our advantage. I can Jump several men at once directly into his compound if that is what we decide to do. I don't know much about warfare, but it seems to me that the ability to get into any location instantly with a well-trained team would be more than enough to give us the advantage."

"You are right about that," said the yellow-furred woman. "If the legendary Morgan Bennett can train you quickly, your help would be invaluable. Since Tyren hasn't been able to find us in the last ten years, he isn't likely to for the next year while you train."

Imber was struck by a pang of guilt again. They were confident in the security of their hiding place and would have no idea what hit them when Tyren's troops arrived. These people obviously just wanted to live in peace, and protect their people. Imber was going to contribute to their downfall.

Imber looked at Allie, and studied the girl's fierce resolve to help, at whatever cost. Allie was willing to travel into the middle of the Highlord's compound, possibly the most dangerous place in the galaxy for her, just to help move men into position. Allie would sacrifice everything for what was right. Imber knew that without doubt.

Imber's father would have admired Allie. He would not have admired Imber for her choices. He would not want her to sacrifice anyone for him, let alone an entire town of innocent refugees. All at once, she made a decision.

"That's not true," Imber said, stepping forward. Everyone paused and looked her way. She took a long breath, knowing she was condemning not only her father, but herself by speaking her next words. "I have been communicating with my uncle, Ambassador Lase, during this trip through a communicator implanted in my hand. He, in turn, has been relaying information to the Highlord. The communicator contains a tracking device I was supposed to activate when I arrived. I have not, and will not. He knows you are in The Shift, but not where. Even with that much though, he'll find you soon. You have to go, find a new place to hide."

Imber stopped and took another breath, looking around. The room was still, her friends were stunned. Allie looked crushed, Raith was shocked, Dav and Artus looked angry. They weren't the only ones, she realized. Many of the council were slowly rising from their seats, expressions of fury and panic on their faces.

"He knows where we are?" shrieked one of the Hgrundewa. "We're ruined!"

"Kill the traitor!" shouted the Sy'hli man, reaching for a pistol at his hip. Several others reached for weapons.

"Wait," said Artus. He was ignored. As the first weapon raised to point her way, Imber braced herself. She deserved this, and she knew it.

"Hold!" Dav shouted. Imber couldn't hear his tone of course, but if his tone was anything like his expression, it was impressive and somewhat scary. His expression was one of fury, resolve, and an unmistakable air of noble command.

The room was still once more, though everyone had simply paused in whatever action or shout they were in the process of and looked in surprise at the boy prince. Dav cast his icy blue gaze around the room. To her surprise, even the Tchratchi leaned back slightly as his steely gaze swept across them.

"There is more to this betrayal," he said firmly. "I will have the full story before any decision will be made against her. Raith," Dav said looking to his friend, "destroy the tracking device."

Dav looked to Imber, and she could see the apology in his eyes. She understood though, and he'd just saved her life so she certainly had no right to complain. Raith came forward and reached for her hand. She met his gaze, and offered her hand freely into his. His expression was also apologetic, but she just nodded her agreement that this had to happen.

"This will sting," he said softly.

"I know," she replied.

Raith gently closed his hand around hers. There was a sharp, electric flash under his grip, and she felt a searing stab of pain through her hand. The burn was sharp, but short-lived as he short-circuited the device in her hand. The deeper pain faded almost immediately, but the skin on the surface of the back of her hand stung badly. As he released her hand, she looked down. A small burned patch showed on her skin just above the device. A small enough price to pay, she thought.

"Have your men take her into custody," Dav said to the Sy'hli man. "Lock her up, but do not harm her. She is to be well taken care of, and closely guarded. If any harm comes to her, by either action or neglect, I will take it as a personal offense and will react accordingly. Am I perfectly clear?"

Again, his expression spoke volumes. Imber was astonished to see the New Council react. They responded to him not like a boy, but like a well-respected prince in full command of his subjects. She almost felt bad that they hadn't reacted that way to Artus at all.

Imber suddenly understood some of the tensions between the two brothers. Artus was the elder brother, and next in line for the Sy'hli throne, but everyone could clearly see that Dav had the knack for command. Artus showed great promise in diplomacy, but he couldn't command the way Dav seemed to when he got a mind to.

The Sy'hli councilman saluted immediately and holstered his weapon. A quick word into a wrist-com as he approached her from around the table and within two seconds, four Sy'hli soldiers entered the room.

Tic, still on Allie's shoulder, hissed menacingly, but Allie put a hand on the jicund to keep her from action. Tic stayed put, but didn't look happy about it. Neither did Allie, for that matter. Imber felt a little better about that. Clearly her friends still wanted to protect her, as much as possible at least.

Imber didn't resist as they clipped a pair of rust-red metal bracelets to her wrists. Imber felt her body seize as the paralyzing cuffs were clamped on, and could barely feel the Sy'hli soldiers' grip as they caught her stiffened form and carried her out of the room.

Whatever happened, she was finished and she knew it. Once she'd been interrogated, there was no way they wouldn't have her executed. Her father, and probably her uncle would both be dead soon as well. In exchange, she had saved hundreds, maybe thousands of innocent lives, and for the first time in what felt like forever was free of guilt.

Imber knew she had done the right thing, and she knew her father would be proud. She only hoped he understood that his death meant his daughter had done the right thing in the end. Goodbye father, she thought and closed her eyes.

CHAPTER FOURTEEN

MARUCK IN THE COMPOUND

Allie was too stunned to speak as she watched Imber hauled out by the Sy'hli. She couldn't wrap her head around what had just happened. For the third time in a matter of weeks, someone she'd trusted implicitly and considered a friend had betrayed her.

Admittedly Gheir had only done it to save his people, and Raith had done it because he was still bound by programming at the time, but seriously, this was getting out of hand. How could she be expected to trust anyone anymore? How could Imber turn on them like that?

She turned her gaze to Dav, who gave her a sympathetic glance before turning back to the council. Dav she could trust, she knew without question. Dav would never turn on her.

He again addressed the gathered adults with nobility and command. She was impressed by his ability to do this, but she had to admit she liked him better when he was laughing and joking. Despite that, Allie was comforted knowing Dav could take charge this way when he had to.

"Members of the New Council," he said, "We have been given new information here. Tyren knows we're in The Shift. He also knows we have the crystal with us, and will send everything he has to destroy us all. The way The Shift seems to work, we have some time before he'll be able to find this hideout, but you must get your people prepared to depart immediately."

"Where will we go?" asked the Uhran who hadn't spoken yet.

"That must be considered carefully and decided by the council," Artus said. "Know that we, all of us, will do anything we can to help. Ambassador Lase has a long history of helping the Resistance, and this betrayal is more of a surprise to us than to anyone. My brother will find the truth from her, and learn what reason she could possibly have to betray us. She fought loyally alongside us in the rescue of Morgan Bennett. We've been given no reason at all to doubt and every reason to trust her. Davrelan is right, there is more to this than we know. When we know the truth, the council must decide her fate. Until then, you must begin preparations to leave. We will leave you to your work."

Artus nodded to the council and turned, heading out of the room. Allie felt her mother take her hand, and squeezed it for comfort. They walked out of the room behind Artus and Dav, but in front of Raith. As the council doors closed behind them, Allie felt tears welling in her eyes.

"Why would she do that?" she asked. "She was our friend."

"I believe she still is," her mother said, leaning down to kiss Allie's head. "She didn't have to tell us about the communicator or the tracking device. She could have simply triggered it and waited until the troops arrived. Her telling us was an attempt to save us from what she'd been helping bring about. Why she was working for Tyren I don't know, but I sincerely believe it was not by choice."

"I don't think so either," Raith said, moving up beside them as the group followed Sinara. Allie was vaguely aware of Sinara telling Artus that shelter had been provided for them all. Allie looked his way.

"Why not?" Allie asked, genuinely curious. "Because you like her?"

"No," Raith said, giving Allie a sidelong glance, "because I read her biometrics. I've known something was bothering her since she joined us, but I've never read any hostility in her toward any of us. She's shown fear, guilt, frustration, and hopelessness, but never hostility or ill will. Whatever made her do it, it wasn't her choice. No way."

That actually made a lot of sense. Imber was so sweet and friendly, picturing her bringing harm to anyone for any reason was incredibly hard to imagine. Dav, her mother, and Raith all believed that she was being forced into it, for whatever reason. Allie's own experience with

Imber just reinforced that thought. Imber wouldn't harm them if she had a choice. Allie refused to believe otherwise.

"When can we go talk to her?" Allie asked.

"Probably not until after the council, Dav, and Artus have questioned her," her mother told her. "For now, we should go get something to eat, and get some rest."

"Artus!" called a voice.

To Allie, the voice sounded like it was trying to be cheerful, but there was something slightly edgy about it. They turned and looked to see a green-scaled man approaching.

"Caranis," Artus said, without enthusiasm. "I knew when we saw Sinara here that you'd be around somewhere."

"Of course!" the scaly man said, forked tongue flashing between his thin lips. Allie fought hard to keep the look of disgust off her face. Something about this man felt... oily.

"I had started to wonder if you were the one who sold us out," Artus said.

Caranis raised both hands in a calming gesture, showing the short, but vicious black claws at the ends of his fingers. Allie decided immediately that she strongly disliked him. Something about him was off, and he had the air of a salesman who would happily sell you his own grandmother for the right price.

"Quite the contrary, Artus!" he said. "In fact, the Coalition Guard came to interrogate me. I freely admit that for the right price I'd have told them anything they cared to know. The trouble is, Sirana had a vision. A few quick words and I knew we had to get out. I called in a favor with Sandro to get us off the station."

"Sandro?" Artus asked incredulously. "Is anyone left alive on Irifal?"

"Oh, probably," Caranis said, waving dismissively. "The point is, Sinara told me that if you and your friends died, so would everyone else."

"You mean the Resistance?" Artus asked, confused. Allie watched the way the grayish-green scaled man's slitted eyes narrowed slightly.

"I mean everyone, Artus. Everyone, everywhere. At least in this galaxy," Caranis said.

For the first time since the man had spoken to them, Allie had no doubt he was telling the truth. She and Artus both looked to Sirana, who nodded once.

"I'm sorry, Artus," she said in her smooth, silken voice, "You and your friends are critical to some event in the future that could mean the complete annihilation of every living thing in the galaxy."

"No pressure or anything," Dav said wryly. Sirana smiled at him.

"Don't worry," she told him, "you have a chance of success."

"That's reassuring," Dav said, unable to keep the sarcasm from his tone. Artus gave him a glare.

"He means nothing by it Sinara, it's just a lot for a boy to absorb," Artus said. Sinara nodded calmly.

"I understand. He is strong willed. This is good, he will need that."

"If his will is what we're relying on, this will be a piece of cake," Artus said with a grin.

"Well my friends, I must go," Caranis said. "Sinara will continue to escort you, but I have an appointment with someone who needs some information."

"Sell us out and I'll kill you," Artus said, in an almost friendly tone.

"You have a lovely day as well," Caranis said in a slightly sinister tone, punctuated by a jagged grin. After a long moment of watching him depart, Allie whispered to Dav.

"I don't like him," she told him. Dav smiled sidelong at her as they started walking again.

"I'm pretty sure Sinara is the only one who does."

"I don't trust him either," she said.

"I do, but only so far as his own personal gain is involved," Dav said. "If Sinara told him he would die if he told anyone anything about us, he'll keep quiet."

They turned a corner and entered what looked like a market square. Shops lined the plaza, and streets headed off in each of the four directions. Portable booths and stalls had also been set up all throughout the space, leaving narrow aisles between them. As she watched, it became clear that these people didn't use currency. They all bartered for their own goods with other goods.

It was interesting to watch one human-looking man trying to trade a stack of green furs to another man with an orange face and a trio of horns on his bald head for three bottles of thick liquid that looked like that pink medicine used for stomach troubles. Allie's attention was pulled away by too many things at once to focus on them for long though.

As she looked at the stalls they passed, seeing all

manner of exotic foods and clothing, and many items she couldn't identify, she found herself feeling suddenly overwhelmed. They rounded another corner and Allie absently bumped into a wall.

Not a wall, she realized as she felt the fur. Slowly, with a building sense of dread, she looked up. When she saw the face at the top of the mountainous body she screamed. It was the kind of scream that people usually reserve for waking up in the middle of the night from a terrifying nightmare.

The colossal Maruck she had bumped into held up one enormous, clawed hand and stepped backward. Dav, Raith, and Artus all had guns out faster than she could follow even if she had been able to look away from the giant monster. Only Sinara's impossibly quick movements stopped a shootout in the middle of the square.

"Be calm," Sinara said firmly as she seemed to simply appear between the Maruck and the others. "This is no enemy. He is a friend."

"A Maruck?" Allie shouted in disbelief.

Not just any Maruck, this was the biggest Maruck she had ever seen. Easily head and shoulders bigger even than Tyren's Maruck general had been.

"No harm," rumbled the huge beast deep in its chest. The words were so low in pitch that they were almost felt more than heard, resonating somewhere deep in her own chest.

"But Maruck are evil!" she cried again. To her surprise the giant Maruck looked hurt.

"No harm," it repeated. "Friends." Allie looked to

Sinara for some explanation.

"He came to us when Tyren took power," Sinara told her. "His people are a race of predators, but their people have been just as oppressed as any other. The difference is that almost all of them have just taken this as an excuse to revel in their bloodlust. Yet not all of them are this way, such as my friend here."

"Maruck fight," the beast said. "but Maruck no hurt people friends," he clarified. Allie was having a hard time understanding this, but the beast seemed completely calm, still holding one hand up in a calming gesture, and having moved back far enough that he no longer loomed over her.

"You don't hurt people?" she asked. The Maruck smiled slightly and shook his head. His enormous tusks were terrifying, but for some reason gave a slightly comical look to the creature when it smiled. She never would have pictured a Maruck smiling before this.

"No," it said. "no hurt people friends of Dgehf." Allie wasn't sure she had actually heard that correctly.

"I'm sorry, did you say Jeff?" she asked. She looked at Dav, who was trying not to smile. The Maruck shrugged.

"Dgehf. Close enough," Dgehf said carefully. He obviously struggled with English, or Sy'hli, Allie had to correct herself as she realized she'd been speaking and hearing Sy'hli for so long she had stopped noticing.

"Well Dgehf," she said trying hard to mimic his pronunciation. The difference was subtle. "I'm happy you don't hurt people. And I'm sorry I screamed. I've never met a friendly Maruck before." Dgehf smiled again.

"Dgehf nice. Girl nice. Dgehf and girl are friends?" he asked hopefully.

Sinara smiled approvingly. Allie took another deep breath. This was not an expected situation and she wasn't quite sure how to handle it.

"Yes, if Dgehf is nice, Allie will be his friend," she replied, still cautious.

Dgehf's smile grew. The huge behemoth stepped forward and held a hand out to her. Allie reached out, hesitating only a moment before taking one of the beast's fingers. Her entire hand didn't go halfway around one of the massive Maruck's fingers. Dgehf very gently shook her hand. She smiled up at him.

"Come along," Sinara said, looking incredibly satisfied, "we must get you some food. Dgehf, you may come by tomorrow and speak with your new friends again if you like." Dgehf nodded.

"Yes. Dgehf visit Allie."

The group moved away. Allie looked back before they rounded a corner, and found Dgehf watching them with a broad, tusked smile. When he saw her look back, his grin grew even bigger, and he waved, massive fingers flapping up and down. She couldn't help but smile and wave back, though that whole encounter had left her bewildered.

Allie had never dreamed that the Maruck were anything other than bloodthirsty killers. Despite his huge size, even by Maruck standards, the massive alien seemed as docile as a teddy bear. He'd even seemed to have his feelings hurt when Allie had said that the

Maruck were evil.

Maybe she could convince Dgehf to go with the strike team when she Jumped a group in to assault Tyren's base. She couldn't even imagine the damage he could do if he were helping the fight. Although he did say he didn't hurt people, so maybe he was a pacifist. Or maybe it was just certain people, since he had clarified 'people friends'. Considering his size, it was probably safer for everyone if he were a pacifist.

Oh well, it was still nice to know that the Maruck was friendly, though it worried her that Maruck could get so big. He was probably a whole massive head taller than any other Maruck she'd ever seen.

"Do I need to worry?" Dav said, breaking her from her thoughts. She smiled at him.

"About what?" she asked curiously.

"Just thought maybe he might try to hit on you. He seemed awfully sweet on you," Dav said innocently. Allie laughed and shoved him.

"Dav!" she said.

He laughed, that bright, open laugh she loved so much. He put an arm around her shoulder, which sent a tingle through her body. He walked that way the rest of the trip to their quarters.

"No," Highlord Tyren said, "do not attack yet. Keep observing and bringing me information. I want this to happen at the perfect moment."

C.A.D.E.-16 barely resisted rolling his eyes. When

was he going to be allowed to go in and destroy the Resistance? This would be an absolute massacre, and he was looking forward to it.

"Yes, Highlord," was all he said however as he closed the channel.

C.A.D.E.-16 had already told the Highlord all about the Ambassador's niece betraying him. He'd taken it surprisingly well, though he might well have expected it. With the threat supposedly identified, their guard would be down to other attack. It made sense, C.A.D.E.-16 was just getting bored.

He wasn't a recon android, after all. He was built to kill, not to take notes and spy on people. The crystal bearer and her friends had a recon android with them, but so far the recon android hadn't detected C.A.D.E.-16's presence. Yet more evidence that getting too close to people just dulled one's senses. Much better to just kill them and stay sharp.

Perhaps tomorrow, he thought to himself. He suspected he knew what Tyren was waiting for, and expected that it wouldn't be more than a day or two. C.A.D.E.-16 could wait that long, if he had to.

CHAPTER FIFTEEN

AN EVENING WALK

Allie slept fitfully. Dreams of all of her friends turning on her one at a time kept creeping into her mind. She awoke tired and feeling no better off than she had when she'd gone to sleep. Everyone else slept quietly, except Raith who had gone to learn the layout of the compound overnight and keep an eye on Imber.

She dressed quietly, slipping on the soft clothes that had been left for her. Allie fully intended to get back into the armored flight suit later, even here she didn't feel safe, but for the moment she just wanted to relax and try to clear her head.

Stepping quietly out of her small room, she went down the hall and through the door at the end into the street. Even Tic, curled up on her bed, hadn't woken up. Allie was somewhat proud of that.

Allie had no idea how they did it, but the ceiling looked exactly like a night sky full of stars, complete with the occasional cloud drifting across it. Their air filtration system down here even managed to replicate a cool night's breeze. If it weren't for the feel of the weight of stone above her head, she could totally believe they were outside.

It couldn't be more than another hour or so until morning, she thought. She knew she would never be able to get back to sleep. Allie was aware that this place was unfamiliar, and that danger was everywhere, but she didn't believe she was in danger of attack here.

She could see Sy'hli guards patrolling periodically, and many other people were out and about on the faintly-lit streets. There was enough light to see by without it being so bright as to be uncomfortable. Just soft and steady, she thought with a contented sigh. It felt good to be just walking, with no goal, no urgency, no fear of being pursued.

Allie walked down the road, taking turns at random, though careful to find landmarks at each turn so she could find her way back. She'd been walking for some time, trying to sort out her thoughts, when a huge, dark figure seemed to appear beside her. She almost screamed, but recognized the figure in time.

"Geez, Dgehf! You shouldn't sneak up on me like that!" The big Maruck gave her an apologetic, toothy grin.

"Dgehf sorry," he rumbled softly like distant thunder, "Dgehf want talk to Allie." That was odd, she thought. Fair enough though, Sinara seemed to trust him and he certainly seemed friendly enough. She couldn't help but touch the shatter gun in her pocket though.

After all, she was now on a dark street alone with a huge Maruck she had just barely met.

"Okay," she said simply. "What did you want to talk to me about?"

"Dgehf smells things," he said, obviously struggling to elaborate, "bad things and good things. Allie smell like good thing."

A brief image of her getting eaten in one gulp by Dgehf passed through her mind, but she shoved it away. She had some prejudices about Maruck, she'd realized yesterday. Prejudices that weren't entirely justified.

Dgehf had been nothing but friendly and didn't deserve to be treated with any prejudice. She knew that eating her isn't what he'd meant, and something in his tone had triggered a bit of nervousness in her for an entirely different reason.

"Thank you, Dgehf. Does that mean you smell bad things around here too?" she asked him.

He nodded, walking with an eerie silence beside her. Nothing that big should be that quiet, she thought.

"Dgehf smell bad things here," he confirmed.

"Have you always?"

"No, bad things come with Allie," he said. She frowned, processing this.

"One of my friends? Do you mean Imber?" Dgehf looked at her blankly.

"The girl who is being held by the council," Allie clarified. Dgehf immediately shook his massive head.

"No, no. Girl not bad. Good, like Allie. Woman good, like Allie. Boys good, like Allie," he said.

Allie considered this. Dgehf also seemed to think

Imber was an innocent. But that meant something else had Dgehf on edge. The only other things that had come here with them were the Rrughn.

"Do you mean the creatures out on the plains below?" she asked. "The ones that Jump?"

"No," Dgehf said with another ponderous head shake, "Just hunters. Not bad. Dangerous, but not bad."

They turned a corner, and Allie noticed a few passersby giving the odd pair some questioning looks. Dgehf positively dwarfed her. She barely reached his thigh. His huge, long arms moved much like a gorilla's would as he walked, fists resting on the ground with each step, and she didn't quite reach his elbows. It probably did look pretty funny. Interesting though, Dgehf seemed to think something evil was around, and that it had come with them.

"Do you know what it is?" she asked. He shook his head again.

"No," he told her, sounding frustrated. "Dgehf not want scare Allie, but…" the big beast hesitated.

"But what?" she asked, encouragingly.

"Maybe let Dgehf watch Allie? Dgehf not want new friend hurt."

She considered this. Dgehf seemed concerned for her safety and wanted to stay close. Allie found that she was touched by his gesture, and by the sweetness of his not wanting to scare her by hanging around. She smiled up at him.

"Thank you, Dgehf," she told him. "I would feel safer if I knew you were looking out for me and my friends. But don't let it interfere with you doing what you need to do, okay? Everyone is going to be getting ready to leave soon, and you'll have to get ready too." Dgehf gave her another huge grin.

"Allie friend," he said simply. Allie nodded.

"Can I ask you a personal question?" she asked after a moment.

She was learning quickly that while Dgehf had a hard time speaking Sy'hli clearly or too accurately, he was understanding it perfectly and seemed to have a great deal more intelligence than expected behind the choppy speech and brutish appearance. Dgehf turned his huge black eyes toward her and tilted his head questioningly.

"Yes, ask," he said.

"Why aren't you fighting alongside the rest of your people, working for Tyren? Why are you different?" she asked.

She still struggled picturing a friendly Maruck, though she had a perfect example walking softly along beside her. Dgehf considered this for a long time as they walked. She could tell he was thinking, he was idly chewing on his lower lip. Allie smiled, but kept her giggle to herself. After a while, he spoke.

"Maruck like to fight. Maruck like to hunt. This is Maruck," he said. She nodded, pretty sure she understood what he meant. He continued, "But Maruck is more. Maruck care for young. Maruck can... nurture. Maruck have close family. Care for family." Well this certainly surprised her.

"I didn't know that," she told him honestly. She really didn't know much about the Maruck.

"Tyren want Maruck to hunt people," he explained in his slow, careful rumble. "Tyren want Maruck to kill. Not for food. Not to protect family. Just to kill. Maruck don't care, just like to kill," he said with a frown. "Dgehf think 'why'? Dgehf like to hunt. Dgehf like to protect family. Protect friends. But kill just to kill? Dgehf thinks is wrong. Animals hunt, and kill. Not too much. Kill to eat, keep from being eaten. Kill to protect family. Dgehf think real hunter like animal. Not kill just to kill. Kill just to kill is... wasted."

"So you chose not to fight for Tyren, with your people," she concluded. Dgehf nodded slowly.

"Chose to fight for family. Dgehf have son, Allie know?" he said, looking back to her. Another surprise.

"I didn't know that," she said.

"Dgehf have son, and mate soon will have baby. Dgehf want son safe. Want baby safe. Son was baby when Tyren in charge. Maruck with Tyren? Not safe. Dgehf want baby learn to hunt. Not kill just to kill. Dgehf think person can choose. Choose to hurt, choose to help. Choose happy, or choose angry or sad. Choose friends, or choose enemies. Sometimes choice hard. Sometimes choice not all yours. If Dgehf can choose, why choose bad?"

"Don't be offended, but that's way deeper than I expected from a Maruck," she said.

"Know many Maruck?" he asked with a twinkle in his dark eyes. Allie laughed.

"Only you," she told him.

"Allie friend," Dgehf said with a shrug. "Dgehf will help Allie. Allie will help Dgehf. Allie choose help, like

Dgehf."

"How do you know that?"

"Dgehf knows. Allie came here."

Simply put, she thought, but a valid point. They wouldn't have come here if they weren't looking for the best way to help.

"I don't know what I could do to help you though," she said.

"Allie help Dgehf. Allie stop Tyren. Tyren stopped, Dgehf son safe. Allie will help. Dgehf will help."

"I will help," she said firmly, putting a hand on his arm.

Dgehf looked down at her again and smiled softly, gently patting her hand with his own, engulfing half her arm. She couldn't help but notice how carefully gentle he was.

Allie walked in silence alongside her large friend for a while, considering. He had brought up a number of good points, and showed her that several of her assumptions were completely wrong. Dgehf was strong, powerful, and dangerous. He was also wise, caring, and willing to sacrifice anything to protect his family.

After a time, she noticed the sun was beginning to rise in the holographic ceiling. Turning around, she began to retrace her steps, before realizing they'd come in a pretty large circle and weren't far from her quarters already. Dgehf continued walking alongside her, quietly and calmly.

He was much better informed than she'd have guessed, she realized. He knew that she was a major player in the fight against Tyren. More than that, he knew she was critical to the plans. He definitely seemed like the kind of friend worth having at your back in a fight. Again, images of the massive amounts of damage he could do went through her mind and she shivered slightly.

Only a few more minutes passed before she came to where she and her friends had been set up for the night. Dav, Raith, her mother, and Artus were all standing outside, talking worriedly. When they saw her, she saw relief flood their faces and instantly felt guilty. As Dav and Raith jogged up to her, she started apologizing.

"I'm so sorry, I hadn't meant to be gone so long," she said.

"Don't do that!" Dav said.

"Seriously Allie, we were terrified something had happened!" Raith said. "Anything could happen, even here!"

"I was perfectly safe," she said with a smile of appreciation for their concern.

Allie actually really liked that they'd both been so worried, though she felt bad for making them worry to begin with. "Dgehf was with me." She patted his arm again.

Dgehf gave them all a big smile. Raith and Dav looked up at the Maruck and back to Allie. Dav shook his head slowly.

"Something about you, Allie. I think I maybe don't need to worry about you as much as I thought I might have," Dav said.

"Oh, don't stop worrying all together," she teased, "I like knowing you care."

"Of course we do," Raith said. "Come on, we have to go meet with the council representatives to talk to Imber." Allie nodded.

"Is she okay?" she asked Raith. He nodded.

"They're taking good care of her, just like they were told to by His Royal Supremeness over here," he said, poking a thumb at Dav. Dav laughed and gave him a light shove.

"Back off, robo-boy," Dav said playfully. Raith grinned. Allie turned to Dgehf.

"You can go look after your son, Dgehf. I'm going to be with my friends here who will look after me. Thank you for walking me home," she said. Dgehf nodded slowly.

"Dgehf will be back," he said as he turned and walked away. Allie watched him go for a moment, then turned back to the others.

"Well," she said expectantly. They both turned and walked back to their quarters to grab their gear. As she drew close, Artus also went inside while her mother fell into step beside her.

"Everything okay?" her mother asked her. Allie nodded.

"Yeah, I just needed to clear my head. Everything is so complicated," Allie said.

Her mother nodded, and leaned down to hug her. Allie stopped walking and turned in to the hug, holding her mother closely for a long moment, obviously a deeper hug than her mother had expected.

"What was that for," her mother asked when Allie finally pulled away.

"For everything," Allie said. "For giving up everything for me, for leaving me with someone who would take such amazing care of me as Katharine did. For staying strong and holding out until I learned about you and could come get you out. For letting me be who I am." Her mother leaned over and kissed her head again.

"Katharine did such a good job raising you that I really doubt I could have done better. I am so proud of the young woman you've become. You're so strong, brave, and bright. You've earned the loyalty and trust of some incredible people all on your own. If things had been different, you'd have made an amazing member of the Order of the Silver Star."

"What is that, anyway?" Allie asked.

"We were a group of crystal bearers and a few others who are gifted in other ways, like Sinara," she said. "We worked to keep people safe. People of all worlds, of all levels of advancement. There were only eight of us, but we were able to do a lot of good. The Order had been around for almost three thousand years before I was invited. There have never been a lot of crystal bearers, only twenty when Tyren took over, and even fewer of the gifted, so the Order was never large. A lot of power there, though." Allie's mother sighed heavily. "Nobody left, though. Just myself and Sinara. Hardly enough to be an Order of anything."

"Don't worry Mom," Allie said reassuringly. She hated seeing her mother in any pain, physical or emotional. Physically she looked so much better after a few days of care, but emotionally Allie could still see the pain, the hurt, the loss, all showing through her once-vibrant emerald eyes. "Once we bring down Tyren, we can rebuild the Order together." Her mother held her gaze for a long moment, a proud and hopeful smile on her face.

"We will," she agreed, "but for now we need to get ready to go talk to the council and see what we can do about helping Imber."

Allie nodded and turned in to her own room. Tic was still asleep, though she woke up when Allie closed the door behind her. Tic looked up, blue eyes bright and inquisitive. The little jicund chirped a question. Allie smiled.

"It's all going to be okay," she said, almost to remind herself.

Tic chirped happily and bounded off the bed and jumped up onto Allie's shoulder for a snuggle and a scratch. Allie spent several minutes enjoying the comfort of her small friend before she changed back into her flight suit.

Dav had told her that putting it into the closet would clean it automatically by morning. As she pulled the suit out, she saw he was right. Wow, that would save a huge amount of time doing laundry, she thought with amazement.

It was odd, but she'd realized that it was the little things she'd found the most remarkable with all the advanced technology. Instantly clean hand towels, automatic laundry closets, sonic showers, all the things that just made it so easy and simple to keep yourself clean and well cared for. The big things like phase drives and arc cannons just didn't impress her as much as a closet that did her laundry for her.

As she stepped back out into the hallway, Tic perched happily on her shoulder, she took a long breath. This was going to be a difficult morning.

CHAPTER SIXTEEN

STANDOFF IN THE SQUARE

The compound where they were holding Imber was very close to the council hall, in front of a large square. There were a large number of people gathered in the open plaza, looking like they were waiting for something. News traveled fast in a rebellion, Allie thought ruefully.

As the group entered the square, all of them back in their armored flight suits, though without helmets, the crowd parted to let them approach the center. The council, all of them, were arrayed along the back of an open area in the middle of the square.

A slightly raised platform had been erected in the center. On it stood two Sy'hli in full battle gear, and Imber, still in shackles and stiffly paralyzed, held up only by the soldier to her right. Immediately Allie knew something was wrong. A quick glance at her companions told her they felt the same.

"What is the meaning of this?" asked Artus as they all stopped on the far side of the raised platform. One of the soldiers put his hand on the pistol at his side. Dav growled softly under his breath.

"Treason, of course," said one of the Hgrundewa councilmen. He stepped forward, looking smug. "Punishable by immediate execution."

"No!" shouted Raith, moving forward. Dav stopped him with a quick extended hand. Raith locked eyes with Dav, and Allie read the quick exchange of communication between the two in their eyes. Not yet, Dav was telling Raith, but soon.

"We agreed that we would have the chance to interrogate her before any decisions were made," Artus said coldly.

"Not necessary," said the councilman, "she openly confessed to treason in front of us all."

"She was not given opportunity to explain herself," Artus argued.

"Not necessary," repeated the councilman. "Guilt was admitted. Punishment follows."

"This is your idea of honoring the laws of the Coalition? Murdering a young girl without allowing her the chance to explain herself?" Artus said, stepping forward menacingly.

The guard wrapped his hand around the grip of his pistol, and gave a slight smile. Artus growled low in his throat at the man. The tone of the growl obviously meant something to the Sy'hli guard, whose smile slipped a fraction.

"Oh, very well. You may ask her whatever you like, but in five minutes' time, her sentence will be carried out," the councilman said.

Allie looked to the Sy'hli council members. They both looked angry, and clearly not at her and her friends. She strongly suspected they'd been out-voted. Artus looked to Allie, to her surprise. He leaned down close as he stepped near her.

"Find out what's going on, and do it quickly," he whispered. "I need to stay back here for a clear shot if this turns ugly."

"We're going to fight to free her?" Allie asked in a similar whisper. Artus locked gazes intently with her.

"Imber is not our enemy. We will do what we must to protect not only an innocent, but our friend."

Allie nodded once, both frightened and determined as she stepped up onto the platform. She approached Imber. The guard touched her bracelets, and Imber's head suddenly fell forward, released from the paralysis.

"Imber!" Allie cried, rushing to help her. She helped Imber raise her head to look at her. Imber smiled her thanks.

"Allie, it's great to see you, but you guys shouldn't risk your own lives or your mission for me. I made my choices," she said.

"I need to know why," Allie said firmly. "Tell me why you were working with Tyren." Imber's eyes shone with unshed tears as she tried to find a way to explain.

"I had no choice," she said softly. "Tyren has my father. He said he would kill him if I didn't do what he said."

Allie paused as the horror of that sank in. Imber had been forced to try to sabotage a group of random strangers in exchange for her father's life. What would Allie have done if Tyren had used her mother that way?

She honestly wasn't sure. It was terrible that Imber had been willing to sacrifice hundreds of complete strangers for her father, but Allie couldn't honestly say she wouldn't have done the same for her mother or Katharine. Or even Dav, or Raith, or Artus, or Imber herself.

And yet, when the moment of truth came, Imber had stepped forward, and confessed her crimes, saving hundreds of people and condemning herself and her father in the process. Allie felt sick, and found herself hating Tyren even more than she already did, though she wouldn't have guessed that was possible until that moment.

"It's okay if you guys hate me," Imber said softly, "I deserve it. I will never forgive myself for what I've done. Now my father is going to die too."

"None of this is your fault," Allie said. "This is all Tyren. We have to stop him, and we need your help to do it."

"Allie, don't!" Imber urged. "Please don't risk yourselves for me! If you get hurt helping me then my trying to save you all was for nothing!"

Allie grit her teeth in frustration. The Sy'hli soldier with his hand on his pistol was focused on Artus, but she knew full well how fast these Sy'hli could be.

"Oh this is ridiculous," interrupted the Hgrundewa

councilman before Allie could figure out what to do. "We shall carry out the sentence immediately. Guard?" he said.

Faster than anyone could move or react, Raith had drawn both shatter guns, raised, aimed, and fired, blasting both Sy'hli guards completely back off the platform. Their own armor protected them from permanent damage, but both were stunned and flat on their backs.

Raith, Artus, and Dav leapt onto the platform, and arranged themselves around Allie and Imber, guns out and ready, aimed at the guards around the platform, all of whom had also drawn guns and were holding them aimed at Allie's friends.

All of this happened before Allie could even scream, leaving her scream sounding delayed and out of place when her reactions finally caught up with the moment, though she was proud she'd caught Imber before the paralyzed girl fell.

"How dare you!" shouted the councilman, angrily stepping forward, though hesitating when Dav's left pistol twitched his way. "How dare you defy the council!"

"The Council of the Coalition is founded on the Code," Artus said, his voice like steel, "and this is not the Code. Therefore, I do not recognize this council as legitimate."

"Preposterous!" shouted the councilman. Grumbles of anger were shifting through the council, and the crowd in general. "We are the council! We make the laws!"

"That also is not in the Code," Artus said. "Imber

will receive a full, fair trial as is her right, or you will have to murder two Sy'hli princes, two crystal bearers, and a diplomatic emissary in order to complete your cold-blooded murder of a single young girl. If that's not enough to give you pause, consider how many of your guards, and your laughable excuse of a council, will fall before we are brought down?"

"This is treason!" shouted the councilman, face turning purple with rage.

"Seems to be going around," said Artus, wryly.

"We will not give in to the demands of…" began the councilman before being interrupted by the deafening sound of static from the ceiling.

The crowd cringed and covered their ears. Allie cringed as well, though had no hands free. Dav, Raith, and Artus didn't so much as twitch. Allie and almost everyone else looked up as the ceiling turned from a scattered image to one that was crystal clear, and all too familiar to Allie and her friends. Highlord Tyren stared down at them from the false sky, a smug, vicious smile on his face.

"Ah, I see my little spy has betrayed me," he said. "Well, I'll enjoy watching her die then. As well as the rest of you. In the meantime, perhaps you'll enjoy a little show I've prepared for you. I'm excited about this one, aren't you?"

His sinister smile widened as the image in the sky panned outward, showing a polished metal wall, and a man shackled to it. The man looked in rough shape, but was conscious. He looked forward, his expression one of a broken man who had lost all hope. It was the look of a man who not only knew he was about to die, but also knew his daughter would follow shortly behind. Imber screamed as she saw the man. Tyren laughed.

"I thought it would be fun for you all to watch what happens to those who betray me, shortly before you are all killed yourselves. You have several minutes of life left though, since this part might take a while," Tyren said holding up a slender electronic device. Imber whimpered, tears pouring down her face.

"We have to help!" Dav shouted to Artus.

"And do what?" Artus said, sounding defeated.

Allie watched as Tyren turned slowly and moved toward the man. It was agonizing knowing none of them could do anything to help him. Imber was about to watch her father be murdered. Allie had a moment of horror where she pictured herself in that situation.

There had been a moment where Allie's mother was the one in danger and Imber had risked her own life to help save her. Allie couldn't stand by and let Imber's father be killed. She'd been wrong, Allie realized, there was someone who could help.

Allie eased Imber to the ground onto her back, and slowly stood, pulling the crystal from her pocket. Imber's eyes were riveted to the holographic sky like everyone else's, as Tyren reached her father. Allie knew she couldn't allow this to happen.

She took a fraction of a second to study the scene around Imber's father as Tyren reached for him, then closed her eyes and pictured the scene as she spun the crystal. Dav saw what she was doing a fraction of a second too late.

"Allie, no!" he shouted, and lunged for her.

Time seemed to slow around Allie as the energies gathered around her. The light built, and she felt the sensation of being pulled in every direction. There was an odd resistance as well, and the faint headache she still had from the rogellium abruptly sharpened.

The whole Jump was subtly different this time, she noticed. More familiar, but more than that it felt smoother, despite the strange feeling of resistance. The pulling felt less like she was about to be torn apart, and more that she was just stretching slightly. The world went dark as before, but only for an instant. Suddenly there was a flash, the pressure in her head was gone, and she was standing behind Tyren.

Highlord Tyren saw the flash and spun about. Clearly he hadn't expected to see Allie standing there. Or the psychotic jicund on her shoulder. Tyren scrambled backward as Tic hissed at him, but bumped into the wall Imber's father was shackled to.

"No! How...?" he stammered, trying to understand. She heard movement behind her, but Tic immediately leapt off her shoulder in that direction, shrieking her battle cry. Allie heard a yelp, followed by a panicked scream and she smiled grimly at Tyren.

He snarled and lunged, but Allie noticed something else different. She could still feel the crystal's energies all around her. They weren't the energies of the crystal, she realized, just the energies the crystal helped focus.

The energy around Tyren was different though. In fact, it was almost a polar opposite. She focused, holding out her hand, and the energies around Tyren swirled and gathered, and pushed inward on him.

The Highlord screamed in pain and sudden fear, falling to his knees. The scream was again one of a thousand distant voices shrieking all at once, and the red haze seemed to rise from his skin again. He tried to move, but Allie just pushed harder. His scream increased in intensity and he curled up on the ground, shaking like a leaf in a storm.

Allie realized with absolute, terrible certainty that she could end this, right here and right now. She knew she could push the energies down hard enough to kill him. It wouldn't even be hard, she realized. Why those energies hurt him, she still didn't understand, but she knew without doubt that they did, and it would be a simple thing to destroy him.

Something stopped her, however. Something about the energies in Tyren nagged at her. Something about them was wrong. She'd seen Dav and Artus and the way the energies moved with them back on the plains of Kobek when she was interacting with the Rrughn, and they looked nothing like what was pressing its way out of Tyren at that moment.

The odd, backwards energy seemed to be tearing itself out of Tyren's body. Tyren turned his face up to Allie, and for a split second, she could see it. In that instant, Allie suddenly understood everything.

Allie could see Tyren. Not the monster who had oppressed a galaxy for over a decade, but Tyren, the older brother of Artus and Dav. She understood without a shadow of a doubt that these were two very different men. The eyes that looked up at her now were pleading, begging her not for mercy, but to finish it. Somehow, they both knew that Allie was going to kill both men if she kept pushing.

The horror of what she now understood and was about to do struck her with all the weight of a world on her shoulders. She recoiled, pulling back both physically and mentally from the man at her feet.

The energies calmed, and the darkness in Tyren ripped back into the body. Physically he looked the same, but she could see that malevolent energy radiating from him again.

Gasping for air, Tyren looked back up at her. These were the old eyes, filled with malice and loathing. This was the Tyren that needed to be stopped. Allie needed to figure things out. She needed to get out of here, to do what she came for and rescue Imber's father. Her hand flashed out, touching the man shackled to the wall.

"Tic!" she shouted. She felt the jicund land on her shoulder an instant later, and she flicked the crystal with her pinkie, her other fingers holding the chain.

"No!" screamed Tyren, trying to lunge for her. Like Dav, he was too late. She focused her mind on the place she had left on Kobek, and felt the pull. It was even easier this time, quicker and almost gentle.

The darkness came, and then the flash of light, and she was standing on the platform again, surrounded by Dav, Raith, and Artus, standing over Imber. Imber's father weighed her down and would have brought her to the ground under his newly-freed weight, if Dav had been any slower. Lucky for her, Dav was super-humanly quick.

He caught the man and eased him gently downward while Allie stepped back. Everyone had lowered weapons and was staring at Allie. She gave a glare of defiance to the council that she was certain could have peeled paint.

Raith knelt and touched the bracelets around Imber's wrists. They instantly snapped open and fell to the ground. Imber wasted no time, she rolled over and embraced her father. He seemed barely able to move, but managed to get an arm around her as both wept openly.

Allie felt tears coming into her own eyes, but pushed them back as she regained her feet. She pushed past Artus to stand in front of the council. Squaring her shoulders and planting her feet, she pointed at the image of Tyren struggling to get back to his feet in the sky above.

"Do you see?" she yelled at the council. "That is what we are fighting to stop! Hatred, prejudice, tyranny, and senseless violence! Cruelty and a callous disregard for life! Fifteen years under his rule and you've become just like him! So ready to take a life, without concern for her real guilt! Without concern for her intent! She saved all of your lives with her confession, and what is your thanks? Immediate execution? How are you better than him? How are you different? All so eager to spill blood for the cause."

Allie took a long breath to calm herself before scanning her gaze across the council. She spoke again, her tone low and hard.

"You all disgust me. I don't want your help. I don't want anything to do with your so-called council. You're all no better than he is." She shook her head and turned back to her friends. "We need to leave. Can we get a ship?" Nobody in the crowd moved behind her as she turned her back.

"Already got ours," Raith said with a small smile. "I sent a drone to retrieve it last night. I spent most of the night repairing it. She's ready to fly. Just say the word."

"You would defy us so brazenly?" asked the Hgrundewa councilman, though he now seemed much less sure of himself.

"There is nothing to defy," Artus said. "Your council is broken and sick. We came here to find allies in the cause against injustice. Instead, we find perpetrators of the same crime. Allie is right. You can't help us."

With that, he knelt and lifted Imber's father. Imber stood slowly, but seemed to hold steady. Allie's mother moved up beside them, taking Allie's hand and giving it a squeeze. The group walked off the raised platform, and straight toward a side road out of the square, where Raith led them.

Tyren laughed maniacally from the screens overhead. "You don't understand, it's already too late for you!" The group paused. That didn't sound good, Allie thought. "Kill them!" he shouted.

For a long moment, everything was totally silent; a heavy, waiting, expectant silence. The pause was long enough that Raith started walking again. Then the screaming started at the far side of the square.

Out of nowhere, a huge explosion rocked the cavern. The holographic images overhead flickered and then vanished in a shower of sparks as the holographic emitters were destroyed. The audio of Tyren's laughter continued for another second or two before cutting out abruptly as well.

Raith started to run, though kept it to Imber, Allie, and her mother's pace. None of the three were a fraction as fast as the rest of the group. Allie ran as fast as she could, her mother and Imber barely keeping up. Dav slowed enough to take up the rear, guns ready as they looked behind them.

The sound of explosions and screams faded into the distance as they ran. For a long minute, Allie thought they were safe. Then the road in front of them erupted in flames. The group pulled up short, backing up from the excruciating heat emitted by the fiery barricade.

A dark shadow appeared in the bright fire, walking directly through the flames almost casually. As he came through the wall, his features became apparent. He looked human, though there was something off in his eyes. He was a big man, as tall as Artus and much broader. His body was tightly packed with chiseled muscle, and his hair cropped so close he was almost bald. A few more steps, and Allie could clearly see his eyes. The irises swirled and shifted in a mechanical motion, glowing an iridescent orange.

"Cade," Raith whispered.

Artus slowly lowered Imber's father to the ground, eyes not leaving the newcomer. All of them slowly drew weapons. Allie had no idea who this was, but Raith seemed to recognize him, and to her horror, was afraid of him.

"Hello, my short friend," the figure said to Raith. "It

has been a long time."

"Not long enough," Raith replied. "I had hoped you were recycled after that disaster."

"Oh, don't be so negative," said the man, moving slowly forward. "Only thirty eight casualties in that little encounter. Nothing like what this one is going to be. I'll offer you one chance to help me clear this little hovel of life. If you refuse, I'll be sure to break you first."

"Don't bother with the threats. I know full well you'll destroy me anyway, given the chance," Raith replied. "Even if I knew you wouldn't, I would never help you hurt innocent people, let alone my friends."

"Pity," C.A.D.E.-16 replied. "Might have been more fun with your help, until I got bored and broke you anyway. Oh well, this will still be plenty of fun."

Allie pulled out the crystal and stepped toward her friends. A blast of yellow energy flashed past. It didn't hit her hand, but it was close enough that the heat scalded. She dropped the crystal with a yelp.

"None of that, now," the menacing figure said with another step forward. His arm was extended and a complex mechanism seemed to have come out of his forearm and latched onto his hand. It was obviously a weapon.

"Enough of this," Raith said. "Artus, get them to the ship. Straight ahead in the hangar on the right. I'll deal with Cade."

"You'll... wait, you'll deal with me?" C.A.D.E.-16 laughed. "Little android, I'm going to turn you into a smoking pile of scrap metal, and all in plenty of time to catch up to and shred your friends. Here, I'll even let them past. Chasing them will be more fun."

C.A.D.E.-16 didn't move, but suddenly the wall of flame vanished. Artus wasted no time scooping up Imber's father again and charging past the figure. Allie followed suit, though she looked back at Raith and hesitated.

"Go!" he shouted at her.

"Play time," C.A.D.E.-16 said with dark excitement.

CHAPTER SEVENTEEN

C.A.D.E.-16

Raith knew he was no match for a Combat and Destruction unit, especially not an Epsilon series. He also knew that this particular android had both the ability and inclination to kill every living thing in the entire hideout, Sy'hli soldiers included, though they might do a bit of damage to it first. He also knew he was faster than the combat android, though only barely.

He lunged forward, fist coming in at Cade so fast that a human eye might have completely missed the movement. The combat android caught his fist without any trouble, stopping his incredible strength cold.

"You upgraded," Raith said, feeling his small hope evaporate. Cade laughed.

"My own design. You're not the only one who can rebuild himself."

The combat android's metal muscles flexed, and Raith felt the metallic skeleton shatter in his hand. He didn't scream, as androids don't feel pain, but he felt every servo break. That hand would be useless without a full rebuild.

Without any apparent effort, the combat android's foot flashed up faster than even Raith could dodge and slammed into the side of his head. He registered the ground leaving his feet, and flew precisely twenty five point four seven feet before slamming into a stone wall with enough force to make his visual processors blur briefly.

He didn't have to survive, he knew that was so unlikely as to be virtually impossible, he just had to delay the combat android long enough for his friends to get aboard the Peacekeeper and off the ground. At the speed of their slowest runner, and the speed Dav could work that ship, they'd be safe in exactly two minutes and six seconds.

Cade's fist slammed into the side of his head and his visual processors blurred again. Raith knew he didn't have that long. He had to figure out a way to delay.

"How did you rewire your power core?" he asked. Cade paused a moment, then laughed.

"I think I even have time to tell you," he said arrogantly. "I hijacked a bio-electric generator from Hgrunde. Jacked my processor directly into it while I rebuilt my power core. Took me a while to find enough tricallium for the new power core first, but I managed."

"How did you keep from short circuiting with the bio-electric generator? The energy wavelength is entirely wrong." Raith stalled.

"Oh, that was tricky. Probably similar to your

technique though. I used a tricallium plate sandwiched between a pair of rogellium crystals as a filter. It only took eighteen seconds to burn out, but I finished rebuilding the power core three and a half seconds faster than that, so it did the job nicely."

"That's brilliant," Raith said, honestly impressed. He wouldn't have thought of that, and it certainly isn't what he himself had done. Cade grinned wickedly. One minute and twenty one seconds left, Raith thought.

"Coming from you, that's high praise," the combat android said. "Not many of us were bright enough to figure out ways to stay alive, between the Infection and the slow death of our power systems. I almost feel bad about having to tear you apart. I am almost out of time though, so I'll just finish with you and then go tear your friends into little pieces."

Cade's fist raised, razor sharp spikes snapping out from his knuckles, then paused. The android looked like he was listening to something. Raith could just make out the communications frequency the combat android was using. His processor was a little scrambled after the two heavy blows though, so he didn't have time to hack into it and hear the message. Cade sighed.

"Oh, fine. I'll come back for you. The Highlord isn't convinced my calculations are correct and wants to ensure your friends don't escape. Don't worry, you can probably hear their screams from here."

Cade grinned, then slammed his fist down into Raith's leg, the sharp spikes tearing into the synthetic flesh and ripping several of his motor system wires. One of the support bars in the side of his knee snapped as well, though that last part wasn't critical Raith knew, he had redundant supports in most of his joints.

Raith's systems almost instantly processed which systems were damaged. He also calculated it would take him eight point four seconds to rewire the knee joint to be able to run again, assuming the combat android left it at the one crippling blow. Cade did stop, knowing he'd bought himself enough time, following orders to immediately pursue the fleeing crystal bearers.

Raith wasted no time and immediately began rewiring the circuitry in his leg to bypass the damaged systems. The blow had torn a large piece of his imitation skin open, making it easy for Raith to access the silver muscle fibers and the coppery wiring beneath. His systems were calculating how long it would take him to catch up. He didn't like the answer. Cade would have them by then.

Knowing he had no other option, he finished his rewire, snatched up his shatter gun and Allie's crystal, and ran at his maximum speed to catch up, hoping his calculations were incorrect, although he knew they weren't. He might be able to get a shot off before the combat android struck, but it would be close, and would depend on which of the group the combat android had been told to destroy first and what order they were running in.

Three... two... one... his systems counted down until he was in sight. He knew he wouldn't be in time. The combat android had reached them. It wasn't using its guns, which is the only reason any of them still lived.

Tyren had probably ordered them torn apart. That

seemed exactly the type of cruelty Tyren enjoyed. The combat android had already raised its spiked hand and was bringing it down toward the back of Allie's neck.

Raith could see something the combat unit had missed, however. Raith may not have reached them in time, but someone else had. A massive clawed hand came from the side and struck the combat unit in a broad swipe with enough force to hurl it sidelong into, and through, a stone wall across the street. The wall crumbled, heavy stone falling down on the android. Allie stopped and looked back.

"Go!" Raith shouted.

"Go!" repeated Dgehf as he and Raith both moved toward the fallen combat unit. Allie turned and ran.

The pile of stone rubble exploded as Cade fired one of his many weapons to clear his path back out. The android climbed out of the pile and locked gazes with Dgehf.

"You die first," the combat android snarled angrily moving forward. Dgehf slammed one fist into the stone ground, hard enough to cause a ripple of cracks to radiate out from his fist. The tunnel shook ominously.

Then he opened his impressive maw and roared. The windows along the street for several hundred feet exploded in a wave with the intensity of the sound, glass raining down in a glittering shower. Raith, still running toward them, saw the look of surprise, and a tiny hint of doubt cross the combat android's features.

In a flash, the combat android raised his right arm and fired as one of his guns snapped out from his forearm and into position. The blast of angry yellow energy slammed into the now-charging Maruck.

Dgehf stumbled, but didn't stop. The look of doubt on the combat android's face grew. Three more shots slammed into the massive beast, but still Dgehf charged.

Faster than any Sy'hli, the combat android leapt, slamming a full-force kick into the massive Maruck's jaw. One enormous tusk broke and spun into the distance with a whizzing sound as Dgehf's head snapped to the side. Cade landed smoothly, and waited for the Maruck to fall. Dgehf's head slowly turned back to face the android. He spat a bit of blood, then spoke one word.

"No," Dgehf said.

Before even Cade's processors could recalculate his next move, Dgehf grabbed him. The Maruck's massive hands enclosed the combat android's entire upper torso, pinning both arms to his side.

Cade strained and slowly began to push the massive hand back open. Dgehf clamped the other hand around his first one, and squeezed with both hands. Raith could hear metal squealing its protest under the strain, but the combat android didn't break. Dgehf growled as he leaned into his crushing pressure.

Raith, having not quite reached them from clear down the street, took his shot, knowing what the combat android would do next. His shot hit the combat android in the face an instant before the weapons built into the android's eyes took effect. The combat android's head snapped back. Raith calculated that he likely bought them two point nine seconds.

"Throw him into that tunnel!" Raith shouted at Dgehf.

The Maruck did as instructed, flinging the stunned android like a rag doll so far down the tunnel that only Raith's advanced visual receptors actually even saw where he landed and slid to a stop. Raith accessed the shatter gun's control board mentally through his contact with the grip, then flung the gun down the tunnel, though not as far as Cade had flown. The hum it usually made while firing was sounding steadily now, and building in pitch.

"Go, Dgehf! Get your family to your ship and get off this planet!" Raith said, turning to run toward where his friends had gone. Dgehf grunted his agreement.

"Tell Allie Dgehf help. Tell Allie is now Allie's turn to help," he said.

Raith heard Cade's scream of rage and knew they had only moments before he was back, though Raith hoped his plan was going to work and they'd have more time than that.

"I will," Raith promised, "thank you."

Dgehf turned and loped down a side tunnel at alarming speed. Nothing that big should move that fast, Raith thought. He looked back to where he knew the combat android was coming from, measured the hum of the shatter gun and calculated remaining time to overload, and turned to follow his friends. Entering the hangar, he was greeted by an unexpected and unpleasant sight. His friends were scattered around the room, behind cover and firing at a battalion of Hgrundewa soldiers.

He drew his remaining shatter gun just as the first one in the tunnel behind him reached its critical point and exploded. By Raith's calculations, it would have happened a fraction of a second before the combat android reached that spot. He heard the tunnel collapsing and smiled.

Cade would have to find a new way around to get to them. If he had accessed the internal layout files like Raith had, which Raith assumed he did when he hacked the holographic sky for Tyren, it would still take him a full eighty three seconds to make it back around to them. Enough time, he thought, though the Hgrundewa complicated things.

Raith had never liked the Hgrundewa. Far too prideful and power-hungry to be reliable. This was probably an attack on Allie and Artus directly for their 'insults'. Allie, Dav, and Imber could reach the Peacekeeper, but Artus, Morgan, and Imber's father would be unable to reach it without having to cross too much open ground under heavy fire. Odds were against them making it to the Peacekeeper without at least one of them dying, probably two.

No chance to get them to the Peacekeeper, and the Hgrundewa were not only too well protected to take out before Cade reached them again, but there were at least twenty more Hgrundewa in these tunnels according to the council's computer system.

They were undoubtedly heading here now, and no way to know how long until they arrived. No time. No way to get everyone safely aboard the Peacekeeper before Cade reached them. Raith saw no other options.

"Dav!" he shouted. When Dav glanced quickly his way, Raith pointed at the Peacekeeper. "Get airborne!"

He raced fully into the room at inhuman speeds, his own shots with his shatter gun carefully calculated to damage visibility rather than people as he ruptured a water pipe above a group of the Hgrundewa, then hitting a stacked pile of cargo crates to one side of another group, which exploded in a white cloud as the ore inside shattered.

Raith leapt just as the Peacekeeper lifted off the ground, the hatch closing. He cleared the closing doorway by scant inches, rolling as he landed. He didn't slow, just raced into the cockpit and sat in his gunner's chair. The others were already in position, Imber filling in as navigator for the moment.

A quick glance at the scanners showed the remaining Hgrundewa pouring in. Artus, Morgan, and Imber's father weren't going to make it. He started to stand to jump back out and help them, but spotted something else.

Eight Sy'hli strike troops appeared almost out of nowhere, leaping the tall stacks of crates and landing among the two groups of Hgrundewa. Instantly, the Sy'hli fell upon the Hgrundewa. Raith smiled. The Sy'hli had chosen to side with their princes. One made it to Artus and spoke rapidly to him. Raith watched on the scanners, but couldn't make out what they were saying over the explosions.

Two of the incoming Hgrundewa carried a huge handheld arc cannon and aimed at the Peacekeeper, firing a massive blast. Dav banked as much as possible in the hanger, which while plenty big enough for the half dozen ships and cargo it held, didn't leave much room for high speed evasive action. The Peacekeeper's wing scraped along the ceiling.

"Dav, go!" Artus shouted over the com after a moment. "We'll follow with our troops here!"

The eight Sy'hli would be more than a match for the forty Hgrundewa, Raith already knew one of the other ships in the hangar was a Sy'hli battle cruiser. He quickly calculated how long it would take the Sy'hli to eliminate the Hgrundewa and knew they'd be safe from Cade, they'd be airborne and gone at least ten seconds before he got there. Unfortunately, the odds of the Peacekeeper dodging the arc cannon that long were much smaller. Raith glanced at Dav, who nodded.

Raith spun the guns around and fired a few precise shots with the ship's arc cannons and the hangar doors exploded, revealing what looked to be a huge volcanic shaft on the other side. He could see light above, though it came in vivid, angry yellow flashes. The storm must still be raging, he realized. Dav wasted no time moving the ship expertly through the hangar doors.

They shot out of the top of the volcano and directly into a storm of epic proportions. Lightning flashed through the air so rapidly all around them that it looked like a strobe light outside the window.

Dav spun the Peacekeeper around like a leaf in a hurricane, dodging bolts of yellow lightning. Banking sharply and rocketing straight up at high velocity, they cleared the atmosphere in seconds and straight into a huge firefight.

Raith quickly scanned the area around the planet. Resistance ships were leaving atmosphere rapidly, but were quickly being attacked by hundreds of other ships that had apparently been lying in wait.

Though all had the huge Coalition emblem imprinted on their hulls, a random collection of ships from a number of races made up a quarter of the enemy ships, and there were at least a hundred Maruck battle cruisers, but none of that was what really concerned Raith. What worried him was the twenty Sy'hli warships. Tyren must have sent every loyal Sy'hli battle cruiser he had, following Cade. How he had found them, Raith still wasn't sure.

One Sy'hli warship could probably handle a dozen of the Maruck battle cruisers, and while the Interceptor could readily outrun them, many of the other Resistance ships couldn't, and there were four other Interceptors in the attacking fleet as well. They were in very serious trouble.

"I don't think we're going to make it out of this," Dav said quietly.

"We're going to do some damage first," Raith promised, firing a wave of plasma bolts at the approaching ships. Every shot connected and did damage to a different ship. A few were crippled, but it would take more than that to make a dent in this mess.

A Sy'hli battle cruiser came up from the atmosphere behind them, screaming past them and straight into a mass of Maruck warships, plasma cannons blazing. Raith smiled. Well that would help, anyway. Whatever flaws the Sy'hli had, cowardice wasn't among them, and battle skill was invariably high among their strengths.

"Wait, don't move," Allie called from her station.

Dav brought the Peacekeeper to a stop as quickly as he could, while Raith kept firing. It was relatively quiet in the ship for a long moment, then a huge number of ships suddenly disappeared from Raith's targeting array, every one of them an enemy ship, in long swaths through the middle of the fight.

In one instant, the Resistance ships suddenly outnumbered their attackers and the enemy ranks were scattered. Every major cluster of enemy ships was gone. Simply gone.

"What just happened?" Dav asked as he kicked the ship back into combat speeds. Raith took out a couple more ships.

"Incoming Shift wave," Allie replied. "I directed it the best I could."

"That was amazing," Dav replied.

"Where did they go?" Raith asked, curious. Several more ships fell. Once the numbers were significantly in their favor, the Resistance was making incredibly short work of the now-scattered enemy.

"I honestly don't know," Allie replied sheepishly.

Tic chirped, sounding somewhat amused. Raith wasn't actually quite sure just how much Tic understood, but sometimes the little jicund seemed a lot brighter than she really should be.

Admittedly, Raith didn't actually know how smart jicund were supposed to be. Jicund were not a common species, and were secretive and hard to find in their home jungle. Keeping one captured for study was far more difficult than it was worth.

"I didn't make the wave, I just split it up so it didn't

hit any of the Resistance," Allie explained.

"That's almost scary," Dav said, though he smiled over at her for a moment as the last of the Coalition ships went down, "but you probably just saved all of our lives, and most of the Resistance while you were at it."

"This is Artus, can you read me?" came a voice over the ship's communication system, though it was heavy with static.

"We read you," Imber replied, the only one not actively participating in the fighting. "Are all of you okay?"

"We made it," Artus replied, the signal breaking every so often. "I took a hit, but nothing a bit of time with a dermal regenerator won't fix. Allie, your mom and Imber's father are both okay. Bad news though, we got clipped by one of those energy waves Allie was talking about as we cleared the atmosphere. According to our sensors, we're right on the edge of The Shift, leaving it now. Where that is relative to you guys, I have no idea. No way to map The Shift."

"I'm so sorry," Allie cried out in horror. "That was my fault, I was trying to get rid of the attacking ships! Are you in the middle of them?"

"No, though a few other ships are on my scanners here. Nothing extremely close, and none of them are ships that could catch this battle cruiser." Raith could hear Allie's sigh of relief at Artus' news. "More bad news though, we're going to have to stay separate for a while. I need you guys to go to these coordinates fast as possible. From where we are, we'll never catch up in time." A set of coordinates flashed onto the navigator's panel.

"What's the situation?" Dav asked.

"The Sy'hli have some intel about Tyren's plans and it isn't pretty. He's working on some kind of weapon near the Lo'riza system. Word is he'll have it finished in less than a week. If he finishes it, the Sy'hli don't think he can be stopped," Artus warned.

"What kind of weapon?" Raith asked.

"We're not sure, but we can't let him finish it," Artus replied.

"I understand," Dav said. Raith could read the worry in his voice, and the nervousness at being in this without his brother for a while. "What's your plan?" It was quiet for a few long moments.

"Diplomatic mission," a new voice answered. "This is Commander Nox, of the Sy'hli Empire. Prince Artus and his entourage are here with me and my crew aboard my ship. Don't worry Prince Davrelan, we'll take good care of them for you. Between Prince Artus, Morgan Bennett of the Order of the Silver Star, and Ambassador Oren, we might be able to convince a few more factions to side with us against Tyren, bring a few more guns to our side."

"I hope so," Dav replied. "Considering the new council's reaction to us, we'll need all the help we can get."

"Roger that," Commander Nox replied.

"Dav?" Artus asked.

"Yes?"

"Be careful. We don't know what the weapon is or what Tyren can do with it. I wish I could go with you."

"So do I," Dav replied. "Keep in touch, but mind your com channels so we're not monitored."

"Understood," Artus answered. "Over and out."

The com switched off. It was quiet for a moment before Dav sighed audibly.

"No help for it, we have to go," he said. "I need to make some calculations with the wormhole network to see how fast I can get us there. A week isn't much time for a trip that long. That's clear across the quadrant. Allie, if you can keep us from getting Jumped around, Imber can get us out of The Shift. As directly as possible please." Imber nodded and turned to her screen. Allie also nodded, and closed her eyes.

Raith listened idly, while his processors ran rampant trying to figure out their odds of escaping Cade for long. The combat android was probably already in pursuit, and definitely shouldn't be neglected in their calculations. He knew not only that series of androids, but he knew this specific android.

Scary was an understatement. Like Raith, Cade had developed a stronger emotional response system than was normal. The combat androids weren't supposed to be emotional at all, but this one was. Emotionally reactive, and completely psychotic.

Cade wouldn't quit, and sooner or later he'd catch up to them again. They couldn't beat him in combat, close or ranged, on land or in ships. Death is what that machine had been built for. Raith needed to figure something else out to deal with him, or they were all in trouble when Cade eventually did catch up.

CHAPTER EIGHTEEN

SHATTERED HAND

It had been two days, traveling at incredible speeds in the Peacekeeper, racing through wormholes and open space. Raith manned the helm any time it was open space so Dav could rest, since Raith didn't need rest of any kind. This was one of those times where Dav was driving, and Imber wanted to take the opportunity to help Raith.

Imber found him in the galley, working on a pair of wristbands. She had no idea what they were for, but it was incredibly tiny, detailed work he was doing on the electronics inside them. She paused, not wanting to interrupt his delicate work, especially since he was doing it all with his one good hand, then reminded herself that he was an android and wouldn't be startled. No doubt he already knew she was there.

She glanced at the broken hand. He'd done some basic repairs with the supplies on hand, but they didn't have the material packs for the crafter to make the tools he needed so hadn't bothered to do more than a quick patch job. Imber had spent the last two days making the replacement parts. They may not have been able to craft the right tools, but Imber already had everything she needed in her gear.

Androids had been a fascination, almost an obsession of hers since she was little. They were so technically complex, but simple and elegant in design. The evolution of androids throughout the galaxy's history was just as fascinating.

She had spent a good deal of time studying android science, and was fully capable of repairing his hand now that she had the parts crafted. She could probably fix his eye too.

Imber had noticed the faint haziness in it that told her his visual receptors weren't functioning at full capacity in that eye either. Whatever had caused that scar on his face had done some damage, though probably not too much. Imber had brought the tools she might need for that as well.

"Hi Raith," she said simply. "Do you have some time?" He glanced up and smiled.

"For you? Always," he said with a wink. Her heart fluttered and she again forcefully reminded herself that he was an android. She sat across from him, setting a small gray case on the table between them. Raith looked at it curiously.

"I have a surprise for you," she said with a smile, opening the case. Raith blinked in surprise as he immediately recognized and understood the purpose of the tools and materials in the case. He smiled up at her.

"You didn't tell me you had these!" he accused, though his pleased smile never slipped. Imber grinned.

"I wanted it to be a surprise. I had the tools, but not the parts, so I had to have them crafted. I can fix your hand now though, it'll be good as new," she said. Raith looked even more surprised.

"You want to fix it?"

"Of course. It'll be easier for me with two hands. Working on your own hand would be more difficult. Not that you couldn't do it, but it really would be my pleasure to help."

"By all means," Raith said, stretching his arm across the table to put his hand in her reach.

Instead, Imber stood and moved over to sit beside him on the bench. It wasn't necessary, she could have done it from across the table, but she told herself that it would be easier without his arm all stretched out like that. Raith didn't comment on the move, just moved his hand over in front of her again, turning slightly sideways so he could look directly at her while she worked.

Imber gently took the hand, giving it a long, close examination. It was weird, she thought, that the synthetic skin was still warm though she could feel the shattered pieces of his metal skeleton beneath the skin. She lay his hand down again palm down, fingers outstretched on the table, then pulled out her first tool.

It was a blue ring of metal, just small enough to cover the back of his hand. She lay it atop his hand, and activated the device. The blue metal glowed faintly, and instantly the synthetic skin on his hand vanished. Not really vanished, she knew, but had phased slightly out of physical space so she could see and move through it unhindered while she worked on his hand. It was a shame the device could only effect one type of material at a time, or it would have been incredibly useful on organics during medical surgery.

She drew two more small tools from the case. One was an ionic extractor, which would let her remove the shattered pieces easily and safely. The other was for disconnecting, welding, and then resealing connectors at the joints in his hand. She began the delicate work.

"I had no idea you knew how to do this kind of thing," Raith told her as he watched her work.

His good hand did the talking, held beside the hand she was working on and moving rapidly in the intricate signed language developed so others could speak to Imber's people non-verbally.

Imber smiled in pleased surprise. She would be able to hold a conversation with him while working this way. Imber hadn't even realized Raith knew the language, though that shouldn't have surprised her.

"It's been kind of a hobby for me for a long time. I love androids," she answered, speaking aloud, though she glanced up at his face for a moment. Raith's grin turned mischievous and she blushed. "Android science, anyway," she clarified, looking back down.

"Either way, I appreciate the help."

"My pleasure," she said sincerely. "If you like, I can fix your leg, and that eye too."

"You noticed the damage to the eye, huh?"

"Hard not to," Imber answered. "That scar points right to it. Don't worry though, I can fix the scar too."

"I'd kind of rather you didn't," Raith signed. Imber paused and looked up at him. He shrugged, looking a little uncomfortable.

"I've spent my life hiding the fact that I was a machine. For the first time, I'm around people who know, and don't care, that I'm not an organic," he explained. "I think the scar looks cool, and I'm kind of enjoying flaunting that I'm not an organic." Imber smiled.

"I understand. We'll leave the scar then, but I do want to fix the eye."

"Please do," he replied. They were both quiet for a time.

"Can I ask you something?" she said suddenly.

"Of course," he signed.

"Why are you helping Allie and the others?"

"Odd question," Raith replied. "Especially since you yourself confessed to your own betrayal to save them all."

"It's different though," Imber said, though she wasn't really sure it was. "As an android, you are programmed to follow the orders of whomever you're programmed to obey. All of the androids that survived the Infection belonged to the Coalition. You fight against them. Why?" Raith chuckled in response.

"That was thanks to Allie, actually. The Highlord was going to recycle me. He mockingly told me I didn't need to follow any orders anymore once the recycler was activated."

"You went into a recycler? There's no way, you'd have been broken down to atoms if you'd been in an active recycler!" she exclaimed, pausing work again as she looked up at him. His grin broadened.

"Allie pointed out that Tyren said it had to be activated, not fully operating. There's a few second delay from activation to full operation. The distinction hadn't even occurred to me," he said, sounding somewhat embarrassed. "Anyway, I climbed in, his idiot henchman turned it on, and I immediately broke the door down and helped the others escape. Not before getting this awesome scar though," he told her with another playful wink. Imber couldn't help but smile.

"That's incredible," she said. He nodded.

"In short, I owe her not only my life, but my freedom. I can go anywhere, and do anything I want. I don't have to answer to anyone. For the first time, I have a real choice. So what do I choose? I choose to fight against the man who used me to hurt others, and in the end tried to destroy me, and help the one who trusted me even knowing I had no choice but to hurt her. I choose to help the one who helped me. She's the best friend I've ever had."

Imber shifted her gaze firmly down, feeling a touch of envy that Allie held that status in Raith's eyes. Only a little bit though, since Allie was a great person, and a great friend to Imber as well. She had single-handedly faced down Tyren and rescued Imber's own father from a torturous death.

It hurt her to know she still had a while before she could be with him, but just knowing he was safe and alive had made all the difference in her world. Allie deserved all the respect and admiration the boys gave her, and then some. She felt Raith's other hand on hers and paused again, looking up.

"Not the only friend, though," he said softly.

Her heart fluttered and she flushed. Imber returned the smile, and held his gaze for a long moment. It was remarkable, she thought, that seeing the metallic scar, his cybernetic hand open in front of her, having all of this evidence directly under her nose that he was a machine, she still found herself drawn to him in a way she'd never felt before.

"I'll take what I can get," she said after a moment. "I don't have many friends."

"Nonsense," Raith argued, "you have me, Allie, Dav, Tic, Artus, and Morgan. Plenty of friends, especially when they're such good ones. Any of us would do anything for you. You know that, right?"

"I do," Imber said after a long breath to steady her emotions.

She truly did know that, and it overwhelmed her. Other than her father and uncle, nobody in her life would have done half of what these people had done for her. "You are all the best friends I've ever had."

"There you go then," Raith said, sounding satisfied.

Imber replaced another joint servo. The tool in her hand hummed and emitted a red light as it fused the joint components to the new support bars on the skeletal frame.

His ability to switch seamlessly between the signed language and the spoken one was impressive, she thought, and sweet of him to do it so she could keep talking with him while she worked.

"Almost done," she said.

A moment later, she'd repaired the last part, and switched off her tools. Turning off the blue ring, the synthetic skin on his hand reappeared. She pulled out another tool, activating it and running it across his hand. Where the tool's band of light touched, the crushed synthetic skin regained its proper color. In a few more moments, the hand looked perfect, just like the rest of him, she thought to herself, feeling the color rising in her cheeks again.

"Try that out," she told him. Raith raised his hand, ran a few quick internal diagnostics, and slowly flexed and opened his hand.

"Perfect," he said with an appreciative glance and a grin. "Seriously Imber, this is top-notch work. I think you did a better job than the scientist who built me to begin with. Maybe I can have you help me with some upgrades later." Imber laughed.

"I'd be happy to," she replied. "We still need to fix that leg and that eye though."

Raith slid the table back slightly, and lay his leg across to one of the chairs to put the damaged knee in her reach, detaching one of the armored plates and pulling up the leg on his flight suit. He'd fixed most of the major damage, but didn't have the tools for the fine-tuning it needed, or the synthetic dermal applicator to fix the torn skin.

"Well you've almost completely fixed this yourself," she said after a close inspection.

"Almost. Just need a tune up and the skin patched."

"Easy enough," she said, and got to work.

"So, question for question," Raith said. "Why are you helping Allie?"

"Similar reasons, actually," she told him. "I was forced to follow orders just like you were, only in my case it was under threat of my father being killed. Allie saved his life, and gave me back my freedom. And all of you saved my life. Tyren is going to keep doing things like this to people until he's stopped. I may not be able to do much, but I'll help however I can." Raith nodded.

"With luck, we'll have this sorted out by the end of the week and we can get you and your father back together and back home to a peaceful life again."

"That's my dream," Imber replied. "All done, time for the eye."

"Are you sure you can fix the eye? That's a pretty complex system, and there's risk of shorting out my memory core, messing around in there," Raith said, now seeming a little nervous.

"Don't worry, I'm familiar with the visual sensory system your model uses," she smiled reassuringly. "Besides, I have a backup unit here I was going to run an echo program on in case something did happen. I can do a quick restore and you'll be right back where you were, only with a fixed eye. Honestly though, my feelings won't be hurt if you don't want me to do it." Raith considered only a moment before nodding.

"It's okay, if you say you can do it, I trust you," he replied. Her smile broadened.

"Thank you, Raith. I appreciate the faith," she told him sincerely.

Imber reached into her case again and withdrew

another small device, which she placed up against his forehead, where it automatically attached. She activated it, a small green glow around the edges lit up. The small readout on the front showing her that it had located his main systems and was set to echo mode.

She put the blue phase ring up over the eye, and the synthetic skin vanished, revealing a part of his metallic skull. Another small tool came up in her hand, and with a few twists of the dial on the side, a panel of the metal skull slid back, leaving the eye and its connected system accessible from the side. Raith's looked straight ahead, head turned sidelong to Imber.

"Imber?" Raith signed with his newly-repaired hand since she couldn't easily reads his lips from this angle.

"Hmm?" she asked, focusing closely on the delicate work.

"If something happens to me in the coming fight, I just want to tell you how much your friendship means to me. Not many people look at me and see a person. I wanted to thank you for treating me like a person."

"Why wouldn't I?" she asked.

"Because I'm a machine," he said simply.

"I'm not sure that's any different. Organics are machines too, right? Just made of different materials and grown rather than built. We function almost exactly the same way though." Raith was still as he considered this.

"I'm not sure it's the same though. Many androids were built that I don't think are people," he signed.

"What's the difference, then?" Imber asked. Raith considered again.

"Feelings, I think. I was programmed for them, but

I'm not sure that makes them any less valid."

"I know they're not less valid. Ours are programmed too, trained into us from birth by experience and biologically built into our systems. Your emotions are structurally built, and then programmed through your AI by experience. Not much difference there." She finished replacing the contact that had been fused by the recycler and replaced the skull panel.

"So to you, I am a person," Raith stated simply.

Imber realized that while rationally her arguments made sense, she had believed him to be a person since the moment they'd met. She could see it in his eyes. He felt and cared about things the same way anyone else would. Android or not, he was every bit as much a person as she was. An incredible person that she couldn't stop thinking about.

She removed the blue phase ring and the backup unit, and gently turned his face toward her. His repaired eye was every bit as clear, dark, and intense, as the other. Only his scar remained, and she found she agreed with him. The scar was perfect. On impulse, she leaned forward and gently kissed his cheek.

"Not just a person, Raith. You're my friend."

CHAPTER NINETEEN

THE HIGHLORD'S VOICE

Highlord Tyren paced angrily back and forth across the bridge of his new ship, the Helios. The core material had been installed and completed, and they were ready for a test. Everything was going according to plan, except for one thing. His brothers and the crystal bearer still lived.

"How is it that two hundred Coalition war ships as well as an Epsilon series combat android are completely incapable of killing one crystal bearer!" he screamed into the com.

"She was accompanied by two Sy'hli princes, eight Sy'hli strike troops headed by Commander Nox, a Theta unit, and a ridiculously oversized Maruck," C.A.D.E.-16 explained.

"One Maruck, two aristocrats, eight soldiers and a non-combat android are enough to stop half my fleet and the most finely tuned destructive weapon in the galaxy?

I begin to think reports of your abilities are seriously overrated," Highlord Tyren growled. "Tell me again why I shouldn't have you scrapped?"

"You still need me," C.A.D.E.-16 replied calmly.

Tyren barely refrained from screaming. The infernal machine was correct, it was still needed. The two princes and the crystal bearer needed to be destroyed, and the combat android was still his best chance of succeeding.

The other crystal bearer had been broken and would be unable to tap into the crystal's energies, so wasn't a direct threat. The girl was showing impressive resourcefulness and power however, and was appearing to be a greater threat by the day.

He also couldn't ignore the continued survival of his brothers. Knowledge of their survival would bring countless Sy'hli out from under every rock to rally behind them to overthrow the Highlord. The Sy'hli had been less than cooperative when he took power, and much of the Sy'hli army had disappeared shortly afterward. If the Sy'hli army resurfaced backed by another heir to the Sy'hli throne, things could go badly for him very quickly.

"Fine, but disappoint me one more time, and I'll have you crushed before I recycle your broken remains," Tyren snarled.

"Yes, Highlord," C.A.D.E.-16 replied. Tyren shut off the com channel.

Things were not going entirely as planned. The girl Jumping in to rescue the Ambassador was unexpected and didn't bode well for the future. Luckily, he'd thought ahead and had rogellium bands implanted in the ship's hull. She'd be unable to Jump anywhere near the Helios, leaving the only means of assault an external one. Against such an assault the Helios would be impenetrable.

The memory of the pain he'd felt when the girl had done... something... to him kept creeping into his mind, sending chills up his spine. He had no idea how she'd done that, but it terrified him to the core. The girl hadn't even touched him. He'd felt sure she would kill him in that moment, and couldn't understand why she hadn't. He knew without doubt she could have. Not killing him was a tremendous mistake, one which would result in her agonizing death if he had any say over it.

She is more powerful than you, came the voice.

"Silence!" he shouted. Preston looked up from where he stood poring over a data tablet. "Not you!" the Highlord snapped. Preston went back to the tablet.

My brothers are more powerful than you, the voice returned, confidently.

"Impossible," Tyren replied with a snarl.

I told you from the beginning that you would not succeed. My brothers and their friends will stop you.

"I will enjoy watching your brothers die screaming," Tyren retorted, hoping to wound the voice.

The voice had gradually grown stronger since his first encounter with the girl's crystal. It had been even stronger since his second encounter with her. The Highlord knew why, and didn't like it. He could feel his weakness, and needed time to rebuild his strength. His control over the voice was slipping.

Your new toy won't be enough to stop them. They've

found the Resistance. Their strength grows by the day. It's only a matter of time before the entire galaxy turns up to tear apart your precious ship.

"The Helios is unstoppable!" Tyren growled.

Not until it's charged. Two days is a long time…

"They were just in The Shift, fool," Tyren snapped.

Nobody could make it from even the outer borders of The Shift to the Helios' present position in anything close to that time. Even a fully charged Helios would have a hard time making that journey in less than a week.

She can Jump the ship.

"She can't control the crystal that well yet. If she could, she'd have Jumped them to the Resistance ages ago, and then Jumped the whole lot of them right onto my base," Tyren was fairly pleased with this logic, because he knew it was true.

That was one of the reasons the crystal bearers were so dangerous, though not the biggest reason. They could bring others with them, and while Jumping a small ship and a small crew was manageable by a trained Jumper, nobody untrained could move more than a couple of people at a time, and no Jumper could land anywhere near rogellium.

You felt her power just as I did when she rescued the Ambassador. No crystal bearer has ever held that kind of power. She's different, and she can destroy you. The voice sounded both smug, and relieved at the thought of the pair of them dying. What kind of deranged fool actually wanted to die, Tyren thought?

He moved to his chair in the center of the room and

sat down. From here he could see every one of the command stations and issue orders. The massive display screen on the far wall currently showed a slowly drifting star-scape.

The Helios was moving, though not quickly. The voice was right, it would be slow, vulnerable, and useless in a fight until he could charge it. Two more days until he reached his destination and could give the Helios a true test of its power.

"You will die," Tyren sneered at the voice.

As will you, it responded with finality.

Tyren wished that knowledge didn't bother him so much. His desperate need for survival was driven by his need for revenge. If he died before he could complete his goal, it would all have been for nothing.

Tyren couldn't let it come to that. He had to survive, so he could kill the rest of them. He didn't care how many others died in the process, everyone responsible for his pain, his internal anguish, would die.

"Not just yet," Tyren told the voice coldly. He stood and moved over to Preston.

"Yes, my Lord?" Preston asked, standing from his chair and bowing deeply.

"How is progress coming in the lab?" Tyren asked.

The voice grew quiet. It always did when Tyren talked about the project he had in the lab. The Helios was a tremendous accomplishment, but was merely a vehicle for the completion of his true plan, which was being developed in the lab at that very moment.

"Excellent, my Lord. The Ymritian scientists have nearly perfected the design. A successful test is expected within the next twenty four hours," the loyal advisor told him.

Highlord Tyren smiled. That, at least, was going perfectly. It would even be completed ahead of schedule at this rate. Once a successful test had been completed, and the Helios was fully charged, they could travel immediately to Sy'hloran, the Sy'hli home world. It was there that he would initiate his true plan. Once it had been set into motion, it would be irreversible and unstoppable.

Then, assuming he survived the final stage of his own plan, he could begin to rebuild his people, so they could become the beautiful and glorious civilization they once were, with no one left to threaten them. On that day, he could die in peace. Not a moment before.

"Inform me the moment we reach the star," he said, turning back to his chair. He sat down and considered the situation and all the information C.A.D.E.-16 had given him. He touched the control bar on the arm of his chair with the tips of his long fingers.

"Klythe!" he shouted into the open com channel.

"Yesh, Great One?" came the rumbled reply, slightly slurred.

"Get in here!"

"Yesh, Great One."

A moment passed, and the huge beast lumbered in. Two other Maruck were with him, he must have been issuing orders to his lieutenants, or pack leaders, or whatever the term in Maruck was.

As they approached, Tyren winced. Klythe was in rough shape. Half his face was swollen and bruised with one beady black eye swollen completely shut, and he walked with a noticeable limp.

The rewards of going up against that blasted Theta, Tyren knew. Klythe looked weak, which made Tyren want to just finish him off just to get it over with. He managed to resist though. Klythe, like C.A.D.E.-16, was still useful.

"One of my brothers is coming here, in a lone ship. Prepare our defenses and arrange half the fleet in protective formations around the Helios. They certainly won't reach us in time, but let's not risk it, shall we?" Highlord Tyren said. Klythe nodded.

"Yesh, Great One," the brute slurred.

One of the other Maruck barely stifled a deep snicker. The Highlord turned his piercing blue eyes on the creature, who shrank back. Despite his size, the Maruck had learned to respect Tyren as a warrior. He was faster and smarter than any of them, and nearly as strong.

"And send the other half to Sy'hloran, I have reason to believe my other brother is heading in that direction. Any Sy'hli battle cruiser without the Coalition insignia should be destroyed on sight."

"Yesh, Great One," Klythe said.

That slur was getting old fast, Tyren thought. For some reason, dermal regeneration technology didn't work on Maruck. Klythe had said once it was because only the weak needed healing. Klythe could clearly use some right about now though, Tyren thought.

He disagreed with Klythe on the point anyway, since he himself had heavily relied on dermal regenerators after his encounter with the little fuzzy demon the girl carried around. He wouldn't have much of a face left without it. As it was, he didn't have so much as a scar. No reason not to use technology for greater advantage and gain, in his opinion.

"Now get out," he said simply.

The Maruck turned and moved toward the door.

"Klythe, send me Harelo," the Highlord called. Just one more piece to put into play. Klythe turned and saluted, then left the room with his two sidekicks. Tyren's thoughts turned inward as he waited.

C.A.D.E.-16 had told him that Morgan Bennett had left on a different ship than the crystal bearer had. That was good, since it meant the girl would get no training from the former Jumper. It was unfortunate that she, and the Ambassador, had ended up on the same ship with Artus however. Those three together would be an incredibly powerful rallying force while recruiting help against him.

The crystal bearer had a girl, an android, and a Sy'hli boy to defend her now. And that blasted purple beast, he reminded himself, touching his face out of habit as he thought about the terrible little creature. They were in an Interceptor, which would make them hard to catch, but once the Helios was fully charged, he'd be able to run them down without difficulty.

The combat android had also told him that the Resistance, while not destroyed, had been scattered by events in the caves of their hideout. With the Resistance scattered, their hideout made public, and many of their number destroyed, they weren't much of a threat either.

Harelo entered the bridge, interrupting his thoughts.

"My Lord?" came the slightly muffled voice as it filtered through his respirator.

"The resistance was better prepared than you told us they were," Highlord Tyren said. "Most of them got away, despite the two hundred ships and the android."

"Forgive me, my Lord. It is difficult to acquire information in The Shift, even with such an excellent spy network as your own."

Highlord Tyren considered this. He'd actually wondered if Harelo might have tipped them off somehow. The Uhran had been acting subtly different since the first encounter with his brothers and the crystal bearer. Tyren was no longer completely convinced that Harelo was entirely trustworthy, despite Preston's assurances that Harelo had done nothing out of the ordinary.

The Uhran had a good point though, it was difficult even to get communication signals through in that region of space, let alone people. The common folk thought it was impossible, but the more educated individuals knew better.

He had pretty much written off the two hundred ships he'd sent the moment he knew they were heading into The Shift however. He had hoped they'd been able to kill more of the Resistance, but no matter. Most of the Resistance wouldn't make it back out of The Shift anyway.

"Very well, but try to do better next time," the Highlord said, trying to sound forgiving. "I believe one of my brothers is heading for Sy'hloran. I've sent half the fleet in that direction, but I'd hate to think that I misdirected my ships. Find out for certain where he is going."

"Yes, my Lord," Harelo replied.

Tyren gestured him away, and Harelo walked back out of the room. This was less an effort to find out if Artus was really going to Sy'hloran, he'd be a fool not to at this point, and more an effort to keep tabs on Harelo and find out if he really was loyal to Tyren.

The Highlord could just kill him of course, but it would be a shame to waste the resource if it turned out Harelo really was loyal after all. Highlord Tyren hadn't gotten to where he was by wasting resources.

"Preston," the Highlord called.

"Yes, my Lord?" asked the small man.

"Keep an eye on Harelo. If you find anything... suspicious going on, bring him to me." Tyren regarded the smaller man. Preston smiled slowly and bowed.

"With pleasure, my Lord."

With that, Preston walked out of the room. Tyren smiled as well. Preston he had no doubts about. That man was small, vicious, vindictive, and ambitious. The Highlord knew that having to share the advisor position with another irked the small man. An excuse to dig up dirt on his fellow advisor and possibly watch him tortured to death later was too much for Preston to pass up. He would do the job, and do it well.

Tyren's hand clamped on the control bar on the arm of his chair against his will, and for a brief moment, the ship's systems began an overload sequence. Tyren concentrated and brought the systems back to normal function, then jerked his hand off the control bar and forced his body back fully under his conscious will.

"You cannot win!" he shouted in fury, trying to bury the fear he felt creeping into his heart.

Neither can you.

CHAPTER TWENTY

STEALTH OR STYLE

Dav watched his display more than the view outside the window. Images coming in from the front were distorted and far too bright, the usual result of faster-than-light travel as the Peacekeeper flew through space with its phase drive activated. The scanner display was far more reliable.

In it, he could see his destination. He couldn't see any details, though they were circling wide, hoping to stay just outside scanner range of Tyren's new ship. Assuming it didn't have some new kind of scanner system they didn't know about.

Nobody seemed to know anything about it, other than the fact that it had some kind of weapon built into it that was supposed to be devastatingly powerful and that Tyren was actively seeking to charge the weapon before encountering any of the Resistance again. Nobody even knew how he was planning to charge the weapon, though a few of the Resistance spies had determined where he was going to do it.

It was on that intelligence that Dav and the rest of the crew were heading toward the system ahead of them. Dav wasn't even sure that Tyren hadn't already charged the blasted machine. There were a lot of risks here, and he didn't like that one bit.

Allie had been very optimistic since they'd left Kobek and The Shift, which Dav couldn't blame her for at all. Since entering The Shift, her power had grown by leaps and bounds.

Some of the incredible things she'd been able to do on Kobek were enough to make even Dav a bit nervous. He knew that if anyone could handle that power it would be Allie. She was the toughest spirit he'd ever met. That wasn't what worried him though.

What worried Dav was the question of where that power was coming from, and where it would reach its limits. No crystal bearer in recorded history could do the things Allie seemed able to do, and nobody seemed to know why. Artus wasn't talking about it. Nobody was, for that matter. That worried Dav too.

He'd always looked to Artus for advice and guidance when he wasn't sure about something. Artus had been different since leaving Earth, however. Dav couldn't figure out what it was, but he'd been moody and uncertain from the moment they'd arrived on Ayaran to rescue Allie.

Dav could still see his strength, his courage, and his determination, but he could no longer see the certainty and confidence he'd once idolized in his elder brother.

With Artus gone on the other ship with Allie's mother and Imber's father, Dav couldn't even talk to him about it this time. He opened the ship-wide intercom channel.

"Coming in fast, we'll be just outside their sensor range in just a few minutes," he said, before switching off the channel.

It was only a few moments later that Allie and Imber came in, Tic chirping happily on Allie's shoulder. Raith had been sitting in his gunner's chair while Dav piloted, though the few glances his way Dav had taken showed he wasn't working on anything related to the weapon's systems.

Dav couldn't figure out what he was doing, though it looked like he was designing some kind of computer chip, and running simulations of its processes. It was all well above Dav's level of technical expertise, so he left it alone.

He wasn't worried, Raith had shown himself to be a loyal friend and Dav trusted him completely. More than that, he really liked the android and had come to consider him a close friend.

He worried about that, too. He knew that whatever Raith had done to rewire his power core wasn't permanent. Nothing was, especially when it basically ran on batteries.

Raith hadn't said how long he had left, though Dav knew Raith's internal systems were constantly measuring energy consumption and that the android would have a precise figure for how long he had left before his power died, and him along with it.

These androids weren't built to last more than ten or

twelve years, and as far as Dav knew, Raith was nearly fourteen, and a rewired core wouldn't last nearly as long as his original system.

From what he knew, a rewired system would actually result in the slow decomposition of the internal systems, and once his rewired power core had drained out, his systems would be so badly damaged that a second rewire wouldn't work. Raith probably didn't have more than another year or two left, from Dav's rough calculations.

He wasn't about to bring it up though. It was a personal matter, and nobody's business but Raith's. Until then, Dav knew full well that the android would do anything for his friends. No time to worry about that now, he knew.

As Imber sat in the navigator's chair, she smiled at him. Dav smiled back, feeling a familiar warm flush to his cheeks. Imber had that effect on him. Allie looked his way, and he turned the smile toward her. She smiled back, but it didn't seem as open and warm as it usually was.

He knew she'd been acting differently toward him for some time, though he hadn't yet figured out why. They'd talked on Kobek, and while she'd assured him that she would always be his best friend, he still felt that distance.

"Are we ready for a fight?" Raith asked.

"Do we expect one getting in?" Imber replied.

"Unquestionably," Dav answered. "Tyren wouldn't let his new ship go playing around in the galaxy without a strong defensive force around to keep it well protected."

"We don't have a force to fight them, what's Plan B?" Allie pointed out.

"I don't think we need to fight them," Dav replied. "They don't know we're coming, and if we come in at full speed, they won't have time to react for a moment after we arrive. If we're quick enough, we may be able to make it into the docking bays before they can even start shooting at us."

"You want to fly into a docking bay at faster-than-light speed?" Raith asked, turning around to stare. "Not even you're that good."

"I know," Dav said, a little hurt, despite knowing Raith was right.

The ship wasn't capable of stopping fast enough for a stunt like that. The Interceptor-class ship was incredibly responsive, but nothing could stop in a two hundred foot standard-length bay from speeds like that without tearing itself apart or slamming into the back of the bay.

"I didn't mean to go in that fast," Dav continued, "just that we fly in as fast as we can right up along Tyren's new ship, and try to maneuver into the bay once we've slowed. If we come in close enough to the big ship, we may not even be noticed before it's too late. Once we're running an internal fight, the four of us can handle almost anything they can throw at us down a narrow corridor."

"True. Pretty big risk though," Raith replied.

"Do we have much choice?" Allie asked.

"Not really," Dav said. "Once he has his new

weapon charged, who knows if he'll even be able to be stopped. We have to stop him before he charges the thing. Unless someone has a good idea for Plan C, I think this is our best option."

"Okay then," Raith said, "Let's do this."

"Allie?" Dav said, looking her way. She looked back over at him. "I'm going to need your scanner data direct-linked to my panel. Flying in that fast is going to be tricky to not hit anyone else, I'll need to know where they are, where they're moving and how fast, or we may end up enjoying a collision at light speed."

Allie nodded, and Dav immediately saw a side panel appear on his display with the sensor-panel's data on it. She was very good at that too, Dav thought, idly wondering if he should worry about that, as well.

"Good news is," Raith added, "if we hit anyone at that speed we won't know it."

"How could we not know it?" Imber asked. "I think we'd notice if we hit something." Raith looked at her.

"Nah, at that speed even a glancing blow would tear us apart, and we'd be destroyed before any of our brains, or processors, could register that anything had happened."

"Oh gee, thanks for that delightful and reassuring thought," Dav said, giving Raith a dark look.

"Sorry," Raith said, looking slightly sheepish. Dav rolled his eyes and turned back to his own display.

"Entering sensor range in three… two… one…" he counted.

The sensor display suddenly registered the region of space they had been told Tyren was moving into. It was a single-star solar system, with a yellow dwarf star similar to the Earth's sun. There were five planets in the system, two gas giants, one ice planet, one small, dense rock too close to the star to be habitable, and one planet that looked remarkably similar to Earth.

An asteroid belt ran just inside the fifth planet out, but they were coming in from an angle that would put them in above the belt. Which was good, because they never would have made it through the belt at these speeds. A moment later, sensors picked up Tyren's ship.

"What the..." Dav muttered.

He had no time to study it. It was less than two more seconds until they were right in the middle of Tyren's fleet of bodyguard ships, alongside the huge, strangely-shaped golden ship.

Dav had managed to thread the needle, so to speak, and came in that fast without clipping any of the mass of ships. There were at least eighty, including seven Sy'hli battle cruisers. The Peacekeeper wouldn't stand a chance in a full firefight.

Dav slowed the Peacekeeper quickly, watching the scanner display for the docking bays. He couldn't see them from here, and something about the golden ship made it impossible for his sensors to penetrate. Tyren must have used rogellium in the support struts, he thought. It would block sensors from penetrating the hull, and prevent Allie from Jumping in. Clever, though it had to be incredibly expensive to acquire and forge that much rogellium.

"Incoming!" Raith warned.

Raith opened fire a fraction of a second before the

guard ships began to shoot at them. Flashes of light from the plasma cannons exploded all around them. Dav's mind kicked into fight mode, his reflexes taking over completely. He was dodging incoming blasts before his brain even consciously registered the shots.

He rolled the Peacekeeper under one of the long, strange arms coming out of the golden ship's hull, just in time as a barrage of plasma bolts slammed into the arm, shielding them from the impact. Ripples of energy came from where the plasma bolts had hit, seeming to be absorbed by the great ship, leaving the golden plating completely unscathed.

Tyren's bodyguard ships had burst into motion, and were swarming around the giant golden ship, setting up a defensive barrier, all of them in line of sight of the Peacekeeper.

"This isn't going to work!" Imber cried. "We have to go!"

"We can't!" Dav shouted back. "They have six Interceptors, we can't outrun them!"

The Peacekeeper flew straight through the middle of an enemy ship just as Raith's shots tore the craft apart, leaving them coming out the other side of a fiery debris field.

That oddly aware, combat-focused part of his mind noticed that Imber's display was showing a text readout of every word they said so she could follow their talking even when she wasn't looking. Dav had no idea when she'd set that up, but he kicked himself for not suggesting it right at the beginning.

"There's the docking bays!" Allie called, sending the

coordinates to Imber and Dav's displays.

"No good," Dav argued, "we can't get in there. We'd have to slow down too much, they'd have us in a heartbeat!"

"Do we have a Plan M?" Raith asked, almost casually.

"Someone always dies in Plan M," Dav quipped back, unable to resist.

"I have an idea," Allie said.

"Let's hear it," Imber called. "Quickly!" she added as shrapnel from one of the ships Raith hit ricocheted off the Peacekeeper's hull, jarring them all.

"How fast can we stop?" she asked.

"I can have us at full stop in two seconds, but like I said, we'll be blown out of the sky if we stop!" Dav said. He knew she had something in mind, but couldn't see how stopping would help.

"Do you trust me?" she asked.

"Yes," Dav said, without hesitation. He knew it was true. If she believed their stopping was the only way, he'd do it, even knowing that stopping would mean their death.

"Fly us past the docking bay again," she told him, "then head out for open space as fast as you can. Only fly until they come after us for a few seconds, then full stop."

"He has rogellium in that ship," Dav pointed out, realizing what she intended.

"Not over the bay entrance," Allie argued. She had a point, Dav had to admit, but that much rogellium would certainly interfere even with a crystal bearer's Jump through a huge opening like the docking bay. Then again, Allie was no ordinary Jumper, he reminded himself. If she felt she could do it, she very probably could.

"Roger that," Dav replied.

Imber and Raith both glanced his way. Dav shrugged as he turned the ship on its side to fly directly between a pair of incoming enemy ships. It was a narrow fit, but the Peacekeeper slid through easily. He banked past the docking bays again. A plasma bolt screamed past close enough to shake the ship.

"Too many of them," Dav muttered to himself as he sent the Peacekeeper into another series of mad banks and turns as he dodged both plasma bolts and ships.

How they kept from hitting each other, he had no idea. Then again, with Raith firing their own cannons like the madman he was, it was possible that the enemy couldn't actually tell if they were hitting their own or if Raith was taking them down.

Dav turned sharply out toward open space again and mentally floored the throttle. The Peacekeeper shot into space far faster than any bullet, even faster than a laser. He rolled and banked to avoid incoming fire, but the move to flee seemed to surprise their pursuers and it took them a moment to reorient.

As they all turned to give chase, Dav abruptly stopped the ship. He could never do that without mentally picturing the screeching of tires, an image which made him smile. As Dav knew she would, Allie was spinning the crystal.

He watched as time seemed to slow, incoming fire on his display gradually slowing down. An instant before three separate bolts hit them, everything on the display changed. He could now see the docking bay all around them. They were sitting perfectly, parked neatly in an empty port in the bay.

Allie had pulled the entire ship and all its occupants along with her in the Jump, and without touching any of the others in the process. Dav had barely felt the usual pulling when they were Jumped. This time, it felt more like what those terrifying Jumping dog-beasts back on Kobek had done. One moment in one place, the next in another.

"Wow," Dav said, genuinely impressed. "Nice parking job." He glanced her way in time to catch her proud, pleased smile.

"Thanks," she replied. "I felt the rogellium pushing back, but it wasn't even that hard. I just needed you to fly by again so I could see what it looked like inside to know where to land."

"Well done," Raith said as well, standing quickly and drawing his guns. "We need to move. They'll pick us up momentarily, and whatever troops are inside this beast will be on their way. We need to find Tyren."

The others nodded, standing and putting on their helmets before drawing their own weapons. Shatter pistols all around, except for Imber's rifle. Dav took an extra moment to slip on his new strike rings.

He'd had to craft a new set, but he felt better knowing if he lost his weapons he'd still be armed. I should have made sets for Allie and Imber too, he thought regretfully. Well, too late now, he knew.

They moved quickly to the doors leading deeper into

the massive golden ship. Even this bay was bigger than Dav had seen before. They probably could have fit the entire fleet outside in it with room to spare, and there had been four of these bays. They had all been empty however, so Dav wasn't sure what Tyren's plan for them was.

Oddly, the entire bay seemed plated in the same golden metal that covered the outside of the ship's hull.

Raith put his hand on the panel by the door, and paused for a full eight seconds before removing his hand. The door didn't open. Dav frowned. Raith could have reprogrammed half the ship in that amount of time. Raith glanced back, looking surprised.

"He's using a completely different system on this thing," Raith said in response to their confused looks. "Nothing is where it should be, and the programming language used is unfamiliar. I'll have to decode the language before I can even open the door, let alone do anything else."

"We don't have time," Imber said. "Stand back."

The group did as they were told. Imber dropped to one knee and leveled her rifle. Dav's heightened sense of hearing could detect the rise of the pitch in the gun's mechanisms as she turned it up to full power.

Raith looked momentarily alarmed as he must have heard the same sound. On his reaction alone, Dav grabbed Allie and spun her away from the door, grabbing Tic from her shoulder and shielding both with his body as Imber fired. The usual hum of a high powered shatter gun firing had risen to a point almost above human range of hearing, and was nearly deafening. Dav felt a concussive wave roll across him.

He held his feet, though only barely. He felt and heard shrapnel hitting him and the walls, floor, and ceiling all around. Turning slowly around once the sound died down, he looked at the gaping hole where the door had been.

Imber's eyes looked just as stunned through her helmet. All three of them looked slowly at Raith as Tic seemed to do a body-parts check of herself. Raith looked distinctly embarrassed.

"I told you I increased their power," he said defensively. Tic gave Raith an annoyed chitter after apparently determining she still had all her appropriate limbs. He shrugged apologetically to her. "Sorry."

"Well, that could be useful, but it looks like we should be careful of aiming outward toward the hull. I really don't want to get blown into space," Imber said, giving Raith a playful wink.

"They have to know we're here now," Allie said. "We should go."

Dav nodded his agreement. He raised his guns and went first through the doorway. With Raith unable to easily access the ship's systems, they didn't have a floor plan to guide them to the ship's command center, where they all assumed Tyren to be.

After a minute, Dav realized the ship wasn't nearly as complex as it should be for something of that size. There were very few corridors, and they hadn't found a single door yet, aside from the one Imber had disintegrated.

Another minute and Dav realized something else

disturbing; not a single soldier had appeared to block their path. What that could mean, he wasn't sure, but it made no sense. Tyren should be doing everything in his power to see them all destroyed right now.

Finally, they came to a pair of doors, one on either side of the corridor. They looked identical, both the same shiny gold the rest of the ship seemed made from. Dav looked first at one, then the other. No difference visible. He instead concentrated and listened. There were voices, behind the door to the left.

"This one," he said, his voice being transmitted to the others through their coms, without fear of being overheard on the other side of the door.

Raith nodded, and moved to the far side of the door, guns ready. Imber took position on one knee where she'd have clear sight into the room. Dav guided Allie right behind him. She was armed, but not trained, and he didn't want to risk her getting hurt.

"Ready?" Dav asked. Raith nodded. All of them turned their heads away as Imber took aim.

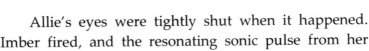

Allie's eyes were tightly shut when it happened. Imber fired, and the resonating sonic pulse from her shatter rifle struck the door. The expected explosion of the door never came. Instead, the pulse echoed back from the door, slamming heavily into the group in a broad wave, blasting them all off their feet. The sound waves hit the far side and bounced back again, slamming into them again before hitting the first side.

The pulse bounced back and forth several times, lessening in power with each pass, but hitting hard enough to toss their bodies back and forth along with it. When it was over, Allie felt like she'd been run over by a truck. She ached everywhere, her ears were ringing, her vision was fuzzy, and her head throbbed.

As Allie slowly refocused on her surroundings, she realized something was wrong. She wasn't lying in the hallway, she was lying in what looked like a laboratory. Not on a table or anything, which was a huge relief, but on the floor by a wall.

It took her a long moment to realize she must have lost consciousness. Several worktables were in the room from what she could see, with numerous technological devices she could never have identified, and vials of various colored liquids or powders everywhere.

Panic overtook her as she realized that her friends could be injured. Tic wasn't even wearing protective gear like the rest of them. Her heart leapt into her throat as the fear of what might have happened to her friends overwhelmed her.

Allie tried to turn her head to check on her friends, but found she couldn't move. It was an odd, very uncomfortable feeling. She could feel her whole body and her senses all worked, though they were still rattled from the backfired shatter rifle blast, but she was completely unable to move. She felt stiff, like all her muscles had locked at once.

A face moved into her line of sight. She recognized Preston, Tyren's weasel-like henchman. Her heart plummeted the other direction. He gave her a nasty grin before the face pulled back. Another face moved into her view. It was Tyren.

"Welcome to the Helios, the grandest ship ever built," he said, with a smug smile.

He knelt down to her level, and fiddled with something at her wrist. She could feel something there that shouldn't be, like a large bracelet. Her mind flashed back to Kobek, where Imber had been wearing some odd kind of shackles that had immobilized her. Without warning, her head was suddenly free to move.

"Tyren!" she screamed at him. He laughed.

"My, you're quite a bit more fiery than the last time we met!" he said, obviously quite pleased with her reaction.

Allie quickly looked from side to side. She could see Dav on one side. His eyes were open, but he wasn't moving either. Imber was on the other side, her eyes still closed. She didn't see Raith or Tic anywhere.

"Where are the others?" she demanded, giving Tyren her best glare.

"Who?" he asked innocently, then snapped his fingers. "Oh of course, you mean the android and the rat?" He reached to a table behind himself and held up whatever he had picked up. It was small, it was fluffy, and it was completely limp. Allie screamed.

CHAPTER TWENTY ONE

THE VANISHING SUN

Tyren laughed again, and dropped the limp purple form back onto the table behind himself dismissively. Allie's scream turned into a sob, torn from her throat. It couldn't be! Tic couldn't be dead!

"As for your android boyfriend, he's over there," Tyren said, gesturing. Allie strained to lift her head enough to see, fighting to keep the tears down enough to retain visibility. Raith was crumpled in a heap in one corner. Standing over him was a big, battered-looking Maruck with a smug, tusky grin.

Allie let her head fall back down as the tears flowed freely. Tic was dead, Raith probably was too. Imber and Dav were just as trapped as she was. Imber hadn't opened her eyes yet, she might be dead as well.

"Did you think I wouldn't be ready?" Tyren sneered, interrupting her hopeless thoughts. "Did you think I wouldn't have prepared for you fools to come back? It was stupid of you to come after me again. You should have gone into hiding. You would have lived longer, though still not long."

"Why are you doing this?" Allie sobbed. "Killing people, your own people, and your own family! Why?"

"Not my people!" Tyren roared. "Not my family! My people were killed fifteen years ago by these pathetic brutes!"

Tyren kicked out at Dav as he said this. Dav made no sound, didn't move at all. Allie looked, and saw that his eyes were still open. She wasn't sure what he was thinking, but he blinked, so she knew he was conscious. She looked back at Tyren and connected something.

"You're not Tyren," she said, several pieces falling into place. Tyren gave her a cruel grin.

"I'm impressed," he said. "You're the first to figure it out. Pity I'm going to kill you soon so that you don't have the chance to tell anyone else. Not yet though. First, I want to show you stage two of my plans. Come along."

With that, he turned and walked out. A large number of Maruck who must have been waiting outside the open door to the laboratory came in and grabbed her, Imber, and Dav.

She made eye contact with Dav as they were carelessly hauled off the floor and carried by the Maruck out of the room. Dav gave her an intense look, but she couldn't figure out what he was hoping to tell her with it.

Allie forced down the tears and tried to look back and see Tic or Raith one last time, but the big Maruck that had been standing over Raith was following and completely obscured her view. The Maruck was big, much bigger than the others carrying her and her friends, though not as big as Dgehf. Allie suspected the big Maruck was the one Raith had taken down with the weird club-gun on Tyren's station.

The thought of her big friend Dgehf brought the tears back. He would help if he were here. The Sy'hli might help as well, if they were here. The rest of the Resistance would likely turn them over themselves to buy some leniency from Tyren, the bunch of cowards.

They were carried across the hallway, and into the doorway across from them. Allie realized the lab had been the room they'd tried to blast into with the shatter rifle. She looked around the new room, and was surprised to see it was the ship's command center. It was the first part of this ship not plated in gold.

This room had almost no metal in it at all, composed mostly of a bright white material that looked like it might be some kind of polished plastic. Preston moved around into her line of sight, between her and the command chair in the center of the room.

"You're going to love this," Preston said, his voice sounding oily and cruel. Allie spat at him. He snarled and lunged, but a voice stopped him.

"Not yet," Tyren said calmly.

Preston stopped like he'd hit a wall. The little man sneered and stepped back.

"Take a look around," Tyren said to Allie. "This is the most glorious creation of technology in the history of mankind."

"The crystals are cooler," she snapped spitefully. Tyren looked at her a moment, then smiled.

"I do have to admit that those crystals are remarkable technology. Not as grand as this though. Besides, there's only one crystal left. See?"

Tyren held up his hand. In it was the device he'd destroyed the fake crystal with back on his station. His other hand came up and dangled the crystal in front of her. Her crystal. He smiled as she thrashed her head trying to get free. He was going to destroy the crystal! The one weapon she had against him!

Tyren dropped the crystal into the device and sealed it. He set it on the floor as he had the last time, and pressed the button. Everyone took a large step backward, Imber, Dav, and Allie dragged along by their Maruck captors.

Allie was too stunned to react. She was losing everything. Raith, Tic, the crystal, maybe Imber. Allie and Dav themselves would likely not be far behind, she knew.

The green light began to shine from the top of the device. As before, the crystal began to refract the light into rolling beams of green light shining up to the ceiling.

Another few moments, and the crystal began to pull the energy into itself. Allie could feel something now, a kind of wrenching in her gut that got worse as the crystal absorbed more of the energy.

She could feel the crystal. Almost like it was reaching out to her, its energies touched her mind. On impulse she focused on the crystal's energy and pushed. The crystal vanished, leaving only the concentrated green energy which promptly exploded in an emerald fireball that rose and dissipated against the ceiling.

The feeling in Allie's gut seemed to explode as well, a crippling pain shooting through her body. If the Maruck hadn't been holding her up, and the shackles keeping her body locked rigid, she'd have collapsed to the ground in agony.

Allie had caused the crystal to Jump blindly without her. It could be anywhere in the galaxy by now. Her crystal was gone, and with it her ability to save her friends and destroy Tyren. Several long moments passed until Allie could breathe again. When she could she glared defiantly up at Tyren. He didn't seem to have noticed the crystal vanish a moment before the small explosion.

"Don't be so dramatic," he told her disdainfully. "Plenty of reason to be angry after watching what comes next, but that? Just a rock. This next part is much better."

He gestured, and one of the men sitting in the seats at stations all around the command center nodded, images flickering on his display too far away for Allie to make out what they were. On the far wall, a massive holographic display sprang into existence.

This system's sun burned huge and bright in the center of the display, almost taking up the entire screen. As Allie watched, she realized it was getting closer. Dangerously close.

"What are you doing?" she asked, unable to help herself.

"Flying into the sun, of course," he replied with a laugh.

"Are you insane?" she asked. She was obviously no expert, but she knew that plasma bolts could melt a ship's hull. A whole star certainly would.

"Possibly," he replied after a thoughtful moment's pause.

He then smiled darkly, and stepped over to the control bar attached to the command chair in the middle of the room. The ship accelerated, the sun in the display quickly becoming too large to fit on the screen.

At least it would kill Tyren too, she thought. That was some comfort. She looked over at Dav. He still looked like he was concentrating on something else. Whatever he was doing, it was going to be too late, she knew.

Allie felt it the moment they crossed the threshold of the star. The ship suddenly began to vibrate faintly. She waited for the inevitable explosion, but it never came. Instead, the ship began to hum. Not the high-pitched pulse of a shatter gun, but a soft, deep, melodic purr.

The holographic displays around the room were going crazy, data and symbols flashing across them at a mad pace. Allie understood none of it, but the men at their stations all around seemed to be very excited.

"It's working!" shouted Preston.

The reaction happened all at once. One moment all the holographic screens were rushing data past so fast it was almost a blur, the blinding yellow light blazing out of the main display, and the ship humming contentedly. The next moment, the screens all stopped, each showing only a full, white bar, the humming went silent, and the display suddenly showed nothing but empty space, distant stars twinkling merrily.

"Perfect!" Tyren shouted, spinning around in

excitement at his success. "Charged and operational! Lieutenant, move to the inhabited world! It's time for a test."

One of the men's screens suddenly changed, and Allie watched the large main display change as the ship turned rapidly. It took only seconds before the small planet appeared in the display, growing rapidly larger.

"Ironic," Tyren said, turning to Allie and Dav, "that the very thing that gives this world warmth, light, and life, is now going to destroy it. You see, this ship is the grandest solar battery ever created. Fueled by the power of their star that no longer exists, this ship can deliver a beam of energy so powerful it can cut straight through an entire world. Of course, the planet would tear itself apart..." he trailed off, malevolent eyes looking at Dav. "This will be more fun when I can hear you scream."

He reached over and touched Dav's shackles. Dav's head turned slowly to glare directly into Tyren's eyes as Tyren released control of his head.

"You'd destroy an entire inhabited world for a test?" Dav said coldly. "Evil isn't a strong enough word. I promise you, brother. We will bring you down."

Tyren leaned close, inches from Dav's eyes. His expression had changed from one of cold satisfaction to burning barely-controlled rage.

"I will destroy every inhabited world before I am through!" Tyren snarled. "Every one of you will die before I am finished! Like you did to my people, I will see yours wiped out."

"We are your people!" Dav shouted back.

Tyren straightened and stepped back again, visibly

collecting himself.

"Don't worry," he said, "this ship is not how I intend to destroy your kind. I have a better plan for that. Much less work. This ship will destroy your home world though, and serve as a delivery method for the third and final move in my perfect game of revenge."

"Revenge for what?" Dav asked, though Allie could tell he was focusing inwardly again.

His lips were turning blue, she realized. Not profoundly, but subtly. His lips were turning blue and his skin was getting paler. Allie frowned in confusion.

"For destroying my world," Tyren said, softly, almost sadly.

"The Coalition..." Dav began, but Tyren shouted, interrupting him.

"The Coalition is a means to an end! They are all cowards and fools, and deserve what fate is coming to them!"

"They won't stand for this," Dav said.

"They won't have a choice. Arm the cannon!" Tyren ordered as he turned away.

Tyren grabbed the control bar again. A hollow diamond shape appeared on the large display, moving quickly to the middle of the planet as a series of numbers and a red status bar appeared on the side. It was a targeting system, she realized. Centered on the world. Tyren glanced back, saw her expression of horror, and smiled slowly.

"Don't worry, the people on this world are complete primitives," he said cruelly. "They can't even travel beyond their own world. The galaxy will never miss them."

"I know there's good left in you," Allie said, hoping to both stall for time for whatever Dav was planning, and maybe even convince Tyren to spare this innocent and defenseless world.

"Good?" Tyren asked as he paused, turning to regard her. "What do you know of it, *human*?" he spat. "Mankind, in all its forms, is a plague! You spread across the galaxy consuming and destroying everything you touch! Entire species are killed for your pleasure, for your food, or for your convenience! You corrupt and twist everything within your grasp, and your technology advances almost by the day to broaden your reach! You kill and destroy, even one another, and for reasons so pitiful that no truly intelligent race would tolerate your existence! All of your posturing and strutting around, spouting nonsense about morality and virtue, good and evil, as if your kind truly knows anything about it! Your hypocrisy is limitless! Your kind have no respect for other human lives, why should I?"

With that, Tyren turned back to the screen. Allie glanced at Dav. His skin had taken on a bluish hue as well, and his eyes drooped. He didn't look well at all, she thought. She glanced the other way to Imber. Her eyes were open, and filled with fear.

"Hold on Imber, we'll get out of this," Allie whispered to reassure her friend. She wasn't sure if it would help, but it was all she could do at the moment. Allie looked back to the world on the display, green land and blue water, white clouds drifting around its sphere, just like the Earth. Numbers flashed on the huge display as Tyren locked onto the planet.

"My Lord!" shouted one of the men on the side of the room.

"What!" Tyren snapped.

"Multiple ships incoming!"

"Have the fleet destroy them!" Tyren shouted.

"They're trying sir, but they're Sy'hli battle cruisers."

"It can't be!" Tyren snarled, looking away from the planet on the screen.

"And one Maruck war ship, but not like one I've ever seen before," added the man. "It's huge, the armor plating looks peculiar, and some of the cannons on that thing look like Tchratchi technology!"

"A Maruck? That's impossible, the Maruck are mine!"

"The Maruck ship is decimating the entire starboard flank, My Lord!"

"No," Tyren muttered. "No!" He was quiet another moment. "You're too late, fool!" he snarled, but sounded like he was talking to himself. Tyren's head snapped back up to focus on the screen. "Just watch," he muttered, again to himself.

Allie cried out as six brilliant yellow beams of light came inward on the display to meet in the center. She realized each beam came in from one of the six long, curving arms on the ship. A sphere of golden light grew in the center where the beams met.

"No!" she screamed.

Tyren lurched to one side suddenly, free hand reaching up to clutch at his head. At the same time, the golden light burst forth from the sphere. The beam didn't strike the center of the planet however.

Tyren's sudden, unexpected distraction had apparently thrown off his aim. The beam struck the planet though, moving in a gentle arc as the targeting system was pushed off by whatever was in Tyren's head and fighting him. A small section of the edge of the planet was struck, the beam slicing through as if the world weren't even there.

Despite the relatively small size of the piece cut off, the chunk of rock launched off the main body of the planet, propelled by a colossal gout of lava as the planet's mantle suddenly found a release for its pressure. From this distance, the lava seemed to almost casually flow out of the world, drifting upward into space, though Allie knew the eruption would be cataclysmic from the planet itself.

Tyren stumbled again, hand coming off the control bar. The energy beams coming in from the arms suddenly cut off, the golden sphere vanishing. Allie noticed something odd. She could feel Tyren.

Not the energies she normally felt while Jumping, or had been feeling all around in The Shift. This was the energy she'd felt coming from Tyren when she'd pushed against him while saving Imber's father. She closed her eyes, and the energies seemed more clearly defined. She could still feel him, and something inside him was fighting against those energies as well.

Tyren suddenly stood, strong and angry, and lunged for the control bar. Allie reached out with her mind and pushed hard against his energies. Tyren flew away from her with such force it looked as though he'd been kicked by a giant. He went straight through the holographic display and slammed against the wall behind it. He shook his head, but looked immediately up to Allie in a hot fury.

"Kill her!" he screamed.

The Maruck holding her clamped one massive fist around her torso and hefted her off the ground. A terrible shrieking noise came from outside the room, like the tearing of metal. "Kill them all!" Tyren shouted, standing up and racing toward them.

Allie's vision began to swim with the pressure of the Maruck's grip. The Maruck hoisted her high, clearly intending to crush her body against the ground. A clattering sound to one side joined Tyren's shouting and the odd sound of ripping metal. Allie glanced that direction in desperation. Dav's shackles had fallen off.

Bursting into motion, though it was slower and less graceful than normal, Dav spun and slammed a vicious uppercut into the Maruck that had been holding his arm. A flash of bright blue energy told her that Dav was wearing his strike rings. The Maruck dropped like someone had flipped his off switch.

Dav landed and stumbled, shook his head, then lunged at the Maruck holding her. Allie glanced the other direction at Imber, whose Maruck captor was raising a massive fist to crush her. Dav struck Allie's Maruck high and hard at the same instant that Allie heard a different kind of shrieking, that of a very, very angry jicund, and the high, sharp sound of a high-powered shatter rifle being fired.

The Maruck holding Imber was struck so hard by the shatter gun pulse that he went right over the top of Imber and slammed hard into the command chair, tearing it completely out of the floor. Allie fell to the ground hard, unable to catch herself as the Maruck holding her let go under Dav's brutal assault.

An instant later, a small, purple figure shot over her like a furry bullet, heading straight for Tyren. Allie felt a smug satisfaction and a glimmer of hope at the yelp of absolute panic she heard from Tyren as he spotted the furious jicund flying once more at his face.

Allie's head whipped back the other way in time to see Raith sliding on his knees to a stop between her and Imber. The lower half of the door into the command center was shredded, showing telltale signs of having been torn apart by jicund claws.

Raith was holding Imber's rifle, and firing rapidly. The soldiers from their stations had drawn guns, but only a couple of them even got shot a off. One hit Raith's shoulder, but though he jerked backward, he fired off two more rapid shots and downed the last two soldiers.

He quickly reached down and touched her shackles, which unlatched and fell off. Immediately, she felt freedom of motion return. Raith did the same for Imber, then handed her the rifle, drawing a pistol. She wasted no time, and climbed to her knees into firing position and aimed at the door.

Allie climbed to her feet and turned toward Tyren. Tic was all over him, a raging force of destruction in a cute and cuddly package. Tyren's panicked efforts to catch and remove the little demon had brought him closer to Allie. She reached out for his energies again and pushed down. Tyren's scream changed pitch, and gained that eerie quality of a thousand distant voices.

Imber began firing behind her, and she heard the sound of many roaring, snarling Maruck pouring into the room. Allie tuned it out and moved closer. Tyren was hers. She had to figure out how to kill whatever it was that had taken him over without killing the man who was truly Dav's brother.

Shouting and snarling behind her, punctuated by shatter rifle bursts told her that her friends were still fighting, but she again pushed the thought out. Tyren was struggling to stand. Tic had realized Allie had taken over, and had released the man, racing over to climb Allie's shoulder.

The jicund perched facing backward, and Allie realized that her small friend was watching her back. She spared a small smile for her loyal friends, then pushed her thoughts into the swirling mass of dark energy.

CHAPTER TWENTY TWO

DEATH OF A SPECIES

Allie staggered at the onslaught of hatred and malice that poured into her mind when she made contact. Hatred far beyond anything a single mind could create. She felt thousands, possibly millions of minds all raging against her thoughts and her energies.

Deep in the middle was one bright and hopeful, though tired and battered mind. When she touched that mind, she knew. She knew everything that had happened to the man who was Tyren.

In her mind, she saw the moment this all began. Tyren along with a younger, perhaps twelve year old Artus and their father. A half a dozen other men stood with them, some Sy'hli, but two of them crystal bearers, on a strange planet. A world devoid of water, devoid of life, but the perfect distance from its sun to be able to support life.

Changes would have to be made of course, but that

was the purpose of terraforming. The device about to be activated would bring about atmospheric changes and introduce the seeds of life to the world. It would take many years for the world to be developed enough to support a colony of Sy'hli, but the process would be begun here today. Hot winds caressed the barren landscape, kicking up swirling clouds of red dust from the flat, dry landscape.

They all wore protective suits and helmets to shield themselves from the hostile atmospheric conditions, one of many reasons terraforming was necessary before this world could be colonized.

"Are you ready for this, little brother?" Tyren asked Artus.

Young Artus smiled up at his elder brother, the hero worship evident in his eyes. Tyren couldn't deny he liked seeing that, but it also made him strive to be the best man he could be, to provide his little brother with the kind of example that a boy with the potential Artus had could follow to reach his full greatness.

"Ready," Artus said.

"In just a moment, the crystal bearers will activate the device," Tyren told Artus as they watched the other men working. "We'll have enough time to get clear before anything dangerous happens, but the initial activation is a sight to see."

"Boys!" called their father.

Tyren winked at Artus and the pair jogged over to where he stood with the other men. As they approached their father, First Seat on the Coalition Council, ruler of the Sy'hli Empire, patron of the House of Tyr'Arda, smiled and embraced his sons.

"A great day, my sons! Today, we bring another world into the fold of the Empire! The colony that will settle here will be a foundation upon which a whole city will eventually grow, devoted to furthering scientific knowledge for the betterment of men and women of all races."

"It's amazing, the way they can change a whole world into a place where people can thrive," Artus said. His awe at the whole process was evident, and it made Tyren smile.

"Remarkable indeed. The science is beyond me," their father admitted with a conspiratorial grin, "but it has something to do with the energy resonance in the crystal keys. The Order of the Silver Star spent a great deal of time and energy building the device that would convert that energy into something that can power the terraforming module. We're about ready to activate the module. Let's move back a bit and watch, shall we?"

The trio moved back, along with the Sy'hli scientists. The two crystal bearers moved forward. The first triggered a few switches on the side of the device while the other drew out his crystal. The second then pulled out his own crystal.

Tyren watched in fascination at the light refracting in the uniquely elegant, unusual pattern through the crystals as the two bearers held the stones high. The crystal bearers began chanting. Tyren knew this wasn't necessary, but the Order of the Silver Star tended to be very ritualistic, so a bit of dramatic flair was to be expected.

After a few minutes, both men brought the crystals slowly down and inserted them into two small ports atop the waist-high device that Tyren thought vaguely resembled a skimmer engine, although with that head-sized blue orb in the center.

The two crystal bearers kept holding the crystals, eyes closing as they concentrated. The blue orb in the center of the device began to glow, the light not filling uniformly, but rather swirling and rippling like sunlight on the surface of the sea, viewed from below.

The light within the orb grew, until it began to reach outside the orb. It still swirled and rippled in a slow, liquid fashion, but now no longer seemed confined by the orb. It reached out first a few inches, curling around the blue orb, the light itself a vibrant blue current in an ocean of air.

Further and further the light reached out. The wind around them began to die out, the swirls of red dust dropping abruptly with the rapid atmospheric changes. The blue shimmering bands of light reached Tyren and his family where they stood. Their father didn't react, so neither did Tyren or Artus, though they both looked to him for reassurance. They waited and watched as the light passed through them harmlessly.

Artus laughed as he felt the tingle from the energy passing through him. Tyren couldn't help but laugh along with him and heard their father do the same. Artus had a laugh that was so bright, so genuine, that others couldn't help but join in.

Without warning, the light tightened in, coalescing in the center of the orb in a vibrant, blue glow so bright that it was nearly blinding. In a silent pulse, the light burst outward again in a uniform ring, racing outward across the landscape and beyond their sight. The endless sea of swirling red dust went mad.

The previously graceful and drifting patterns of the patches of red dust suddenly began lashing and snapping around as if a thousand tiny hurricanes had suddenly sprang into being.

A small tornado of red dust slammed into the group of Sy'hli. Tyren felt himself almost knocked off his feet. It didn't feel like wind, more like a physical shove. The force yanked and tugged at him, taking him completely off his feet.

As he hit, he growled in pain. A small, but jagged rock jutting out of the ground had torn completely through his suit and cut into his arm. Instantly, Tyren felt more than heard a sound like a million distant screams all crying out in pain tearing through his mind.

Artus had fallen as well, though the bigger men had retained their footing, if only barely. Tyren rolled over to cover his little brother, shielding him with his body.

The chaos seemed to last forever, the wind, sand, and dust lashing at them in a fury before abruptly stopping. The pressure instantly went away, the screaming winds vanished, and the storm seemed to die in the span of a heartbeat. What was left was stillness, silence, and clouds of red dust drifting slowly to the ground, moving no more.

"What was that?" the Emperor demanded.

Tyren knew this wasn't supposed to happen. He had seen terraforming activations before, and it was never like that. He stood and reached down to help up his younger brother, then winced at the pain in his arm. He helped his brother up with his other arm, then clapped a hand over the tear in his sleeve and the wound beneath it.

"I don't know," replied the lead scientist. "Nothing in the terraforming module should have caused that storm."

"Did the process work?" the Emperor asked. One of the other scientists already had a small device out and was scanning the atmosphere.

"Perfectly," he answered. "Atmospheric pressure and conditions are adjusting at expected rates. Chemical content will follow shortly as the process continues. This world should be habitable in twenty cycles."

In the background, the machine continued to pulse steadily as the crystal bearers retrieved their crystals.

"I want a full investigation into that anomaly," the Emperor told the men. "Have the Order of the Silver Star help, it might be something wrong with the crystals."

"Right away," replied the lead scientist.

"Let's go." Tyren and Artus followed their father as he turned and headed back to the ship.

The wound on the back of Tyren's arm had stopped hurting, though it itched like mad. He scratched at it idly, looking up at his father's back as they walked up the ramp.

We killed them all, the voice came clearly to Allie's mind, pulling her out of the memory. Her mind was in a quiet, calm place, alone with another mind.

Their entire species, their whole world. The voice was

filled with regret, bitterness, and pity. *It was an accident, of course. We had no idea that they were life forms. Silicon-based, how could we possibly have known? On our world, sand is mostly silicon based. Life is carbon. Everyone knows that. Our terraforming device killed them all. The only survivors of their species entered my body for protection.*

Allie felt sick as she began to fully understand.

They took control slowly. First it was just little thoughts. I didn't even realize they weren't my own. By the time I understood, it was too late. They were strong, and many. I became a passenger in my own body.

"We have to try and help them," Allie said to the voice, to the real Tyren.

No, said the voice, *it's too late. They've become consumed with hatred and revenge. In the beginning there were other thoughts, like sadness, regret, longing. Not anymore. Only anger, only hatred, only cruelty and malice. You have to destroy us. What they have planned is cataclysmic, on a universal scale. If you don't destroy us, all life is lost. All life.*

"I can't," Allie said, though she felt the truth of Tyren's words. "I'd be responsible for the extinction of a species, and the death of the brother of two people I care for more than anything!"

If you do not, I will be responsible for the deaths of all life in the universe. What they have planned won't stop with our galaxy. It will spread at the speed of light across our universe. It will take billions of years to reach the ends of the universe, but it will be unstoppable, and inevitable.

"I can't kill you!" Allie shouted back, angrily. "I won't!"

Do it, Allie! For me, for you, for Dav and Artus, for all your friends! Do it, or you'll all die!

Allie felt the swirling mass of angry, hateful voices pressing closer. She felt the pressure against her mind as they battered at her shield of energy. Allie knew she didn't have much time.

Do it!

Allie cried out in frustration and desperation as she grabbed the mind of Tyren and pulled it close. Wrapping her thoughts around it like a shield, she drew in the energies that she no longer seemed to need the crystal to feel. Pulling them into a tightly focused ball of energy encircling her, she pulsed, exactly as she'd seen the device do in Tyren's memory.

The voices all around went insane, screaming and gnashing in pain, rage, and desperation. Allie's own scream drew out for longer than she had breath. When it was done, all was silent.

Slowly, she opened her eyes. She knelt on the floor of the control room, cradling Tyren's head in her lap. His eyes fluttered slightly, but didn't open. She couldn't feel the hostile energy around or in him anymore. Truthfully, she wasn't sure she felt anything in the body of her best friend's brother. Surrounding them was a circle of red dust, lying still on the ground.

Looking up, she realized why it had gone silent. Allie's friends all knelt, hands atop their heads. Even Tic sat on Dav's shoulder, hissing softly at the horde of

Maruck all around them. Her friends didn't seem injured, so she couldn't understand why they'd stopped fighting.

And then she heard the chuckle. Her head whipped back behind her to see the huge, battered-looking Maruck directly behind her, holding one of those awful club-guns pointed directly at her.

He was too close, she realized. None of her friends could reach her or help her before the beast fired his weapon, probably taking her head clean off. They had given up to save her life while she'd been lost in Tyren's mind.

All that she had done, all that she had gone through, how close they all came, only to lose in the end. It wasn't fair, she thought, feeling her last traces of hope trickling away. She was exhausted, in her mind, her body, and her spirit. Too many losses, too many stolen chances, too much crushed hope. Allie didn't think she could take any more anyway.

Then she saw something to stoke that dying ember in her spirit, rekindling her hope. Her heart practically leapt at the sight. In the back of the room a Maruck was entering behind the virtual horde of Maruck already there.

This was no ordinary Maruck, however. He was massive, immense even by Maruck standards, towering above the brutish behemoths all around. This Maruck was special. This Maruck was her friend. Slowly, she smiled.

CHAPTER TWENTY THREE

IN THE BETWEEN

Allie watched hopefully as Dgehf entered the room. He walked in silently, but with an air of powerful menace, directed very clearly at the Maruck holding the gun to her head. As he reached the back line of Maruck, they began to notice him.

The first of the Maruck glanced behind as he approached, and did a sharp double-take. Its beady black eyes went wide, showing white around the edges. Allie hadn't even known they had white in their eyes at all.

The brute stumbled back, bumping into his neighbor, who promptly also took notice. The effect rippled through the crowd, the Maruck all backing away slowly, but with definite need to be out of Dgehf's way. Allie heard many of them muttering his name.

The movement and sound caught the attention of the over-sized Maruck behind Allie, who looked up from her at the approaching monster. Her captor was still a long moment, then spoke a single word.

"Dgehf," it rumbled. The name carried a great deal of weight in her captor's mind, and she thought she heard traces of fear in the tone.

Dgehf moved to the middle of the room where he stopped. The rest of the room was still and quiet, a heavy tension filling the air with the same physical oppression as a hundred thousand gallons of water filling the space.

"Klythe," Dgehf growled.

"Traitor," Klythe grumbled in the growling language of the Maruck. Allie understood it perfectly.

"Coward," Dgehf replied. Klythe snarled his anger at the insult.

"Klythe challenge," growled the brute behind her. Dgehf looked Klythe over, studying the battered warrior. He sneered derisively.

"Klythe broken," Dgehf spat.

"Klythe challenge!" Klythe roared.

Dgehf considered, then nodded once and lowered into a threatening stance, huge hands open, fingers outstretched, showing black claws the size of daggers.

Klythe dropped his gun and roared, a deafening, rumbling sound like a rockslide right next to Allie's ears. For a moment, she thought she might be deafened. Then Dgehf roared and she knew she hadn't been deafened yet.

Dgehf's roar sounded like a sustained explosion, making Allie's skull feel like it was going to rattle right out of her head. She screamed and covered her ears with both hands. Even the surrounding Maruck seemed shaken by the sound.

When it was over, she could see the other Maruck rumbling nervously, casting anxious glances to one another. They were all backing up, opening the middle of the room.

None of them seemed to mind when Allie's friends stood and backed up along with them. It was odd, seeing her friends now standing casually amidst the horde of Maruck warriors. Only Dav went the other way, circling around Dgehf quickly and darting between the two angry beasts to grab Allie and Tyren, dragging them both to the side just as Klythe charged.

Even as far away as she was, Allie felt the impact when Klythe collided with Dgehf. The two titans slammed into one another, clawed hands swinging. Klythe connected solidly on Dgehf's jaw, knocking the bigger Maruck's head to one side. The impact sounded like cannon fire.

Dgehf snarled, one huge hand coming up to enclose Klythe's throat. With a bellow of rage, Dgehf hoisted the smaller Maruck completely off the ground and slammed him hard to the floor. Klythe threw another blow at Dgehf's elbow, jarring the joint hard enough to force Dgehf to let go.

He rolled back to his feet and lunged again, but Dgehf deftly sidestepped him. As Klythe spun around to attack, Dgehf brought his fist upward, swinging it like a long hammer. Klythe's huge feet left the ground as the blow connected beneath his jaw, sending him up and backward, rolling several times before regaining his feet.

With surprising agility, Klythe lunged forward and leapt up, huge tusked mouth gaping as he lunged for

Dgehf's own throat. Dgehf's fist stopped the move cold, coming down fast and hard, and dropping Klythe to the floor again. The Maruck general hit the ground like a dropped cement truck. He didn't move again.

Allie watched the other Maruck's reactions with morbid fascination. They all stared at the still, fallen body of their powerful leader, then slowly looked up at Dgehf.

Dgehf lowered himself menacingly again, one fist almost eagerly thumping the floor and gave a slow, threatening growl, casting his black glare around the room. The other Maruck all slowly and carefully set down their weapons and held up their hands in surrender. From behind them, a full squad of Sy'hli strike troops calmly entered the room, weapons in hand.

Allie was about to jump up to help fight them, but the Sy'hli showed no hostility at all. The Maruck all moved back against the wall as the Sy'hli herded them away from her friends. Two of the Sy'hli moved up to Dav and bowed, removing helmets.

"Your Highness, we are relieved to see you well. Your large friend was right to bring us," one said. Dav smiled broadly.

"I'm glad to see you, and I very much appreciate your help. Has Tyren's fleet been eliminated?" he asked.

"Yes, Your Highness. Between our ships and your Maruck friend's over there, they weren't much of a challenge. It looked like someone had done some serious damage to the fleet already before we got there. Your doing, I assume?"

"My flying, Raith's shooting," Dav said, gesturing to Raith, who returned the smile.

"Is everyone okay?" Allie interrupted, looking around.

Tic chirped, bounding down from Dav's shoulder and leaping into her arms. The others all nodded, coming over to her. She cuddled the little jicund happily, who purred with complete contentment. Tic seemed a little rough, but not seriously injured.

The blast had probably just stunned her and Tyren was too focused on her to notice the jicund was still breathing. Allie looked Raith over carefully. He looked okay.

"I'm fine," he told her. "The shatter gun ricochet shorted out my motor control systems, so I couldn't move. Took me a while to reroute the processing functions."

"Your timing was perfect," she told him gratefully. He winked at her.

"As always," he replied.

Allie saw movement to one side, and looked toward Dav. He was reaching toward Tyren who was beginning to stir. "No!"

"He's killed billions," Dav argued, staring at his brother with not justice, but vengeance in his eyes.

"It wasn't him," she told him.

"Of course it was! We've all seen the things he's done and tried to do!"

"It wasn't him," Allie repeated. "It's a long story, but he was being controlled by another creature. Or colony of creatures, actually."

"What?" Dav asked, looking at her in confusion and frustration.

"This," she said, gesturing at the red dust on the floor and on Tyren's clothes, "is actually a colony of alien parasites. I'll fill you in on the details later, but your brother hasn't been your brother for a long time."

"I..." Dav began, pausing as he looked at his brother and tried to process that. "I want to believe that, but I know what this man is capable of. We can't risk letting him go free."

"So lock him up until we can prove his innocence," she told him.

Dav took a long breath, and let it out slowly. He looked up at her, his vivid blue eyes drawing her in. His eyes showed anger, frustration, confusion, sadness, and helplessness. She reached out and took his hand.

"Your brother is a good man. I've seen his mind, his thoughts. He loves you and Artus, and has been fighting against the parasite's control the best he can. He tripped Tyren back on the base and saved my life, he moved Tyren's aim when Tyren was trying to destroy that planet..." she glanced at the display, knowing the planet was doomed anyway.

Despite just having a piece cut off, the volcanic backlash would be cataclysmic. Even if they might possibly have survived that, the destruction of the system's star would effectively kill everything in this system in a very short time anyway. Allie resolved to have Dav call in as many ships as they could find that could get here in time to rescue anyone they could from that planet as soon as possible.

"You're right," Dav replied after a long moment, pulling her gaze back to his. "There's more going on here, and we'll reserve judgment until we can prove one way or the other what it is."

Dav stood and grabbed Tyren, hauling him easily to his feet as the man groggily began to regain enough focus to figure out what was going on.

"Lock him up. And the Maruck," he told the Sy'hli.

Their commander saluted and they began to escort the Maruck and Tyren out of the room. A few of the Maruck looked like they were ready to resist, but a sharp, low snarl from Dgehf convinced them otherwise.

"Dav, how did you get out of those cuffs?" Allie asked. Dav looked a little embarrassed.

"I convinced the cuffs I was dead and that they were wasting energy by keeping me immobilized," he replied.

"Wait, what?" she asked, not understanding.

"I dropped my metabolic rates. Breathing, heart rate, body temperature, that kind of thing."

"You can do that?" she asked incredulously.

"Apparently," Dav replied with a wink. "Once the cuffs sensed my systems go cold and still, they deactivated."

"How do you survive that?" Allie asked.

"This might sound weird, but the primitive ancestors of the Sy'hli were hibernators," he told her with a laugh.

"So that's why you can sleep so late on Saturday mornings!" Allie teased him.

"Hey!" he protested. Allie noticed Dgehf heading over and turned to face him.

"Allie help," Dgehf said, coming over to her. He gave her a huge smile. She couldn't help it, she ran forward and hugged him. It was something like hugging a furry tree. His huge hand patted her back with exceptional gentleness.

"Dgehf help," she told him in response. "Thank you, your timing was perfect too."

"Dgehf think Allie need more help. Dgehf bring Sy'hli, they want to help prince."

"I'm glad you brought them. Now we don't have to worry about what to do with the other Maruck, or the fleet outside. How did that big one know you?"

"Klythe," Dgehf explained, "leader of Maruck. Dgehf once leader of Maruck, but Maruck want to side with Tyren. Dgehf not want to help Tyren, Dgehf leave."

"They all seemed pretty afraid of you," she said, remembering the looks on the Maruck's faces when they recognized him. Dgehf's grin turned slightly scary.

"Dgehf is... legend," Dgehf said, a little smugly. Allie laughed.

"Over now?" Dgehf asked her. She nodded, looking around at her friends.

"I think so," she said, taking a deep breath as she realized that it was. It was finally over.

"Guys?" Imber called. They looked her way and she pointed at the big display.

The piece sliced off the planet had broken into several smaller fragments, and was now drifting slowly around the planet, trailing a stream of volcanic debris that was cooling rapidly in the dead of space. The world itself looked covered in ash. None of this is what caught her attention however. They were moving toward the planet, quite rapidly.

Raith dove for the control bar. He held it for several long seconds, then glanced at the others and shook his head.

"I can't crack the system fast enough. We have thirty seconds before we hit the planet. It will take me at least that long just to decode the system and another several seconds to stop us."

"There has to be something you can do!" Allie insisted, her frustration evident. She was having a strange sense of déjà vu. Last time we faced Tyren, didn't we end up in a space craft careening helplessly toward a planet, she thought? Every time they seemed to be coming out ahead, something else happened.

"Tyren coded it," Raith told her. "He was holding the control bar the whole time you were doing whatever it was you were doing to Tyren. He must have set the course and locked it in. I'm breaking the code as we speak, but we don't have enough time. I'm sorry." The others exchanged glances.

No, Allie told herself. She wasn't going to let this happen. They'd been through too much to lose now. She had Jumped an entire ship before. More than once. Admittedly this ship was a great deal bigger, but it was the same in principle, right?

Allie knew she didn't have the crystal anymore, but for whatever reason, she could still feel the energies and seemed able to manipulate them. She closed her eyes and placed a hand on the floor where she sat. This really was a déjà vu moment, she thought.

"Allie?" Dav asked.

She ignored him. This was going to take a lot of

focus. She concentrated on the traces of energy she felt. She reached as far out as her mind would reach and pulled the energy to her. The amount she gathered was intense, and she felt it burning in her mind as she struggled to contain it. The energy pulled against her, too much brought into one place. It began to fluctuate wildly. Mentally, she pulled harder and tightened the energy around the ship.

"Allie?" Dav asked again, more urgently?

Allie didn't know where to take it, except back to the last place she remembered seeing the ship, where the star for this system used to be. She pictured the stars as they looked from that place, and then pushed hard on the swirling mass of energy she had gathered.

She felt the slowing of time, and the pull. This was different though, painful. Far worse than even her first Jump. She felt like every cell in her body was being torn apart at once. Allie tried to scream, but couldn't seem to force her body to breathe.

It seemed to take forever before it stopped, and for a brief instant, there was something there, something watching her in the Between. Only an instant, then it was gone.

After several long moments, she could hear someone shouting her name. She was passing out a lot lately, she thought in that odd, detached part of her mind. Allie resolved to work on that.

"Allie! Allie!"

It was Dav. She'd recognize that voice from a million miles away. She opened her eyes. The light was all too bright. She felt something warm on her lip and reached up to touch it. Her fingers came away stained red with blood. Her nose was bleeding.

"Are you okay?" Dav asked, the concern in his voice evident.

"I'm fine," she lied. "Are we safe?"

"Yes and no," Raith told her. "You managed to Jump the Helios, and I have us stopped."

"And...?" Allie urged.

"Something about that Jump managed to rupture the containment field holding in that star's energy," Imber told her. "The ship is leaking energy fast, and Raith figures we have about twenty minutes before it reaches a critical point and explodes. Possibly to the degree of a supernova."

"So we didn't save anyone on that planet after all," Allie said softly. The others looked down.

"I'm sorry," Raith told her. "We did everything we could. We have to go now though, or we'll join them."

CHAPTER TWENTY FOUR

AFTERMATH

Dav had already sent the Sy'hli away with the prisoners back to their ships. He knew the Sy'hli battle cruisers had plenty of brig space for the prisoners, and was more than happy to let them deal with them.

Tyren worried him, but he also knew that the commander would be taking Tyren back to Sy'hloran for trial. He brushed red dust off his suit and scratched at a small cut on his cheek. It wasn't bad, just enough to itch.

He knew what Allie had told him about Tyren having been controlled. He believed her of course, but it wasn't easy to let go of the resentment and anger toward his eldest brother, a man he'd met only when he was an infant and whom he'd grown up believing had murdered his parents. The Sy'hli would be thorough in trial though, and he knew they would test the dust. If they had a sample, he realized.

"Come on, let's get to the ships. I want to get a

sample of the dust for the Sy'hli council first though," he told the others.

He helped Allie up, glancing at the blood on her lip. The nosebleed hadn't lasted long, but it worried him. She'd pushed too far this time, and they both knew it. No surprise, the crazy girl had Jumped the entire massive ship, lined with rogellium, and all of its occupants several hundred thousand miles away, all without a crystal.

Dav hadn't the slightest idea how she had done it. Jumping a ship that size was impossible. Jumping anywhere near rogellium was impossible, let alone actually bringing the stuff with you when you Jumped. Jumping without a crystal key was impossible. Speaking every verbal and written language instantly was impossible.

In short, Allie was one big web of impossibilities. His concern for what was going on with her was only growing. As they left the room, Dav went across the hall to the lab.

"I'll be right back, I need to grab something to contain a sample of that dust," he told Allie. She nodded, and waited in the doorway for him.

Dav entered the lab, and moved toward the back. He picked up a small vial. As he turned and walked back out, his arm reached out and grabbed another vial, a golden vial, without either his conscious direction or awareness, and slipped it into a pocket in his combat suit.

Moving quickly back into the command center, he went to the scattered red dust on the floor and scooped some into the vial, sealing it tightly. Standing and returning to Allie, he gave her a smile. She smiled back, and they headed for the Peacekeeper.

The Sy'hli were already leaving the bay, their battle cruisers moving quickly, but precisely into formation as they exited the Helios. Dav jogged alongside Allie up the ramp into the Peacekeeper and up to his favorite seat. Sitting in the pilot's chair, he quickly activated the engines and brought the ship off the bay floor, closing the back ramp. Falling into place behind Dgehf's massive Maruck war ship, he followed them all out of the Helios.

Dav glanced at Allie, who felt his gaze and looked back at him with a smile. His attention was pulled sharply back to the ship's display when they moved through the bay doors and were instantly struck with a barrage of solar energy pouring off the Helios.

His systems also registered a huge surge in gravitational pull. The leakage of the Helios' systems seemed to be releasing massive amounts of matter as well, though not as much as the star it had absorbed would have.

He immediately accelerated the ship to get away from the solar energy as quickly as possible. At the rate the energy leakage was increasing, it would be intense enough to melt the hull in another minute or two. Definitely time to go.

The Peacekeeper shot through space, following the Sy'hli cruisers. Now that Tyren and his weapon had been stopped, technically Artus was now ruler of the Sy'hli Empire. Once they were clear and further away, he would have to reach out to Artus and fill him in on the situation.

A flare from behind shook the ship. It wasn't the full explosion, but that was imminent, he knew. He activated the ship's phase drive, sliding slightly out of phase with normal matter to exceed the speed of light. The pressure and gravity from behind vanished almost instantly as they cut through the empty space. The Sy'hli fell into an honor guard formation around the Peacekeeper. Dav grinned.

"Well this is cool," he said.

"Yeah, it's been a long time since I flew with a guard," Imber replied. He glanced over at her and took a moment to absorb her smile.

It was over, he realized. Tyren was in captivity, his weapon was destroyed, his plan undone, and the Sy'hli were once again rallying behind their ruling house. They had all survived, for now, and were heading to the Sy'hli home world. Life was going to get back to what it should be.

The Sy'hli government would use its power in the Coalition to help undo as much of the damage Tyren had caused as possible. Dav and Artus would once again be able to live in their true home, in peace and without fear of being hunted.

It would probably take generations to undo all the damage Tyren caused in less than fifteen years, but that was always the way it went. It was always harder to fix something than it was to break it. The difference was, fixing things was far more worthwhile.

Imber would go back with her father and uncle, Raith would do whatever he decided he wanted, and Allie would go back to Earth with her mothers, both birth and adoptive. At that thought, Dav's heart sank. He couldn't stay on Earth now, it wasn't really his home. Besides, Artus would need his help to rebuild the Sy'hli Empire and fix the problems in the Coalition.

Allie's home was Earth. She had been born and raised there, among her people, with someone who loved her. She now had two of her own kind there who truly loved her and would take care of her.

She had no reason not to go back there and live a peaceful life, which is what she'd clearly said was all she wanted. Back to algebra and geography, back to middle school and bullies like Lacy Briscoe, back to combustion engines and short-range space travel.

Dav wasn't sure he could do it, even if Earth had been his home. He'd completely fallen in love with space, and the freedom of interstellar travel. He adored the diversity of all the myriad races all living and working together, and was fascinated by the technology.

He was so excited to get back to his true home, to the life he was supposed to be living, free of fear and hatred, free of the limits of a single planet. Despite all of that, he was sad. He knew it was Allie that he would truly miss. There wasn't much else about Earth that he would really miss. Maybe cheeseburgers and superhero movies, but that was about it.

Dav looked back at Allie. From here he could only see the back of her head, unless she turned to face him, but it didn't matter. She'd been his best friend as long as he could remember. Desperately, he wished it could have been more than that, but now that she knew he wasn't human and they both knew their homes were hundreds of light years apart, that wasn't possible any more. It really never had been, Dav thought to himself.

He shook his head and went back to his display as Imber sent him a string of coordinates and a navigational course to get to Sy'hloran. He changed course, mirrored by the Sy'hli honor guard and the huge Maruck warship at their tail. He switched on the com system and used the system to link up to Artus in the ship he, Morgan, and Imber's father Ambassador Oren had left Kobek in.

"Artus, come in. This is Dav and the crew of the Peacekeeper."

There was a long silence on the other end. At this distance there would be a delay between each message, but this was a good deal longer than that. Dav was just beginning to worry when the reply came.

"Dav!" Artus said. His voice was clear and strong. "What's your status?"

"Our status is 'totally awesome', big brother," Dav said with a grin.

"Tyren's weapon?"

"Destroyed. Tyren is in custody, along with a number of his Maruck, heading to Sy'hloran. We're all okay, thanks to our incredibly amazing skills. Well, that and the timely arrival of Dgehf and a squadron of Sy'hli battle cruisers."

"Seriously? That's excellent!" Artus replied.

"Allie's super powers have stretched from improbable to impossible, by the way," he added, grinning over at Allie, who stuck her tongue out at him, but she couldn't suppress her smile at his teasing.

"What about Preston and Harelo?" Artus asked. Dav

paused. He had completely forgotten about them in their rush to get off the ship.

"Their situation is unknown. Preston was on the Helios, Tyren's ship, but I didn't see him after the fighting started, and I never did see Harelo," Dav finally explained.

"Preston is dangerous," Artus pointed out. "We'll have some troops look for him. Harelo needs to be found as well, though I suspect if he's okay, he'll come out of hiding as soon as it's clear that we've won. Well little brother, we sent you to stop a weapon while we went to Sy'hloran to gather support for the war, but it looks like that was unnecessary. With Tyren in captivity and his power broken, there may not be a war at all any more."

"Sorry to make you waste the trip," Dav told him.

"Don't be! We've been enjoying some lovely diplomatic dinners here on Sy'hloran for the last day and a half," Artus said with a laugh.

"Save me some dessert. Looks like it will take us just over a week to reach Sy'hloran though. We'll have a few days there and then we can take Allie back home with her mother." Dav glanced at Allie again, who had turned to look at him as he said that last. He couldn't read her expression.

"Sounds good. We'll be sure to have a welcome home party waiting for you when you arrive. The political climate here is very favorable. There was apparently a reason that Tyren wasn't living on Sy'hloran. There's a lot of hostility toward him here. We've got plenty of support for taking over the head chair of the Coalition Council."

"Glad to hear it," Dav replied. "That makes our jobs a whole lot easier."

"Ready to help rule a galaxy, little brother?"

"Not hardly," Dav replied with a laugh.

Absently he reached up and scratched at the irritating cut on his cheek. He'd have to get Allie to use the dermal regenerator on him again. This time he'd make sure not to make her upset while she was using the cleaning device that close to his face.

"Too late, it's on us," Artus replied teasingly. "We could have just left Tyren in charge."

"Not hardly," Dav repeated.

"Okay then, as the two responsible members of the House of Tyr'Arda, it's on our shoulders."

"Actually there's kind of a long story about that," Dav said. "I'll let Allie explain it all when we get there, but the situation with Tyren is far more complicated than we though."

"Dare I ask?"

"Like I said, I'll let Allie explain when we get there."

"Okay little brother." There was a short pause, then Artus spoke again. "Do me a favor, and put those Sy'hli soldiers through their paces trying to keep up with you. Commander Nox says his men could use some brushing up on their high-speed maneuvers."

"Roger that. Over and out." Dav said with a laugh.

He'd put them through their paces, all right. If any of them could keep up, he'd be shocked. He made a mental note to keep them from getting too far behind though, just in case they hit more hostile Coalition troops who hadn't gotten the memo that their boss was no longer the boss.

Not only was it fresh news that Tyren was no longer in power, but many of the people who would know about it over the next few days would still be loyal to him. And Preston was still out there, with access to all of Tyren's plans and contacts. Preston didn't have the political backing, but that certainly didn't make him harmless. Far from it.

There was also that combat android from Kobek, he knew. The android would still be pursuing them under orders, whether Tyren was still in charge or not. At least until he was destroyed or given orders from Artus, who would shortly become the ranking member of the Coalition Council.

It was important that they make it to Sy'hloran before that android caught up with them or it would get ugly fast. If they knew his com channel, Artus could give him orders remotely and force him to turn himself in peacefully. As it was, it would be a race to see if he caught them before they made it to Sy'hloran.

Dav doubted the android's ship, whatever he had escaped Kobek in, could catch up with them, but that was assuming the android was going directly for them and not seeking an intercept course to Sy'hloran.

He wasn't sure how informed the android was, but if he was anything like Raith, it was better for him to just assume that the combat android knew just about everything.

In short, Dav knew that while the struggle against Tyren was over, there were a lot of battles left to win before the war was truly over. It was mostly cleanup at this point, but many lives would still be lost. Hopefully the Coalition would stand down quickly once they realized they were no longer under Tyren's thumb. Most of them would, Dav believed.

The most important thing was that for the time being, Allie was safe. He looked over at her again, Tic curled up on her shoulder, Allie idly stroking the purring jicund. There wasn't much time left, he knew.

In two and a half weeks, he would be returning her home. He would spend as much time with her as possible before that, but knowing he was going to have to say goodbye was killing him. Dav didn't see any other way. This really was the end, for everything about his former life. He only hoped it was worth it.

OUTBREAK

They'd been in space again for three days. During that time, Allie and her friends had spent a lot of time together, just relaxing and enjoying one another's company. They had played several games around the table in the galley, something so distant from the events of Allie's recent past that it seemed almost alien to her, as though simple pleasures like games were no longer part of her life.

They had to be, she knew, in order for her to return to a normal life. Allie would truly miss Imber, but she needed to go back with her father and Allie with her mother. Hopefully she could use Dav's systems to keep in touch with her once they all made it back to Earth. Maybe she could even come visit from time to time. She certainly hoped she would.

Allie and Imber were preparing for bed in their bunk while Allie's thoughts drifted back and forth between

Dav and Raith. She had figured out that Imber really liked Raith, which made her both jealous and relieved, since she knew Imber had no designs on Dav.

She worried about it though, since she didn't think an actual relationship could work between Imber and Raith, with him being an android. He wouldn't age, he wouldn't die, while she would slowly grow old and eventually pass away.

"Are you returning Tic home to Ayaran before you go back to Earth?" Imber asked, pulling her free of her thoughts.

Allie froze. She hadn't even considered that. Tic was such a huge part of her life now that she'd completely forgotten that Tic was quite obviously an alien and there was simply no way she could keep the jicund on Earth without putting her at extreme risk of capture and probably dissection.

"I hadn't even thought about that," Allie said softly, the realization of what she'd have to do hitting her all at once. "I have to though, I can't bring her back to Earth." Tic deserved to be back in her jungle anyway, with her family, assuming she had one.

"I'm sorry, I thought you'd already thought about that," Imber said apologetically. "It's a shame Earth is so sheltered, or you could bring her there. If you were living on any of the friendly Coalition planets it wouldn't be a problem at all, since it's only one jicund. You might have problems if you brought two, invasive species and that kind of thing, but just one shouldn't be an issue."

Allie thought about this. She had to go home, didn't she? Of course she did. Katharine was there, her home was there, her school was there, her life was there. Even Dav would be there. She'd only come along on this second trip away from Earth to help Dav stop Tyren. She didn't belong out here any more than Tic did. They both belonged at home.

"Yeah, that is too bad. I can't though, too much to leave behind on Earth. My whole life is there."

"I understand," Imber answered. "Dav will miss you," she added. Allie froze.

"What do you mean?" she asked slowly.

"Dav and Artus," Imber replied. "They have to go home too."

"To Earth?"

"Of course not, to Sy'hloran," Imber said, slowly realizing what Allie had thought.

"Dav grew up on Earth," Allie argued.

"Allie, I'm really sorry. Dav is a member of the ruling family of the Sy'hli Empire. He can't just pack up and go live someplace else. He has political and diplomatic responsibilities, especially in the aftermath of Tyren's rule. It's going to be his life's work to try and fix the damage Tyren inflicted on the galaxy. He can't do that from Earth."

Allie sat down heavily on her bed. Imber was right. Allie had been so stupid. How could she have just assumed that now that Tyren had been stopped everything could go back to the way it was? It was childish and foolish to think that way. Dav had responsibilities on Sy'hloran, and Allie had responsibilities on Earth. Didn't she?

She had Katharine, but Katharine could come live

someplace else too, right? Allie realized her mother may be more comfortable off Earth as well, and may also have diplomatic responsibilities as a crystal bearer.

It occurred to Allie that she was also a crystal bearer and may have greater responsibilities off Earth as well. Her abilities could prove invaluable in helping to undo Tyren's mess.

If she and her mother lived on Sy'hloran, she could still be close to Dav, though physical distance wasn't a huge factor either, she realized, since she could Jump anywhere he was to visit him whenever she wanted. That wasn't quite the same though, and she knew it.

Could she responsibly go back to living on Earth as a normal human, ignoring her gifts? Not using them to help the galaxy, as these gifts were obviously intended? She had so much power, and it seemed to be growing all the time. Allie knew she could do a lot of good with her ability. Her mother might be able to teach her to See where she was Jumping so she could Jump places she'd never been before.

Not using her gifts to help when she knew she could would make her indirectly guilty for many bad things happening. Like walking past a dying man on the street, who had obviously been attacked. Not helping would make her just as guilty of the man's death as whomever had attacked her. Allie had a moral obligation to use her gifts to help as much as she could.

The more she thought about it, the more she realized that Katharine and familiarity with Earth truly were the only things drawing her back. If Katharine could come to Sy'hloran too, she could learn to love a new place to call home. If that world was anything like Dav and Artus and the mind she'd felt from the real Tyren, it would be a beautiful and wonderful place.

Allie would have to discuss all of this with her mother when they met up on Sy'hloran. Having thought about making her life a grander one of both adventure and aid to those in need, with Dav by her side, she was having a hard time imagining anything else.

She had no delusions about her and Dav actually ending up together, he obviously liked Imber whether she liked him that way or not, and he had never given her any indication he was at all interested in Allie herself that way.

Either way, she wanted Dav in her life, as her best friend, no matter what. It looked like that actually might be possible. She could spend her life helping others, surrounded by all of her friends.

"You okay?" Imber asked, sitting beside her.

Allie looked at her new friend. She really was beautiful, her heirlines elegant and distinguished, her face open, honest, and pretty. She couldn't really blame the boys for being captivated by her.

Allie couldn't resent her for it though. Like all her friends, Allie had come to love her and couldn't imagine thinking badly of her. They had been through too much together so quickly for little things to get in the way. Allie leaned over and hugged her.

"I think so," Allie replied. "I really think so."

It was late, and everyone but Raith was sleeping. The Highlord sat up slowly in bed. He technically shared the bunk room with Raith, but since Raith didn't sleep, he was never back here.

He wouldn't be able to take full control of this body while it was awake for a while yet, it would take some time to regrow all of his former strength. The boy's mind was strong, stronger than his former host Tyren's mind had been. It would take a delicate hand to wrest full control from him.

Until then, the Highlord, as he chose to still call himself, would bide his time, wait, watch, and learn. He had already learned that Harelo was a traitor. Preston hadn't been able to uncover any evidence of Harelo's treachery, to the Highlord's surprise, but he had seen the truth of it in Dav's mind when he entered his body.

The difficult part would be hiding his presence from the brat crystal bearer. How she'd Jumped without a crystal, he had no idea, let alone how she'd done it to a rogellium-laced ship of that size. Her energies had nearly destroyed him.

If a small trace of the colony hadn't managed to escape while she was attacking, his entire species would be extinct. After that, the Jump had nearly killed him again. The girl was simply too dangerous to allow to live.

She would die, painfully. There was a degree of irony in the situation though, and things might even work out better this way. In this body, he would be able to murder Artus and the brat girl Allie in such a way as to stare them in the eyes while he did it. Their looks of surprise and betrayal would be glorious as he slid the blade between their ribs. He had decided to kill them both in such a personal manner, knowing they deserved it for what they had done.

The blasted android and the Ambassador's daughter were going to die as well, but his hatred was pinpoint sharp and focused on the brothers and the girl who had nearly killed him. Their deaths would wait though, they would wait until the perfect time.

"C.A.D.E.-16," he said into the holographic communicator he slipped from beneath the bed. There was a pause, and the android's image sparked into life above the handheld unit.

"This is not the Highlord's channel, face, or voice. How do you have this com?" the android replied.

"I am the Highlord, fool," snapped the Highlord. "Security code J-26754-PR-24-Alpha."

"Code confirmed," replied the android. "Is there a change of orders?"

"Yes. Do not hunt down and kill the girl. Instead, move in secret to Sy'hloran and remain in hiding until further orders."

The android didn't look happy, but the Highlord didn't care. He knew full well the combat androids weren't stealth units, that's what the Thetas were for. He no longer had a Theta, however. The Theta would be destroyed soon as well, but the Highlord was considering letting the Theta watch all of his friends die first. The combat android could help with that, since he could more than handle the recon android.

"Yes, my Lord," replied the android, the com channel switching off. One more quick call, the Highlord thought with a smile.

"Preston," he said, activating the appropriate coded channel. A moment later, Preston's face appeared.

"You!" shouted the advisor.

"Oh stop that," the Highlord said in disgust. "I am your Highlord."

"You are the enemy!" retorted Preston. "I will trace your call and have you assassinated!" the Highlord smiled. Something he had always liked about Preston was his viciousness.

"Save the hostility for the real enemy, or I'll make sure your death is slow and painful. I may even send you back to the Daneris Nebula where I found you and leave you there to rot."

"My… my Lord?" Preston asked, visibly shaken.

"In the flesh. New flesh, I admit, but in the flesh nonetheless."

"What are your commands, my Lord?" he asked, face pale and tone shaky.

"Find Harelo. Kill him. Then contact the Blackstar and tell the Captain I have a job for him."

"As you wish, my Lord," Preston said, his cruel smile coming back. The image winked out as the Highlord turned off the com.

The Highlord stood and moved out of the room and into the hallway. Touching the panel beside Allie and Imber's door, he turned off all of the lighting in both the hallway and the room beyond.

He opened the door and slipped silently into the room. None of the occupants stirred. Even the jicund remained comfortably asleep, secure in her feeling of safety with the brat girl.

One thing to be said for these Sy'hli bodies, he thought to himself, they were incredibly powerful physical forms. Agile, stealthy, and strong, and they had incredible vision. Even without any light in the room, this body could see in energy spectrums outside regular light.

Without a noise, he made it to Imber's closet, carefully opening the door. In complete darkness, he cautiously removed the cap of the golden vial and poured a tiny amount of the liquid within onto the shelf at eye level, quickly re-sealing the vial and closing the door.

Stage three was now active, he thought to himself with satisfaction. This was just a small taste of it, of course. He intended to release the bulk of his ingenious creation in a form that would spread more effectively, but this would be a nice start. Something for his enemies to enjoy as he completed the last of his plans. He would have liked to use the Helios as the carrier of the virus, it would have been more poetic, but this would work out nicely as well.

This would work out much better actually, he thought. With the fools thinking they had won, nobody would even be looking for him. He could take his time and plan carefully. Nobody would know he was there until it was too late.

The virus suspended in the liquid wouldn't become active until it was touched by light, at which point it would become the single most deadly virus the galaxy had ever seen. Nothing would survive. Nothing except himself.

He had already taken the antidote, a single dose hidden in the cap of the vial. It was the only dose ever made, and the only man who knew how to make more was dead. His own immunity assured, he wanted Allie and Artus to watch as the people they cared about fell victim to the virus.

Shortly after watching their friend Imber die a terrible death, he would kill them himself and watch as the light faded from their eyes. Struggle as they may, the Highlord would win, in the end.

COMING SOON

STARJUMPER LEGACY

BOOK THREE
THE PLAGUE OF DAWN

CHRISTOPHER BAILEY

NOVEMBER 2015

ABOUT THE AUTHOR

Christopher Bailey lives in Washington state with his amazing wife, happily raising their first child. Working professionally with children for more than twelve years has helped him develop a fondness for children's literature, and a frustration for the lack of good stories for older children that are completely family-friendly.

Inspired by an argument between two children in the school where he worked, he decided to write his first novel, "Starjumper Legacy: The Crystal Key". In answer to that argument, magic and science are one and the same, only divided by level of understanding. The real truth is that both exist in our world today if you only take the time to look closely enough.

With half a dozen more novels already in the works including the exciting conclusion to "The Starjumper Legacy" trilogy, he looks forward to the chance to publish many more stories yet to come and hopes his readers enjoy reading his stories as much as he enjoyed writing them. The adventure continues...

CPSIA information can be obtained
at www.ICGtesting.com
Printed in the USA
FSOW02n0005091015
11959FS